"A fast-pace̶ The story captured this reader from the very first page, and is a must read for paranormal romance fans."   —The Romance Readers Connection

"Well paced and lightly written, mixing magic, romance, and humor to good effect . . . perfect for lazy summer afternoon reading."
—LoveVampires

"This paranormal romance overflows with danger, excitement, and mayhem; however, whenever things become too stressful, a healthy dose of irony or comedy shows up to ease the way. Tate Hallaway has an amazing talent for storytelling."   —Huntress Book Reviews

"A truly enjoyable read if you like a jaunt into the paranormal . . . and enjoy humor as well as the more serious side of life!"
—WritersAreReaders.com

"What's not to adore? . . . Tate Hallaway has a wonderful gift."
—MaryJanice Davidson, *New York Times* bestselling author of *Undead and Unfinished*

"Tate Hallaway kept me on the edge of my seat . . . a thoroughly enjoyable read!"
—Julie Kenner, *USA Today* bestselling author of *Demon Ex Machina*

"Will appeal to readers of Charlaine Harris's Sookie Stackhouse series."   —*Booklist*

"[Hallaway's] concise writing style, vivid descriptions, and innovative plot all blend together to provide the reader with a great new look into the love life of witches, vampires, and the undead."
—Armchair Interviews

The Vampire Princess Novels by Tate Hallaway

Almost to Die For

Almost Final Curtain

Almost Final Curtain

A VAMPIRE PRINCESS NOVEL

TATE HALLAWAY

New American Library
Published by New American Library, a division of
Penguin Group (USA) Inc., 375 Hudson Street,
New York, New York 10014, USA
Penguin Group (Canada), 90 Eglinton Avenue East, Suite 700, Toronto,
Ontario M4P 2Y3, Canada (a division of Pearson Penguin Canada Inc.)
Penguin Books Ltd., 80 Strand, London WC2R 0RL, England
Penguin Ireland, 25 St. Stephen's Green, Dublin 2,
Ireland (a division of Penguin Books Ltd.)
Penguin Group (Australia), 250 Camberwell Road, Camberwell, Victoria 3124,
Australia (a division of Pearson Australia Group Pty. Ltd.)
Penguin Books India Pvt. Ltd., 11 Community Centre, Panchsheel Park,
New Delhi - 110 017, India
Penguin Group (NZ), 67 Apollo Drive, Rosedale, North Shore 0632,
New Zealand (a division of Pearson New Zealand Ltd.)
Penguin Books (South Africa) (Pty.) Ltd., 24 Sturdee Avenue,
Rosebank, Johannesburg 2196, South Africa

Penguin Books Ltd., Registered Offices:
80 Strand, London WC2R 0RL, England

First published by New American Library,
a division of Penguin Group (USA) Inc.

First Printing, May 2011
10 9 8 7 6 5 4 3 2 1

 REGISTERED TRADEMARK—MARCA REGISTRADA

LIBRARY OF CONGRESS CATALOGING-IN-PUBLICATION DATA:

Hallaway, Tate.
    Almost final curtain: a vampire princess novel/Tate Hallaway.
        p. cm.
    ISBN 978-0-451-23311-0
    1. Teenage girls—Fiction.   2. Vampires—Fiction.   3. Witches—Fiction.   I. Title.
    PS3608.A54825A55 2011
    813'.6—dc22   2011004453

Set in Minion
Designed by Ginger Legato

Printed in the United States of America

For Shawn and Mason

Acknowledgments

As usual I must thank my editor, Anne Sowards, for all her work in making this book that much better, and my tireless agent, Martha Millard, for making it all happen. A hearty three cheers to my writers' group, the Wyrdsmiths, for their critiques, suggestions, and support. In particular I have to thank Naomi Kritzer and Sean M. Murphy, who are the best and most dependable beta readers any author could hope for. Also, a shout-out must go to Maggie Jackson, my emergency teenager. My partner, Shawn Rounds, also performed the hero(ine)'s labor of proofing the final draft and continues to be my plot muse extraordinaire. Thanks also to my son, Mason, though he did his best to get Ima to play video games instead, for reading the galley of *Almost to Die For* and recounting all the funny lines to me out loud. It was an inspiration.

Almost Final Curtain

Chapter One

Rumor spread through Stassen High on whispers and tweets. Mr. Martinez, the drama coach, was spotted talking to the lead singer of Ingress—the one and only Nikolai Kirov.

My boyfriend.

Actually, Nikolai and I were only kind of seeing each other, since I was also "betrothed" to Elias Constantine, a vampire knight, but there was no explaining that to the cluster of giddy girls that swarmed around me like I was the queen of the world, and not just Anastasija Parker, the vampire princess of St. Paul.

"Come on, Ana," pleaded my sometimes BFF, Bea. "You must know *something*."

I couldn't believe Bea was encouraging this lot to harass me. Of course, unlike me, she enjoyed being the center of attention. Normally, she and I were part of the outcast clique, and most of our interaction with this gaggle of cheerleaders and jocks involved slushies and slurs that conveyed their deep misunderstanding of the nature of Real Magic.

Bea and I were witches.

Well, to be precise, she was. I couldn't cast a spell if my life depended on it, and believe me, there were times that it very nearly had. Being half vampire dampened my access to that particular source of power. But there were other kinds of energy I could tap. Our coven mostly tolerated me because of my abilities, but it was complicated.

Kind of like my relationship with Nik.

"He's so cool," one of the cheerleaders sighed. There was a wistful gleam in her eyes, the kind I'd seen in the eyes of a lot of the groupies that hung around Ingress after the shows. "Are you really dating him?"

"Yeah. I mean, kind of."

The worst part was that every time I stumbled over the exact nature of my relationship with Nikolai, I could see the hunger flare behind their gazes. Inevitably, the desire was followed by a measuring look full of jealousy and wonder at what I could possibly have that attracted a college boy in the hottest local band in the entire Twin Cities.

I wondered the same thing too.

"She is, no 'kind of' about it," Bea said to the disbelieving sneers. "Nikolai is completely smitten."

I couldn't tell for sure, but I thought I heard a bit of envy in Bea's voice too. The bell rang, saving me from protesting that sometimes I worried that his intense interest in me might have more to do with the fact that, in his spare time, Nikolai was also a vampire hunter. Or, at least the apprentice to the local vampire hunter, his dad . . .

Did I mention it was complicated?

By lunch, I told Bea I couldn't take it anymore. Even though we didn't have a pass, we took our sack lunches and sneaked out to eat them in her car. Bea had this giant boat of a vehicle. It had bucket seats and smelled like your grandpa's aftershave. Of course, she'd added the MY OTHER CAR IS A BROOMSTICK bumper sticker and the dream catcher dangling from the rearview mirror.

I breathed a sigh of relief when the doors clicked shut . . . but too soon.

"Text him." Bea poked me in the arm. I shot her a frustrated grimace and almost got out of the car, but she said, "Come on. If you have some information, the grapevine will take care of the rest."

She had a point. If I had some crumb to toss everyone, they'd forward the news around themselves without constantly having to harass me. Bea clicked the key into lock position so we could watch the time and listen to the radio—the car was so ancient, it didn't have a way to play MP3s. I dug through my backpack for my phone. Of course, it had to be off during school, and it took forever to power up.

"You should get a cell made this century," Bea said with a snort.

"Hey, it was cheap, and it's not like it's rotary—or whatever Mom says"—I twirled my fingers like she always did—"where they had to wait for the zero. I don't know. I never understand what she's talking about. Okay, it doesn't have a cord, at least."

"Might as well, at that speed."

When my phone finally finished turning itself on, I was surprised to see I already had a text from Nikolai.

"Hey, he wrote," I said, showing the phone to Bea.

"Oh! Open it!"

We put our heads together to peer at the tiny screen. With a gush of anticipation, I hit Accept. Seconds passed as the stupid phone deducted the minutes, and then finally the text appeared. It read: "Guess what? We R doing the music for your spring play. Try out! More 2nite."

Bea and I looked at each other and read the note again. "I thought we were doing *My Fair Lady*," I said to the equally confused expression on Bea's face. "Do you suppose Mr. Martinez decided to do *Jesus Christ Superstar* again or something?"

In my freshman year, Mr. Martinez caused a big splash with the production of *Jesus Christ Superstar*. He rented a couple of real helicopters, which landed on the school lawn and poured out actors dressed like soldiers, who proceeded to "occupy" the school as the Romans had Judaea. It was the kind of production that got everybody—from the cheerleaders to the dirtbags—jazzed about theater. "Great Goddess, I hope not. There's only one female role in that whole stupid musical. Let's hope it's *Hair*."

"Maybe he's going to do *Rent*?" It was a well-known fact that Mr. Martinez was fabulously gay and liked to push the envelope a little, but even so, it would be a bit avant-garde for him to pick any musical written after the 1970s. "Can you imagine? Like, who would even try out to be the drag queen?"

"Lane might," Bea suggested. "He likes to be out there and doesn't care what people think."

I shook my head. "The parents would totally freak out if Martinez really did *Rent*. Half the characters are HIV positive."

"Yeah, that's kind of retro when you think about it," Bea said, pulling out a tuna sandwich from her bag. "Who worries about AIDS these days?"

"Well, they should. It's not like they cured it," I pointed out, digging through my own sack in search of a bag of carrots. "But the play is kind of dated, and I don't know the music; do you?"

"Yeah, and here's what's weird: Mr. Martinez has only been showing us every production of *My Fair Lady* for a month. Why would he pull a bait and switch now?"

I shrugged. Bea and I had drama class together at the end of the day. Most of the theater types took drama as an elective, and well over half of us were in each school production, even if it was only as stagehands. In fact, it was sort of assumed that if you wanted to be in a play, you needed to take Mr. Martinez's course. It wasn't a requirement, you understand, just how it worked out, and Mr. Martinez made no secret of it. So he often spent class time reviewing recordings of professional versions of that season's show. By this time last semester, I was so sick of *Macbeth* that I half considered being truant just so I wouldn't have to see one more performance of it. "I kind of hope he's decided on a rock opera of some sort," I admitted.

Thing was, I couldn't see myself as Eliza Doolittle, the lead in *My Fair Lady*. She was supposed to start off as all rough-and-tumble and end up some kind of well-heeled British lady. So not me.

With my mismatched eyes and superpale skin, I had a much easier time with roles like one of the Wyrd Sisters in *Macbeth*. I was awfully freaky-looking to be romantic-lead material. The only other speaking female role in *My Fair Lady* was the nanny, who sings along with the song about dancing all night. My stick figure did not scream matronly either. Bea's kind of did, but I knew better than to point that out.

That was just the way it always was, wasn't it? Bea hated her curves and dark wavy curls; I envied them. She felt the same about my ramrod-straight hair and matching twiggy nonfigure.

But we didn't talk about that. We didn't talk about much of anything, in fact. Instead, she and I spent the rest of lunch lost in our own musings about the play, although as I ate my pastrami on rye, my mind wandered back around to Nik. Having a locally famous rock-star boyfriend did strange things to my ego. At the shows when he shouted out to me or came over to talk at breaks, I felt superspecial. I could sense all the eyes jealously staring at me, wondering who I was to garner such attention from someone as awesome as him. Meanwhile, while he sang, I had plenty of time to check out the competition and most of the time I fell short in my own estimation. There were college-age women drooling over Nik, some of them looking like rock stars themselves.

I figured it was only a matter of time before he dumped me for someone closer to his own age, someone more willing to, well, you know, help him live up to that rock-star reputation. Okay, just between us: we hadn't had sex yet. I wasn't ready. I was just sixteen, and really, we started dating only last fall, and trust me, with everything else going on while I was discovering that I was some kind of vampire princess, well, I was distracted.

Plus, there was Elias.

How do I explain him? He's a vampire. But vampires are nothing like what you expect—they're more like blood-drinking elves, except from hell. Literally. Only, the real hell isn't the one in the Bible either. It's older and stranger and, apparently, deeply hierarchical. Elias is a knight and acts like he's from the Middle Ages too, with a lot of bowing and touching romantic gestures like that. My dad's the local vampire ruler, but Elias is the one who makes me feel like a princess.

And thanks to this one battle between True Witches and vampires where I accidentally on purpose bit him, we were betrothed—which normally meant "engaged to be married" in medieval times. I had no idea what it meant to vampires. Luckily, there didn't seem to be any rush in the vampire community to push Elias and me toward the altar. It seemed more like a peace-treaty thing that involved him "courting" me a lot.

Totally off the subject, but the whole courting stuff was made of win. It involved a lot of flowers and being the center of manly attention, minus any pressure. I don't even know if vampires have sex like we do. Well, they must sometimes, or I wouldn't be here. But they were kind of another species. Though I know they have all the same parts, since I'd seen Elias naked—a lot. See, vampires liked to run around in the buff. Weird. But even so, Elias never even kissed me once. Maybe the whole biting thing was their version of sex.

I'd eaten only half my sandwich when Bea pointed at the dashboard clock. "Oh noes!" she said in mock seriousness.

But we'd be tardy for real if we didn't hustle. I jammed everything back into my bag, in the hopes that I might have time for a snack during free period. Otherwise, my stomach was going to be growling all through the rest of the day.

We got yelled at by Ms. Yang, the hall monitor, when she spotted us sliding in the side doors. But Bea was fast on her feet and came up with a convincing lie to keep her from sending us to the assistant principal's office. Plus, as Bea talked, I felt a slight hum in the air. She'd cast a glamour spell to keep Ms. Yang off our case.

Parting ways in the hall, I headed off to history, which was on the second floor and way in the back. I thought I'd be able to make it in time, but I miscalculated, forgetting about my sudden popularity. Three cheerleaders stopped me by the water fountain. "So I heard—," one of them started with a snap of her gum.

I cut them off. "Nik told me his band is going to do the music for the school play." They started to open their mouths to beg for more details, and I waved them off. It wasn't like they were going to try out for the play, was it? Or were they? OMG. What if all the cheerleaders and jocks auditioned? No, the thought was just too horrible, so I blurted out, "I'm sorry; that's all he said. I've got to go."

I scooted in the door a half minute after last bell, which meant I missed more class time going back down to the office to get a tardy slip. As I waited with the other deadbeats for the secretary to fill out the form, I sighed. Times like this, I wished I had Bea's powers. Zap! No more tardy!

Mr. Shultz accepted my pass with a kind of suspicious grimace when I got back to class, like he thought that somehow I'd forged the note, even though he was the one who'd sent me off to fetch it.

I took my seat and tried to ignore all the irritated glances. This was honors history, after all. My colleagues had no patience for anything they perceived as bad behavior. As quickly and quietly as I could, I got out my textbook and flipped to the current unit.

Slavery.

I stared again, as I often did, at the picture at the beginning of the chapter. It was an artist's rendition of an auction block. I got a strange shiver down my spine.

Once upon a time, according to Elias anyway, vampires were

slaves to witches. The First Witch created some kind of talisman to bind their will to hers. The power of this thing, whatever it was, kept them in thrall for millennia. And thus it was, until the vampires discovered the artifact and plotted to steal it. Then it got lost or something—I don't know. Anyway, vampires were free now, but still kind of held a grudge about that whole stolen-from-their-homeland-and-used-as-chattel thing.

No surprise, right?

Ever since we started this section, I'd been trying to ask Elias what it was like. Every time I brought the subject up, though, he'd get all tight and quiet, and then suddenly find some excuse to be elsewhere.

My only conclusion was that it must have been awful. And yet here was Mr. Shultz trying to explain how human trafficking was profitable and made a kind of business sense back then.

"Isn't it still profitable?" asked Lane. He was being intentionally provocative, but his point was valid. It wasn't like slavery didn't exist anymore. But if I knew Mr. Shultz, he'd find a way to make Lane's outburst into homework for everyone.

"Excellent point, Mr. Davis," Mr. Shultz said. "Perhaps we should all do a little research into current examples of human trafficking? How about a ten-page paper due Wednesday, for extra credit?"

There were a few groans, but in truth we were the students who lived for extra-credit projects. Do you know how many points an A-plus in an honors class bumps up your GPA? We were all competing to be valedictorian in two years, after all. I pulled out my notebook and wrote down the specifics for the paper. It could be fascinating, I thought. It was an intense subject. I wondered how much Mr. Shultz would freak if I did mine on vampires and witches.

I shook my head. He'd probably think I was making it up and give me no credit.

After class, Lane tugged my sleeve. As Bea pointed out, Lane was the likeliest candidate for a boy who might be willing to play a drag queen. It wasn't because he was particularly gay; he just liked to shock people. He was tall and gangly, like he hadn't quite filled out the body he suddenly had. His just-over-his-ears sandy brown hair was stylishly bed-headed. I thought he was kind of cute, but he was a little too artsy for me. When we'd talked backstage in the past, I never understood his music references and hated every movie he claimed to admire.

"Are you really dating a rocker?" he asked.

I rolled my eyes. Apparently, not even Lane was immune to the gossip. I would be so glad when Stassen High forgot about me again and went on to the next new thing. "Yes, Mr. Davis. I am. Why do you ask?"

"Well, Ms. Parker, it seems my hopes to accompany you to the Spring Fling have been dashed. I am beside myself with grief."

I could never tell if he was being serious or not. That was the other thing that always bugged me about Lane.

Luckily, I waited him out long enough and he started talking again before I embarrassed myself by being flattered. "Seriously," he said. "I never figured you for a heavy metal chick. I always thought you had more class."

Oh, nice. But at least these kinds of passive-aggressive insults were standard operating procedure for Lane. I knew what to do with them. "No, not really," I admitted with a sweet smile, as though he'd given me the biggest compliment. "Sorry to cut this scintillating conversation short, but I have study hall and, thanks to you, I need to spend my time in the media center doing research. Bye-bye!"

I waved toodle-oo to Lane's baffled expression and headed off to the library.

On my way, my gaze was attracted to a very fine male body bent to retrieve something from the bottom of his locker. Trim waist, broad shoulders, taut abs—in short, a body to die for. As he straightened, I started to smile into . . . the ruggedly handsome face of Matthew Thompson, soccer star and homecoming king, who randomly flipped me the bird. Okay, I guess he had just cause, since a few months ago I *did* lick blood off his face in gym class. That was awkward, especially since, even now, I could taste him. My stomach growled.

He seemed to hear the sound, and so I licked my lips seductively and flounced past like some kind of vamp vampire.

When he was out of sight, I sighed deeply.

Why were all the guys in this school such *jerks*?

After checking in with my homeroom teacher and showing her my Honor Society pass, I headed to the library. My plan was to find a nice quiet place in the stacks to hide away. Let's face it, I was just not made to be a popular girl. The only time I liked being in the spotlight was onstage. There, it was scripted. Someone much wittier than I was came up with all the lines, and I knew how it was going to end before it started. In real life, you never knew what was going to happen. Real people never acted predictably.

The librarian waved at me when I came in. I saw Matthew Thompson settling in at one of the big tables with his math tutor, James, a senior and his class's most likely valedictorian. I ignored the "come here" wave from Thompson. I mean, he did just flip me off, and anyway, I was sure he just wanted to find out about the rumors, and he had plenty of other sources—like half the cheerleading squad.

I slipped into the stacks with a sigh. Long ago, I'd discovered that way in the back, near the dusty poetry section, there was one of those old-fashioned study carrels. It had a built-in overhead lamp that no longer worked and a slot for papers, and was shaped sort of like a voting booth so that when you leaned in over your books, you had the illusion of complete privacy.

With a glance around to see if I was truly alone, I pulled out the uneaten half of my sandwich and surreptitiously tucked it into the overhead slot. I took out my cell phone and turned it on so I could watch the time. Believe me, it was easy to lose track back here.

A half hour later, I had finished up my sandwich and tomorrow's math assignment. I was just about to tackle English reading when a tap on my shoulder made me yelp. Guiltily hiding my crumbs, I peered over my shoulder to see if it was the librarian come to chew me out.

Nope. It was a vampire.

They're easy to identify once you know what to look for. They really do have pasty white skin, for one thing—at least if they're white to begin with. This woman was a very pale shade of Asian, but the absolute dead giveaway, if you'll pardon the pun, was the cat-slit eyes. Her features were enviably porcelain fine, and her black hair fell arrow straight, almost to her knees. Though her clothes were modern, there was always something uncomfortable in the way vampires wore them that made them look out of place, otherworldly, alien.

Plus, she curtsied. Who else but a vampire would do that

anymore? "A thousand pardons for disturbing you, Your Highness. My name is Khan, and I have come to request a boon."

It must be an important favor, because normally vampires didn't go out in the daytime. A thought occurred to me. "Did you come through the sewers or something? Is there an underground connection to the school?"

The idea both thrilled and scared me. I mean, how cool would it be to sneak into the library after hours? But then it also meant vampires had easy access at any time. I wasn't sure how I felt about that.

No, I lied; it totally freaked me out.

"Yes, Highness, but I don't have long." Khan looked over her shoulder then, like she expected someone to be chasing her. "Please, I need your blessing to pursue my dream."

Sounded harmless enough, but I was suspicious. Most of the time when vampires approached me for courtly things, Elias or my dad was around to give advice. I mean, what did I know about vampire politics? What if this "dream" of Khan's was to assassinate my dad? It wouldn't be the first time someone tried to kill him. "What is this dream of yours?"

"To break my betrothal contract and marry the one I love," she said, with a proud lift of her chin.

"You can do that?"

Khan smiled slightly. "Not without royal permission."

So I didn't *have* to be betrothed to Elias. This was news. No wonder she didn't want to ask in front of him or my dad.

I considered her request, trying to decide if I was going to regret allowing it. But, try as I might, I couldn't see any harm in letting her marry the man she wanted. "If I say yes, this isn't going to start a vampire civil war or anything, is it?"

Khan looked surprised by my question for a moment, but then laughed. "No, Your Highness, it's not."

"Why not ask my dad, then?"

She frowned, as if not sure what to say. "I don't wish to insult the king. . . ."

"But . . . ?" I prompted. I had to admit, Khan had my full attention. Despite the fact that my dad showed up at my doorstep last fall and demanded I come with him to be the princess of the vampires, it wasn't like we were close. In fact, when I refused to choose sides, he seemed to have lost interest in me. I didn't get invited to court or any of the reindeer games.

Khan pursed her lips, and for a moment I thought she wouldn't tell. Then everything spilled out in a rush. "His Royal Highness is a sexist pig who hasn't had an updated thought about women since three thousand B.C.!"

Oh. Okay. Well, that might explain why my mom, the über-feminist Queen of Witches, didn't last long in a relationship with him. I wanted to ask Khan to go into more detail, but my cell phone beeped, reminding me I had only a few more minutes of free period left.

"Done. Permission granted. Whatever I need to say. You have my blessing." Besides, this was totally romantic, right? "Go be with the one you love."

She curtsied her way out, profusely thanking me the entire way. By the time she disappeared completely into the shadows of the stacks, my cell phone beeped more anxiously a second time. Time to get to drama class!

I packed up my books, feeling like I'd handled Khan pretty well, considering. I mean, it would have been nice if I'd gotten an instruction booklet to go with the whole princess gig.

On my way out, Thompson bumped into me. Like, as in nearly tripped me, which I guess was his sort of Neanderthal way of being friendly because he smiled and said, "I'm thinking about trying out—you know, for the play."

I didn't mean to, but I laughed. It was just as I feared. Mr. Martinez had managed the miracle of making not only *me* cool for the day, but theater as well. Everyone and their dog wanted to be in the show. Even a guy like Thompson. Unbelievable.

Thompson actually looked a little hurt by my reaction, but he covered it with a cough. "Whatever. You're one of those theater people. You got any advice?"

I looked up at his square jaw and chiseled cheekbones. He was handsome if you ignored his knuckle-dragging personality, and I could see him acting in a Renaissance Festival troupe that involved bashing people with a stick, but as suave Professor Higgins? No way.

"You *do* know that theater involves singing and dancing and costumes and makeup, right? I mean, the whole thing is a little bit gay for you, Thompson."

"Maybe I'm some kind of undiscovered talent," he said.

"Yeah, undiscovered all right." Okay, that might have been a little mean of me, but if you knew the kind of shit I had to put up with after the whole face-licking incident, you'd be on my side. Trust me, it was nowhere near as cruel as the things Thompson and his buddies had said to me. "Look," I continued, trying to explain as carefully as I could. "Acting seems easy, but that's the magic of it, okay? Looking easy—when it's not. You can't just wake up an awesome actor one day. If I were you, I'd save myself the heartbreak and just buy your tickets for the front row instead. Trust me, there's no way you're going to get a speaking part."

The thing I wasn't going to tell Thompson was that any boy who tried out usually got into the show no matter how bad he was, because we were always hurting for male bodies onstage.

"Is that a prediction, witch?" Of course, the way he said that last word, it sounded more like the one that started with a *b*.

I flashed him my patented evil eye—which, given my one blue and one brown, was honestly fairly spooky. I'd creeped myself out with it in the mirror. "Count on it, asshole."

Thompson looked ready to hurl more insults, but Bea chose that moment to slide up between us and take my arm all ladylike. "Is this brute bothering you, Ana?"

The air hummed with the electricity of a spell revving up. So I quickly said, "Nothing I can't handle, Bea."

"You sure I can't zap him?" She waggled her fingers at Thompson menacingly, and he shrank away. He'd been the victim of her "zap" before. Her spell had made him unpopular for twenty-four hours, which was tantamount to a death sentence to someone like Thompson.

"I'm sure," I said. "Come on. I can't be late to class again."

As we walked through the hall, my mind kept returning to the conversation with Thompson. At Stassen, theater held a strange place in the school hierarchy. My clique included the kind of weirdos that thought quoting Shakespeare's dirtier bits was hilarious, true. But thanks to stunts like the one Mr. Martinez was pulling now, where he brought the cool to drama, we weren't always outcasts.

That was just me, and my own special brand of dorky. I was still considering this when we met up with my other sometimes BFF, Taylor, whose real name was something much more African sounding. She was Somali and usually wore a *hijab*, a scarf that covered her hair and neck. Since she was Taylor, however, hers were incredibly sparkly and tended toward loud, outrageous patterns. Today's was neon green with golden glitter.

"You look fabulous," I told her.

She beamed. "And I know a secret. You're going to die when you walk in," she teased.

Bea shushed her.

And I thought, *Oh no, now what?*

I anticipated the excited chaos of everyone's chatter, but not the sight of my sometimes, kind-of boyfriend perched on the edge of Mr. Martinez's desk. On other guys a peasant shirt with poet sleeves looked dorky and pretentious. Maybe it was Nikolai's half-Romany blood, but he not only pulled the fashion off—with leather pants, no less—but bumped it up to wicked hot. Plus, he had those tumbled, let-me-just-fix-that-stray-bit-for-you locks that always threatened to fall in front of the most gorgeous, deep amber eyes any girl has had the pleasure of losing herself in.

I started to say hello when he sauntered over and planted an amazing peck on my cheek—in front of EVERYONE.

"Aw," the entire class sighed as if they'd rehearsed it. Judging by the way Bea and Taylor smiled at me, I figured they had.

"Now, now, none of that," Mr. Martinez chided sweetly, as my cheek burned bright red where Nikolai's lips had brushed it.

I slunk into my seat and tried desperately to blend. Thankfully, most everyone was staring at Nikolai like God himself had materialized in the front of the classroom. Meanwhile Mr. Martinez looked kind of like the smug magician that had conjured him.

"In case you can't guess, I have a little bit of a surprise for everyone today. But there's more—"

My stomach lurched at the thought of something else; I was beginning to think I couldn't take any new excitement. Before Mr. Martinez could say anything, the loudspeaker beeped, indicating an incoming announcement. We all quieted as best we could, given the rock star in our midst. The principal came on and told everyone there would be a special assembly in the gym in a half hour. Bea looked at me to see if I knew what was going on. I shrugged and shook my head. Everyone stared at Mr. Martinez for an answer.

"I'm sure you've all heard the rumors that Ingress will be performing the music for our spring play. What you don't know is that Mr. Kirov and I have spent some time composing new arrangements for *My Fair Lady*. His band is going to give the school a taste of my vision for the production. He'll be singing a very much updated version of 'Get Me to the Church on Time.'"

Oh my Goddess, how hilariously weird was that? Not to mention mortifying! My boyfriend was going to be crooning a song in front of the entire school about wanting to get married. Everyone was going to be watching my reaction! Could I just die now and get it over with?

Plus, Nik kept glancing at me. I tried to smile back, but I couldn't help feeling very childish, sitting in the second row, third desk, like some stupid little high schooler. In my version of the universe, Nik would never see me like this, here. How juvenile did I look? Why did I have to pick today to wear my ratty *Sailor Moon* T-shirt?

Luckily, after a brief introduction to the class, Nikolai excused himself to go help his bandmates set up in the gym. Mr. Martinez did his best to try to impart some wisdom in the intervening time, but everyone's eyes—except mine—were glued to the clock, counting down the minutes until we could all head down to the gym.

Jinny, the girl in the seat behind me, tapped my elbow. When I turned to see what she wanted, she quickly passed me a note. When I gave her the "Who sent this?" look, she nodded in Taylor's direction.

Hiding it in my lap, I unfolded the paper. It read, "You look ready to barf. Are you okay?"

Oh, the things I could write back. Yes, I'm sick of all the stuff about Nik, and, oh, a vampire visited me during study hall, how are you? But that would just weird Taylor out. She was my friend, but she was a mundane. The only stuff she knew about magic or vampires came from those MMORPGs she loved. So, instead, I scribbled, "Just overwhelmed. Thanks for worrying about me. I'm okay."

Folding it back up, I contrived to pass it back to Jinny, who rolled her eyes at the hassle of having to be the secret communication conduit yet again. I watched the progress of the note, but the intercom beeped before it made it halfway back to Taylor. Everyone leaped out of their seats. Mr. Martinez indicated we should all be orderly and calm, but I could barely hear him over all the babble.

Taylor, Bea, and I found a way to stand next to one another in line so that we'd be sure to be seated together. I was really, really glad Nik wasn't around to see this. Standing in orderly rows was the opposite of cool, and I was pretty sure you never had to queue up like this at the U of M, where Nikolai went to college.

Mr. Martinez tapped me on the shoulder on my way out the door. "Surprised?" he said with a smile.

"Oh, yeah," I said, trying to keep sarcasm from creeping into my voice somewhat unsuccessfully. "This is just great."

Mr. Martinez was usually pretty good at understanding what people were really saying, but this time what I meant bounced off him like with a typical adult. "Do you want to sit in the front? So Nikolai can see you?"

"Oh, could I?" When he looked ready to make arrangements, I waved my hands to banish the idea. "No, seriously, I don't want to distract Nikolai, you know? I'm sure he should concentrate on the music and stuff or whatever."

Maybe Mr. Martinez finally saw the horror in my eyes, because he blinked and seemed to suddenly understand. "Oh, yes, right." He nodded. "Well, I hope you enjoy the show. I think it's going to be awesome."

I worried when teachers thought things were going to be "awesome," though most of the time I trusted Mr. Martinez not to be a complete idiot. Bea nudged me with her elbow, reminding me to hurry along and not lose my spot next to her.

"I wish you were a True Witch," Bea whispered in my ear once we were in the hall. "I'd help you conjure up an invisibility spell."

It was surprisingly sweet of Bea to think of it. I told her so, especially since the impulse to hide was against her outgoing nature. "Can we sit in the back?"

"We can try." Bea sounded disappointed, though.

Taylor flashed me a "You can't be serious" frown.

"You guys could ditch me," I suggested, and I actually meant it. I didn't want to spoil their fun.

Mr. Martinez cleared his throat for quiet in the halls. I felt my cheeks burn brighter. Could I feel more like a kindergartner?

Mindful of Mr. Martinez's watchful eye, Bea shook her head at the idea of separation.

Taylor mouthed, "We'll work something out."

At the gym we found a spot that satisfied all our requirements. Our class was stuck in the middle of the bleachers, but the three of us ended up at the very top row. For seeing the band, they were choice seats, but people would have to crane their necks to stare at me, so maybe they wouldn't bother. I could only hope.

The excitement was pretty palpable. I heard Nikolai's name whispered on a lot of lips, which was just odd. I mean, I knew that Ingress was the new it band. There was talk of a record-label deal, and they'd gotten some radio play on the local stations, but when I was hanging with them, it all seemed so normal, you know? They weren't this big freaking deal. They were just guys (and one gal) that sucked up most of Nikolai's time and gave me grief for not having my driver's license yet.

Stevie, the band's drummer and only girl, peeked out from behind a makeshift curtain. She saw me and waved. The crowd went wild. Heads spun trying to see who'd wave back, so I didn't. I just smiled and nodded, trying to make it look like I might be talking to someone else.

But it didn't work. Fingers pointed. People stared.

At this point I might as well lick Thompson's nose. Again.

Bea patted my thigh. "Poor baby. You're too cool for school."

I shot her a sharp look. "What's that supposed to mean?"

"You don't even know when you have it good, do you?"

"I don't like everyone gossiping about me."

"So don't listen to it. At least *you* have a boyfriend."

Did I mention that Bea had set her sights on Nikolai before I "came out" as the vampire princess at my Initiation? Yeah, well, she had, and she hadn't entirely forgiven me for stealing her man, as it were—even though it'd been Nik who'd pursued me, not the other way around. I wondered what she'd say if she knew I had not one but two guys in hot pursuit?

"He's superhot," Taylor agreed with a sigh. She leaned her elbows on her knees, her *hijab* sparkling in the overhead lights. "My dad would freak if he knew we were listening to 'rock and roll' at school." She did the air quotes and a pitch-perfect mimic of her dad's gruff, heavily accented voice.

I nodded in sympathy, though obviously my folks weren't Muslim. My mom had been pretty strict for a long time, though, about whom I kept as friends. When she thought I was going to be a witch, it had been almost unbearable how little I got out to do anything other than study spell craft. Maybe she'd been afraid I'd run into vampires.

Speaking of which, I looked around to see if I had an honor guard. Lately, I'd been noticing kids at school with a strong supernatural aura. Not that I could actually see auras—that was Bea's kind of magic. But I'd catch people looking at me in a way that didn't seem entirely human, though I thought they must be, if they were trailing me around school in the daylight. Vampires did have regular human, uh, companions they used to watch over them as they slept, and I got the feeling it was these "Igors" I saw trailing me from time to time.

I wouldn't put it past my dad to keep an eye on me. He was kind of creepy like that.

Well, maybe that was unfair, but I found it sort of unnerving how much my own father approved of and encouraged my "engagement" to Elias, who was who knew how much older than me. Dads were supposed to be overprotective and go apeshit when you dated *anyone*, much less some zillion-year-old vampire from hell. Not that I had any real experience with dads, mind you, but I knew how Bea's dad could be and I watched TV.

Of course, my dad was from hell too. I guess that made me a hellion—for real. Man, how weird was that?

The gym reverberated with a chord struck on an electric guitar. All talking stopped, as if by magical command.

The lights went out. We held our breath. When they came back on, the curtain was drawn and the music began.

You wouldn't think so, but it was exactly how Mr. Martinez said it would be. It *was* awesome.

"Get Me to the Church on Time" never sounded so cool.

Ever.

In fact, Nik's song was so epic that I got over my natural shyness and stayed behind after the dismissal bell rang to help the band pack up. Even though hanging around meant I had to watch everyone—even guys like Thompson—fawn all over my boyfriend. I noticed people looking at me differently too, like they wanted to be me.

If they only knew.

That was when I spotted them, the Igors. They hung back by the bleachers and their eyes never, ever left me. But the look they gave me had nothing to do with jealousy or envy or any of that. Their gaze was watchful, protective, and serious.

They could have just been class weirdos, but they had the patented stare, and, well, Igors generally had a different standard of personal hygiene. They always managed to look slightly unwashed. Vampires had a penchant for sleeping underground, and Igors followed them around like puppies. From personal experience I can tell you that after a couple of scrabbles through the St. Paul underground, you stop looking perfectly all together. I think it's all the sandstone. Grit gets everywhere, and the caves are incredibly damp—they made my hair go gross and clumpy.

Nik noticed the focus of my attention.

I felt a spike in power. Nikolai revved up his psychic blade, the weapon he used to kill vampires. Even though I couldn't use magic myself, I could feel when energy was afoot. I raised my hands to calm him. "They're human," I whispered.

He didn't look so sure, and his power continued to buzz beside me like an electric current, making my skin prickle.

I pointed at the half windows near the roof that flooded in natural light. "Human."

"Freaky vamp junkies," he muttered, dropping his power with ferocity as he shoved his guitar into its case.

My mouth twisted into a frown. It wasn't that I didn't agree with his evaluation of the Igors, exactly, but these were my people. Well, my people's people, at any rate. This was why Nikolai and I weren't exactly a hundred percent.

Nikolai's liquid amber eyes flicked over my face, and he shrugged. "Sorry. No offense."

I should have said, "None taken," but, well, I *was* kind of insulted. The Igors made my skin crawl, the way their glassy eyes gaped at me. But they were there to protect me. From people like Nik.

The residue of his magic stung my skin. I rubbed my arm. "Yeah, hey, see you later," I said, grabbing my backpack. "I'm going to miss my bus."

"I said I'd give you a ride," he shouted, but I pretended not to hear him.

The Igors followed me out.

The Igors, who blended naturally at school, stood out like the proverbial sore thumb now.

I'd completely missed the school bus, no surprise. But I always had emergency change to take Metro Transit, otherwise known as the city bus. I guess the transit part included light rail now, but St. Paul didn't have a train yet. All those were over in Minneapolis.

The point was, it was me, a concrete bench, and three Igors standing around, looking awkward.

They kind of hung back, but it was pretty obvious that they fully intended to escort me all the way home in their sinister yet sort of sweetly protective way. So I turned to the nearest one. His complexion was waxy and pale, and blond hair hung limply to his shoulders. He wore a washed-out, stained, pale blue T-shirt that matched his scummy jeans. His eyes darted this way and that, trying to avoid my gaze, but I asked him anyway, "So, uh, can you feel it?"

I rubbed my arm where the proximity of Nik's power had scorched me; the Igor stared blankly.

I pointed to my arm. There was no mark, so I supposed I looked foolish trying to show invisible prickles. "Does the hunters' magic sting you?"

"We would be terrible guards if so," he said, staring at the gravel clumps he kicked with black Converses. "And remember: it is not *us* he hunts."

It was true; Nikolai's magic was keyed to one thing only—vampires. Unlike me, the Igors were entirely human. His blade wouldn't harm them.

"Um, good point," I said, because I felt I should say something, but truthfully, the thought that Nik's sole magical purpose was to kill vampires put me in an instant funk.

I slumped down onto the bench. Spring had come early to Minnesota. Global warming, probably, but as we liked to say, can't complain, especially when it meant the crocuses were up and the sun warmed the air to nearly sixty degrees at the tail end of March. Part of my Midwestern brain rebelled at the idea of no snow at this time of year, but the other side relished the freedom of having to wear only a light jacket to keep off the slight bite of cold breeze.

The smell of wet grass and moldering leaves added to the feel of spring. Birds chattered as they darted heedlessly through the traffic in pursuit of mates.

The weather made it hard to hold on to the blues, but my grim entourage helped. I caught the distinct whiff of sewer from someone's clothes. I sighed. I always kind of hoped being a princess would come with a better class of hangers-on. My ladies-in-waiting were a bit grimier than I'd prefer.

I was so caught up in my mope that I didn't notice the car until I heard the Igors' angry hiss. Looking up, I saw Nik's ancient, rust-encrusted Toyota rumbling in the no-parking zone of the bus stop. The door swung open, and he leaned over the passenger seat to shout, "I thought you were avoiding me. Get in."

The Igor I'd chatted with put a warning hand on my shoulder. I was kind of surprised by his touch because they usually kept their distance, avoiding drawing attention to themselves as much as possible. It was a major breach of the usual protocol for one of them to actually interfere like this.

Nikolai saw the Igor's hand on my shoulder, and his lips instantly curled into a predatory snarl. "Stand down, junkie," he warned, and I felt it again, that searing spike of energy welling up in him.

Unconsciously, I flinched. My reaction only made the Igor's hand tighten.

Nik looked ready to come out of the car. I was sure there would have been a fight, except the bus blared its horn, protesting the car blocking the bus lane. Nik motioned at me to get in. I stood up to obey.

But as I got closer, I glimpsed the dark fire in Nikolai's eyes, and I turned and hurried onto the bus instead.

I barely found a seat before my cell phone rang. "What is *wrong* with you?" Nik asked before I could even say hello. "I thought you'd be really pleased to see me today. I only took the gig for you."

That was a lie. I mean, I'm sure I played a large role in his decision, but it was clear the band was going to get great publicity for this charity stunt. Still, despite my personal embarrassment, it was pretty cool that his band was willing to come to my school to perform, so I told him, "This isn't about the stupid school play."

There was a long moment when Nik said nothing. I even checked to see if we'd been disconnected, and was about to see if he was still there when he said, "Now I know something's seriously wrong. 'Stupid school play'? Who are you and what have you done with the real Ana Parker?"

He was trying to make light, but I wasn't in the mood. Even though the lady sitting next to me had earphones in both ears, I whispered into the receiver, "You're so quick to pull up that freaking blade. You know it hurts me."

More silence, only this time it was much deeper. When he finally spoke, his tone was clipped. "Actually, I forget. I don't think of you as one of them."

"Well, I am 'them.' I'm their goddamn princess." A person with a better-honed dramatic sense, like Bea, for instance, would have snapped the phone shut at that moment and ended the conversation. But I wanted to hear what Nikolai would say to that, so I waited. The more the silence grew, the more I started to regret my words. I didn't really mean to come on that strong. "Goddamn" was a little harsh, and Nik was sort of apologizing in a backhanded way when he said he forgot I was a vamp, and—

And I should probably say something, because I wasn't sure he would.

"Maybe we need to talk about this stuff," I said hopefully. "You know, really air everything out."

"Yeah," he agreed gruffly.

"How about you drop by tonight after eight and we can go somewhere?"

"Sure," was all he said, and I didn't need the powers of a True Witch to sense the looming breakup.

"Okay, cool," I said without enthusiasm. Well, at least I had solved one of my problems—no one would be jealous that I was a rock star's girlfriend anymore. "See you then. Bye."

Well, way to screw that up, I thought as I closed the phone and tucked it into the front pocket of my backpack. I almost pulled it back out to text Bea, but I wouldn't get much sympathy from that corner. I could always send a "he's all yours," but I shouldn't get her hopes up. After all, I didn't know for sure it was over.

It just felt like it.

Tell me again why boys were such jerks?

Chapter Two

If Nikolai knew the real reason I told him to drop by at eight instead of earlier, things between us would've definitely been over—no conversation.

I was expecting Elias at the house.

Nikolai couldn't stand Elias. Elias wasn't just any old vampire. He was like the prince's personal guard or something. Anyway, he was incredibly powerful, and Nikolai and his dad, the vampire hunter, desperately wanted to bag him.

I left the usual signal for Elias—a red sock dangling from the windowsill—to let him know I was "receiving," which was his courtly way of saying that it was safe to come by. I wished, however, we had a more elaborate system, like my striped Wicked Witch of the West stocking to say, "Watch out for Mom—she's in a bad mood," or a black one to indicate, "We have to keep this short because the hunter's apprentice is coming at eight."

I'd have to hang out all three tonight. For some reason, Mom was crankier than usual. She completely freaked out over the fact that I'd taken the city bus home. Why didn't I call her? Did I want to worry her to death?

I tried not to roll my eyes the entire time she talked. Who knew that six minutes later than usual would be such a big deal? Especially since most Wednesdays she worked so late at the university—running one of her women's spirituality groups— that I was usually asleep when she got home. That was the whole reason I had Elias come by on Wednesdays in the first place.

Mom also despised Elias. It was more than just the protective-lioness thing—my mom was the Queen of Witches. Thanks to that whole former slave/owner thing, vampires and witches didn't get along. At all.

Next to Nikolai and his dad, Mom was vampire hater number one. She refused Elias entry over the threshold, so when he came courting, he sat in the top branches of the giant spruce outside my window. Vampires liked hanging out in trees for some reason—hell elves, I'm telling you.

Anyway, I couldn't figure out why mom threw such a snit fit. I'd taken the bus home a bunch of times before. I suspected the real reason for her ballistic mood was the Igors. Mom probably caught sight of them before they disappeared into the underbrush of our neighbor's garden. The lots were wide here in Crocus Hill, and many people took advantage and planted small forests for privacy. Our neighbor claimed to be green, but I think he was just lazy and didn't want to mow, and thus, it was a perfect place for the Igors to go to ground. Mom liked to pretend that I didn't have an "honor guard."

Let's get real—Mom liked to imagine I wasn't a vampire princess at all.

Anytime anything happened that reminded her, snap!—she

became Ms. Cranky Pants. Dinner had been frosty. I was just as glad to escape to my room upstairs, doing homework and waiting for Elias.

I glanced out the window. It was warm enough to have the storm windows up. It was too early in the season for crickets, but the birds heralded the sunset with muffled chatter. A woodpecker added a staccato beat to their symphony by pounding noisily on the telephone pole. The breeze held the promise of rain and the delicate scent of the neighbor's apple blossoms.

I tried to concentrate on my history chapter, but my gaze bounced over the words and flicked instead between the cell and the window. I picked up the phone and tried to will Nikolai to text. Setting it back with a sigh, I peered into the gathering darkness for a sign of Elias.

"Trouble?" he asked, the nearness of his voice startling me. Leaning forward, Elias's pale form seemed to materialize out of the tangle of branches just beyond my window. His inky black hair was cut short, above the ears. The style always seemed a bit militaristic to me and not very vampy, and when I asked him about it, he said it was a close approximation of what was popular when he was brought across the Veil.

As always when he was using his vampiric powers, Elias's pupils were bright yellow, and cat-slit. Once he'd settled in, they'd return to their normal color, a captivating stormy gray. I'd never had the courage to ask which was his real eye color.

He pointed to my phone. "Are you expecting news?"

"Probably not," I said, setting the cell aside. "Nikolai and I might be fighting."

At the mention of Nik's name, Elias pulled back into the shadows slightly. I was sure he was trying to hide his expression, but the darkness served only to make him look more sinister. "It would be my deepest pleasure to defend your honor if my rival has besmirched it in any way."

Elias always talked like that. Sometimes it took me a few minutes to parse out what he was really trying to say. "No, you can't go beat him up." I smiled once I had. "And he might not be your rival anymore either."

"Oh, most unfortunate," he said. Though he'd pulled back so that his face was now completely hidden, I totally heard his unconscious smile at the thought.

"You're the worst liar, Elias Constantine." I flicked off my desk lamp and used my feet to wheel my desk chair over to the window. I leaned my elbows on the sill. From this position and with the lights off, I could see Elias more clearly.

He leaned his back casually against the trunk of the tree, his long, trim legs stretched across the branches like a lounging panther. Though vampires weren't fond of clothing for some reason, in deference to me he wore a nicely fitting black T-shirt and similarly colored jeans. His feet, however, were bare.

"Aren't you cold without boots?"

"The Mother is birthing. I tread lightly."

Did that make sense? I guess it did to a witch, at least metaphorically speaking. The earth was pregnant with new life in spring, so he walked gently. Respect for nature was one thing that vampires and witches had in common; they were both Goddess worshippers. But this was the first time I'd heard real evidence of the vampire side of it.

"Ostara is my favorite time of year," I remarked, referencing the Wiccan celebration of spring equinox, which had just passed. My mom would never call herself a Wiccan because her brand of witchcraft was much older, but to blend, we followed a lot of their customs.

Elias nodded. "Soon everything will be in bloom."

We fell into a silence and I tried, in vain, not to glance at the spot on my desk where my phone sat.

"You seem very agitated, Ana," Elias said when I returned my attention to him. He sat up straighter, swinging his feet around so that they dangled off the branch. "What did you and the hunter's apprentice fight about?"

I tried to shrug it off like it was no big deal, but I found I couldn't look him in the eye as I said, "Oh, you know, the same old—the honor guard, the fact that I'm a freaky half vampire, and all that."

Though he said nothing for a long time, I could feel the heat of his eyes on me. Finally, I looked up. He was staring intently. His eyes had gone all catty again, and his lips pressed into a thin, serious line. "I would hold you if I could."

With a graceful leap, he was on the roof. His footfalls were so soft, they sounded no louder than the rattle of a strong wind. I craned my neck, trying to figure out what he was up to.

All of a sudden, he hung upside down in front of me. I gasped in surprise to see him like that. With a deft movement, the screen snapped off its runners. There was a magical echo, like when a sudden shift in altitude makes your ears pop. I only hoped that my mom didn't sense the slight breach in her defenses.

After stashing the screen somewhere above, Elias reappeared with his arms outstretched. "Come," he said. "I can lift you."

I looked down at the ground and the two-story drop. I knew vampires were stronger than your average bear, but he was in an awkward position hanging over the edge of the sloping roof; what if we slid?

"The stars are out," Elias said, his fingers wagging impatiently. "Please, Highness, join me on the roof."

Steeling myself, I reached out the window and took his hands. His skin was warm against mine, and I felt a slight magical tingle at his nearness. I got up on my knees, with much of me hanging out the window. I felt myself waver, but his grip was strong and firm. He directed me to twist around. Then his hands were under my arms and I was airborne. I felt a momentary dizziness, but it was just a short boost, and he released me to stand beside him on the rooftop.

I lost my breath in the excitement, and it came back in a rush at the view of the carpet of stars above and my neighborhood spread out below. From this vantage point, I could see the dark ribbon of the Mississippi River in the valley and the cluster of bright downtown lights.

The air cocooned me in damp coldness, but instead of shivering, I felt exhilarated. "It's beautiful."

Elias said nothing, just held me. He was much taller than me, and my head nestled perfectly under his arm. Tentatively, I slipped my hand around his slender, taut waist. Heat exuded from his body, and I snuggled closer. Bare, silhouetted treetops, dotted with buds, lay like a lattice in front of everything. Across the river, traffic was a line of flashing lights, which we watched in companionable silence.

"I'm sorry for your pain," he said quietly, once we'd settled to lie back against the roof tiles to stare up at the specks of stars in the night sky. "But I'm not sorry that you're who you are. If you weren't the princess, we would never have met."

Our fingers entwined and he gave my palm a reassuring squeeze. My body was hyperfocused on Elias's nearness. I felt the slight touch of his legs against mine, the rough calluses on his palms, and the heat of his skin.

My mouth twisted as I tried to find words. I should agree with Elias's sentiment, at least. I really *liked* Elias. But my life had been so much simpler before I knew about my dad and vampires. "Uh, yeah," I said finally.

"You don't sound convinced, my lady."

I loved it when he called me that. It was so old-fashioned and sweet. "It's not that," I assured him. "It's all this other stuff."

Wisps of clouds threaded in front of the thin silver crescent of the moon. The shingles on the roof pinched my back slightly, but the feeling of being high above everything eclipsed any physical discomfort.

"Other stuff?" he prompted.

"Nikolai, you know, and—" But I trailed off because I didn't know how to explain what it was like to be half vampire, half witch, but not enough of either to really fit anywhere properly.

Before I could say something more articulate, Elias pulled his hand away. "You're in love with him, aren't you?"

"It doesn't matter. It would never work."

The instant it was out of my mouth, I knew I'd said the exact wrong thing. I should have denied being in love with Nik; had I really just agreed that I was? At any rate, Elias sat up, steepling his hands on his knees. His entire posture was agitated; if he were a cat, his back muscles would have rippled.

I pulled myself upright too. I thought about touching his shoulders, but decided I didn't want to see him flinch away from me. "I mean—that is, what I meant to say was I don't know how I feel about Nik. It's so complicated."

"I see." His tone was cold, distant.

A smarter person would have stopped talking, but I didn't know how to close the rift I sensed opening between us and I desperately wanted to fix it. I didn't want to lose both Elias and Nik in one day! "I feel the same way about you. Not the complicated part—well, actually, you are complicated—but what I'm saying is . . . uh, I like you."

I thought it was a pretty intense admission, but the hot glance he shot me implied he thought I was full of shit.

"No, really, Elias. I do." I tried to infuse my words with the weight of everything I couldn't say. "Why do you think things are complicated with Nikolai?"

This softened his gaze a bit. "Are you saying you fought about me?"

"Well, no. It was more about the vampire thing as a whole, and the honor guard in specific, but you're a big part of that."

"Ah." He sounded distant again.

When was I going to learn how to talk to guys without completely messing everything up? "Let me try this again," I offered.

From his reluctant smile, I think Elias would have let me make another attempt, but of course, at that very moment Nikolai's Toyota pulled up in front of my house.

We both recognized the car immediately.

He was early! I opened my mouth to offer an explanation, but the look on Elias's face stopped me.

"What is *he* doing here tonight? This is supposed to be our night."

"Um," I started, but how could I explain in a way that didn't end up with me duplicitously planning two dates in one night? Anyway, Elias was having none of it. He stood up. With inhuman bounds, he leaped the distance of the roof. In seconds, he was standing next to the tower's cap, one hand resting against its peaked, conical roof. Elias stared down at the car, as if still hoping it belonged to someone else.

Below, I could hear Nikolai's car door slam shut. In the quiet of the night, the sound of his bootheels on the sidewalk reverberated loudly.

"It is him," Elias confirmed through clenched teeth. "Perhaps we should test this junior hunter's skill."

"Wait!" I shouted to Elias, but it was too late. He launched himself into the air. Like some unholy bird, he stretched out his arms, as though they could slow his descent. In midair, he flipped over and tucked himself into a tight ball. He landed in a predatory crouch in front of Nikolai. I swear I could hear his snarl from this distance.

For his part, Nik shouted in surprise and anger. He stumbled back, plastering himself against his car.

Elias uncurled himself slowly, deliberately. "You intrude on my territory, apprentice."

"Your 'territory'? I don't think so," Nikolai growled. "You don't belong here. Not with Ana, not on earth. Make one move, demon, and I'll send you straight back to the hell that spawned you."

Like a stab to my own heart, I felt Nikolai's blade surge into life. I could almost see its orange flame flickering around his fist.

Elias had the good sense to stand perfectly still.

I held my breath. I had to stop them somehow.

Before I could call out, the front door slammed open on its

hinges. I nearly leaped from the roof in surprise. Mom stuck her head out. "What's going on out here?" Her power shot up, cold and hard, when she recognized who stood on her sidewalk. "Vampire," she hissed. "Strike him dead, Kirov."

"No!" I shouted. "Don't you dare!"

Heads swiveled in my direction. Just as I'd hoped, Elias took advantage of the resulting confusion. With speed too fast for a human eye to track, he dashed from sight. Not being human, however, I noticed his slight hesitation. Before he disappeared, our eyes met, and without words, I knew how much it disturbed Elias to leave a fight—to leave me.

"Ana?" Nik said at the same time as Mom's confused, "What are you doing on the roof, honey?"

More important, how was I going to get down?

I looked over at the tree.

It would take a superhuman jump, but, well, I had the ability. I just had to allow that part of me to surface.

"I'll get the ladder," Mom was shouting.

"Where did the vampire go?" Nikolai asked no one in particular as he scanned the street. "Damn, they're fast."

"I can get myself down," I said, even though Mom was already starting toward the carriage house/garage. I closed my eyes and let the nighttime surround me in an embrace. I surrendered to its call, and when I opened them again, I was sure my pupils changed to catlike slits, because I could see everything as though it were the light of day. Fangs descended with a flash of pain. My body felt light and . . . in tune, somehow, with the very fabric of nature.

The tree pulsed with a life of its own and seemed to reach out to me. I took a running jump, and fell into its awaiting arms.

They caught me easily, and seemed to lead, like a stairway, to the ground.

Before Mom had even reached the backyard, I landed on the soft, richly scented grass. "Sorry," I whispered to the tender shoots I'd crushed underfoot.

Nikolai's eyes were wide, and his fist stayed clenched at his side. With my vampire sight, his blade burned white-hot. I could see its pointed tip jutting from the center of his knuckles. Power sizzled through his aura like tiny flashes of lightning.

Raising my hand to shield my eyes from the intensity, I turned my head.

"Is this why you invited me here tonight?" he asked, his tone remarkably calm, almost sad. "So I could see you, like this, with him?"

Okay, Ana, don't mess it up this time.

I squared my shoulders and faced him. His aura continued to crackle. But if I didn't look at the blade shimmering in his hand like a small sun, I could meet his gaze without blinking. "That wasn't the plan, but—you know, we should talk about this." I waved my hand to indicate my face and the fangs and the crazy cat eyes I was sure he noticed, even in the dark. "I feel like it's coming between us."

Mom came around the corner. She squeaked and dropped the ladder with a clang when she saw me standing there. "How did you get down? Please tell me you didn't . . ." Her hand flew to her mouth, as she took in all that was my fabulous vampire self. "Oh, Ana! Don't stand there looking like that!"

She made it sound like I was on the front lawn in my underwear. Mom was looking at me with undisguised horror.

My hands on my hips, I spun to tell her what I thought about all that, but Nikolai spoke first.

"It's all right, Dr. Parker," Nikolai said, using Mom's honorific the way Elias called me "Highness." "It's under control. I just came by to ask Ana out for a malt."

A malt? What was this, the 1950s?

"Oh, that sounds delightful," Mom said, instantly forgetting her horror at seeing me all vamped up. It kind of freaked me out, the way Nik and my mom interacted. It was so clear that my mom wanted Nikolai and me to be together, like a normal couple, that she pushed to the point of being . . . well, icky. Plus, she sort of fluttered around him. Like, she was all into him. I was doing my best not to gag, when my mom added, "Do you need some cash, Ana?"

I rarely refused the offer of money, even at a time like this. I had my hand out, but once again, Nik interrupted me before I could even start.

"I've got it covered, Dr. Parker."

"Please, Nikolai, call me Amelia."

Please don't!

"I'll have her home before eleven, Amelia."

Ugh! He did!

Nikolai opened the car door with a rusty squeal. He gestured all gentlemanly-like for me to take a seat, as if I'd already agreed to this ridiculous malt.

"I'm not sure—"

"Oh, go ahead, sweetheart," Mom said, pushing her round glasses up on her nose. She might be the most powerful witch in the Midwest, but she still looked like a frumpy college professor.

Her blond curls spilled out from a makeshift bun. The fabric of her olive cotton skirt rode up a bit, and there was a greasy smear where she'd balanced the ladder against her ample hip. "You can even stay out to midnight, if you're going to be with Nik."

Whom, five minutes ago, you were telling to kill Elias. "I have homework."

"Do it in the morning," Mom offered sweetly, if somewhat insincerely. I could see it pained her, the teacher, to even suggest such slacking.

"We do need to talk, Ana," Nikolai reminded me gently. "Please."

It was the "please" that did it. I felt the fangs click back into concealment, and the night dimmed around me. With a sigh, I slumped into the passenger side of Nik's Toyota.

Apparently Nik was serious about the malt. We ended up in a booth in the back of Snuffy's on Cleveland. The restaurant had an honest-to-goodness lunch counter, a jukebox, and red vinyl-covered seats. Photos and framed newspaper articles featuring local sports stars from the seventies to the present day adorned the wall.

"Okay, this is surreally *Leave It to Beaver,*" I said, taking another look at the retro decor. "What are you up to, Nikolai Kirov?"

"I just really wanted a malt," he said with a shrug. It was striking how much like a traditional vampire Nik looked. Under the fluorescent lights, his pale skin had an almost greenish cast. His hair was long enough to tie back, though he usually let it fall loosely to his shoulders. The studded leather jacket amped up the bad-boy vibe.

In contrast, Elias, the actual vampire, usually tended toward business-casual.

Weird.

After a gum-snapping waitress in her forties took our order—was this place for real?—I watched Nik studiously avoid me. He played with the corner of the paper place mat, instead, folding and unfolding the corner.

"My eyes are back to normal," I assured him. "You *can* look at me."

He leaned back against the booth, the leather creaking as he crossed his arms in front of his chest. Despite what I said, he stared at the watch on his wrist as he spoke. "Things are getting intense at home. You know, after I turned eighteen in October?" He sneaked a look at me, but didn't wait to see my reaction. "Papa wants me to 'graduate.'"

He didn't mean from college, and I knew it. "But you can't! You have to kill a vampire to do that."

His sharp glance and a nervous check around the room made me realize I hadn't said that as quietly as I probably should have. I wasn't too worried. I'd hung around with Taylor's friends when they talked about ax-murdering trolls encountered in computer games and no one ever looked twice. "I know," he said, keeping his voice pitched low. "But I can't hold him off much longer."

"You're going to have to," I whispered harshly. "You can't kill my friends."

"Now they're your friends? I thought they were just your 'people.'"

I didn't want to get into petty semantics. I struggled to keep my voice down. "You can't kill anybody. It's not right."

Nikolai bowed his head, running his fingers through his hair. "I have to do something, soon."

"Why don't you tell your dad the truth? Tell him you don't want to be a vampire hunter."

He looked up at me then, his amber eyes flashing dangerously dark. "Because, Ana," he said. "That's *not* the truth."

I pressed my back stiffly into the vinyl of the booth, trying to absorb what Nikolai had just said. When my brain couldn't process it, I dumbly asked, "Are you saying you *want* to be a vampire hunter?"

He went back to fiddling with his place mat, as I tried to remember to breathe. My understanding had always been that Nikolai's family expected him, as their only son, to take up his father's paranormal vocation, but that Nik had his own feelings about the whole affair—even before we became involved. Had he changed his mind? I watched him intently, trying to read the answer in his posture, his movements.

Nikolai scratched the back of his neck, considering. He let out a measured sigh. "Look, I don't know, Ana. I was serious about what I said to Constantine earlier. Vampires don't belong here. Ask him and I'm sure he'd tell you he'd rather be home, beyond the Veil. You know as well as I do that their whole culture is based on homesickness."

He seemed to want an answer, but all I had was a shrug. That jibed with what little I did know about vampire culture. Elias had told me that they based the hierarchy of their society on what they remembered of the place they'd been stolen from. The First Witch had ripped them from their home, and once on this side, it took a magical death at the hands of someone like Nikolai's father to send them back.

Still, I didn't see vampires lining up to throw themselves on Nik's psychic blade.

"So you're just performing a public service?" I couldn't quite keep the snark from my tone.

"Wouldn't the world be a better place without vampires?"

I might have had a smarter comeback if I hadn't had my own doubts about being half vampire. Instead I pulled the paper wrapping from the straw and looked over at the kitchen as if I suddenly cared how long it took them to make my chocolate malt.

"You see my problem," Nikolai said, as if my silence meant I agreed with him.

"But I don't," I said. "If it's really just that simple—that the vampires don't belong here—why doesn't the Council of Witches concoct a spell to send them all back? Tidy up their problem, as it were?"

The waitress came with our drinks. She put out tall glasses and shook the malts from the metal containers. The smile she gave Nik and me was sly, like she thought we were a cute couple.

Once she left, Nik returned to my question. "I suspect you're part of the reason." To my confused look, he added, "No one knows what will happen to you if they do something like that."

I shook my head. The ice-cream drink was so thick I used a spoon to take a bite, and then I waved the tip of it at Nik. "Vampires have been around since the first goddess cultures in the Stone Age. My dad came over under one of the Ramses pharaohs. Witches could have solved their vampire problem well before I was born."

"The talisman was only lost a few decades ago. They were useful to the witches before."

Before. It was a much more loaded word than it seemed. *Before* the secret war, *before* the vampires contrived to steal the mysterious talisman that kept them in thrall, and *before* it was lost to both parties—or hidden; I was never sure.

"And," I said, slurping a big mouthful of malt now that it was soft enough, "there are those vampires who have stayed loyal servants. No one wants to lose their 'useful' slaves."

Nikolai grimaced at his glass. "Yeah, there's that."

I was glad that it seemed that we both found that idea distasteful. "It's weird," I said, taking a long sip of my malt. "I've never understood why anyone would stay with someone who used to, you know, *own* them."

Nik lifted his shoulder. "Vampires had been our slaves for thousands of years. It was the life they knew. I suppose it was comforting for some to stay."

"Sounds like the party line," I said with a sneer.

"How do you explain it?"

I couldn't.

But there was a lot I didn't understand about vampires. The "loyal servant" faction was the reason I had an honor guard. Occasionally, one of them tried to kill my dad, and a couple of times last year, at least, they went after me.

I think that was the other reason my mom hated seeing the Igors trailing me; it reminded her of the problems in her own camp. If someone in the coven was sending servants to assassinate my dad or me, they weren't playing by the rules of the truce.

I never could figure out why anyone would want my dad

dead—or deader, anyway. Okay, so Khan thought he was a sexist or whatever, but he always seemed okay to me. It wasn't like I saw evidence of his provoking witches all the time.

"You know, if you guys would just leave the free vampires alone, there'd be peace," I said, pushing my malt glass away. Since awakening the half-vampire part of me, I noticed it didn't take much food to fill me up. "What is your beef with them, anyway?"

Nik seemed to have lost interest in his malt as well. "You're serious?"

"What?"

"Your dad is a menace, Ana."

"In what way?" I meant the question to be sincere, but from the way Nik frowned, I must have sounded a bit defensive.

"He incites his people to violence against us. Why do you think the coven recruited my dad from Russia?"

Actually, I'd never considered that they had. I always thought that Nikolai's dad moved to America for the same reasons Taylor's family did, because this was supposed to be the promised land for immigrants. I guess that seemed silly when I thought about it that way. "Uh," was my only intelligible response.

"Most covens in America don't need hunters. Your dad has made the Midwest region extraspecial."

Maybe if Nikolai hadn't sneered at that point, I would have reacted better. "My dad?" I sputtered. "Maybe your dad fed you a load of bull. Did it ever occur to you that maybe your dad was brought over to threaten mine?"

Nikolai's jaw tightened. "It's getting late. We should get you home. We don't want your mom worrying."

"Don't be like that," I said, following him as he made his way to the cash register with the bill. "I didn't mean to blurt that out," I added, which was true, even though I did think it was possible that Mr. Vampire Hunter might be a bit biased against my dad. "Whatever."

I chewed on my lip as he paid up and we walked out to where the car was parked along the street. I was trying to decide how to put what I wanted to say. I sat for a long time before buckling up, and finally gave up on diplomacy. "It really bothers you— what I am—doesn't it?"

He didn't say anything, and I'd have to turn on my vampire eyes to read his expression in the darkened interior of the car.

Even I knew that was a bad idea right now, so I just kept talking. "You used to say it kind of made you feel, uh, turned on dating one of the 'enemy.' I guess that's not working so much for you anymore. Maybe we should take a, you know, break."

It was hard saying "break" like that even without the "up." Just the thought of not seeing Nik on a regular basis made my stomach drop. I'd miss him. Worse, I knew that there were so many other *normal*, uncomplicated girls waiting for just such an opportunity to pounce. I suspected once I let him go, I'd never see him again. But how could I blame him if he wanted something simple like that?

I blinked back the tears forming in my eyes, and busied myself with the seat belt.

His hand touched my thigh lightly. There wasn't the instant magical awareness like with Elias, but my body tingled in a very physical, *human* response.

"Maybe we should."

Chapter Three

To my credit, I held it together until I got home. Mom was surprised to see me back before ten, but I offered little explanation beyond "I'll tell you later." Even that came out kind of quivery, so I had to dash up the stairs.

When I made it to the safety of my room, I shut the door and flung myself on my bed. There I let the floodgates go. I cried until I left wet spots on my pillow.

"I wish it were still fashionable to challenge him to a duel." I nearly choked at the sound of Elias's soft voice at the window. "Though it pleases me to see an obstacle removed, I never relish your pain. A curse upon him who casts aside your affection so callously."

"It's not like that." I swallowed a sniff and palmed the tears from my cheeks. "It was a mutual decision. Kind of."

"Do your tears bear false witness, then?"

It took me a second to figure out what he meant, and then I shook my head. "No, I'm crying because it still sucks to break up."

"Indeed. And I still hate him."

Despite everything, that brought a slight smile to my face. "You would no matter what, Elias."

"True enough," he agreed. The night had grown darker, but the streetlamp across the road illuminated just a hint of his pale, fine-boned cheek beneath a canopy of pine needles.

I was sure that if I was up for it, Elias would happily listen to me complain about Nikolai all night. I wasn't in the mood. Plus I didn't really have anything against Nik, not really. He was a vampire hunter's apprentice. I was a vampire. End of story.

All I wanted to do was wallow. Maybe even stereotypically inhale a pint or two of mocha ice cream, and listen to sad, weepy music on my iPod.

"Hey, it's really cool that you waited up for me and everything, but I want to, well, be—"

He didn't let me finish. I heard rather than saw him shift on the branch as if readying to leave. "Of course, my lady, you must have time to grieve alone. Though my main intent was to watch for your safe return, I also came with a message. Your father wishes to speak with you about the matter of an engagement you broke. I'll stall him as long as I can. Though you know your father—he won't wait forever, and this is a matter of some urgency."

I blew my nose in a Kleenex. "What are you talking about?"

"Did you give Khan permission to break her engagement?"

"Yeah, I guess I did."

"It was foolish. Her marriage had been arranged to strengthen relations with the Southern region's prince. The boy she loves is a loyal servant." Elias spat the last words like they were such a foul concept that they were literally distasteful.

What did I care if Khan loved a servant or a human? "Look, it was romantic," I said, feeling my heart go all wobbly again. A tear sneaked out of the corner of my eye.

"Ah, I understand," I heard him sigh in the darkness. "Yet, I believe I shall let *you* explain your actions to your father, the prince."

Given how willing Elias usually was to insert himself between me and any conflict, this probably meant Pop was pretty angry. "Whatever. I can handle Dad."

I thought I heard a chuckle as he left in a rustle of pine needles.

A knock on my door made me jump. "Honey, are you talking on the phone to someone? Can I come in? What happened with Nikolai? You seem kind of upset."

Kind of? Yeah, that was the understatement of the year. "Go away, Mom."

"I don't mean to intrude, but is everything okay with you and Nik? You came home awfully early. Did you fight about that vampire? You know I've told you not to have him around here."

Technically, she'd said "in the house," but I didn't want to get into yet another fight about Elias and vampires tonight. "Mom, seriously, I don't want to talk about it. Not right now."

"Okay, honey. Should I bring up some hot chocolate or something?"

My lip trembled. "Yeah, that'd be nice."

Of course, I knew it was all part of her devious plan to get me to talk to her, but it totally worked.

In twenty minutes she was sitting on the opposite end of my bed. She sat cross-legged with her back against the metal frame and a steaming mug of cocoa resting on her knee. My laptop playing Taylor Swift's "Teardrops on My Guitar" on a constant loop was the only illumination. I hugged the box of tissues to my chest as I tried to talk through the sobs. "It's a break. Not a breakup. At least I hope so."

"Well, that's not so bad," she said, taking a sip. "Maybe he needs a little space."

I rolled my eyes. "Don't be dumb, Mom. There must be, like, a thousand girls waiting to date the lead singer of Ingress." She looked confused, so I added, "You know. Older girls."

She adjusted her glasses. "What's Ingress again?"

This was why Mom was rarely my confidante. If it didn't involve million-year-old goddess cultures in Anatolia or wherever, she had no clue. "Nik's band."

"So this is about groupies? I thought you were fighting about vampires."

"We *are* fighting about vampires; the groupies just make this whole thing that much worse. A break means the exclusivity clause is off, you know? Do you think a guy like Nik isn't going to jump on the opportunity to—?" I stopped because I was stumbling into embarrassing territory, and I could see the lightbulb flicker to life behind Mom's eyes.

"Cat around?" she said.

I was glad the dark of the room hid the heat on my cheeks. "Yeah, something like that. I don't really want to talk about this anymore." Mostly because I was afraid she'd start trying to explain birds and bees and condoms again.

To my surprise, Mom nodded. She stretched her legs, and then stood. "Try to get some sleep. There's school tomorrow."

"Okay. Uh, thanks."

"You're welcome, sweetie. Believe me—I understand that

men are complicated. You and Nik will work things out. I have faith."

I frowned at that. Hadn't I just explained why we wouldn't?

She headed down the stairs, with a little "It'll be okay" wave. At least my awkwardness at talking with Mom briefly overwhelmed the ache in my heart. I snuggled under the comforter, and pulled it up over my head. I fell asleep humming the refrain of "Teardrops on My Guitar."

I woke up to rain pouring from dismal gray clouds, matching my mood perfectly. Thankfully, Mom was already off at one of her college gigs, so I munched my cornflakes silently, watching the rain streaking like tears down the glass.

Our house was way too big for the two of us, but Mom had inherited it from the Parker witches. Grandma and Grandpa had been dead as long as I could remember, but we lived with their memories and leftover stuff inside a gigantic estate in the trendy Crocus Hill neighborhood. The Victorian was more than a hundred years old, and every burst of wind caused its joints to creak and crack. This morning, especially, with thunder rattling the windows, the rooms felt cavernous and huge. Lightning threw long, flickering shadows across the expanse of the dusty, unused parlor, down the golden hardwood hallway, to glitter on the glass beads of the heavy chandelier above my head. I sat in my customary chair in the corner of a dining room set that could easily seat twenty. The noise of my spoon clanking against the bowl was the only sign of human habitation.

With a heavy and resigned sigh, I padded on stocking feet to the kitchen. There, I put my dishes in the sink and then wandered out toward the door to get ready for school. I found my bright yellow raincoat in the closet by the door and an umbrella in a wicker basket near the coatrack. Shouldering my backpack, I headed off to the bus stop.

Umbrellas were so stupid. They never really kept the wind from sneaking under and spattering your face with wet. The fourth time it bent backward, I gave up on it and collapsed it. Thus, my hair was completely soaked by the time I found a seat on the bus next to a shy, first-grade girl with thick braids and frog eyes on the hood of her rain jacket. The weather subdued the usual raucous mood, and we bounced along glumly, everything smelling of moistness. The older kids' gossip had already shifted to a new topic—apparently someone had done some kind of typical high school prank—and so, thankfully, no one asked after Nik or Ingress.

I read my history chapters as the bus shuddered from stop to stop.

When we got to Stassen, I waved good-bye to the little girl. She rewarded me with a big white smile.

Bea and Taylor waited by my locker. My Converses were completely soaked, and the rubber treads squeaked on the polished linoleum floor. When I saw my friends, I considered dashing into Mr. Knutson's art room to hide, but Bea saw me and waved.

They both looked so happy; I felt miserable.

Taylor hopped up and down on her toes with excitement. "You didn't text us!" she admonished. "How did it go with Nik last night?"

"Oh, great," I said as casually as possible as I dialed the combination to the lock. "We broke up."

Though I quickly buried my head in my locker, I could almost see their horrified double takes in the pregnant silence.

"You're not serious," Bea said. "This is a bad attempt at a joke, right?"

"I thought he got this gig with the musical just to hang out with you," Taylor added. "Why would he break things off?"

I shoved the books I needed for the next couple of periods into my backpack, and then pronounced, "Boys are stupid."

"Yes, but they're so cute." Bea smiled, the wheels clearly turning over her plan on how to make her move now that Nikolai was free. Bea had always had a crush on Nik.

"I thought older guys were supposed to be more mature," Taylor said, sounding honestly confused. "He always seemed so into you. What changed?"

Bea and I exchanged a glance. She knew about the vampire/hunter/witch problem, but Taylor was our nonmagical friend. All the mystical stuff was supposed to be secret.

So I shrugged and offered up something I hoped she'd understand. "His dad is Russian, you know. I guess they're kind of traditional. There's a lot of pressure for Nik to follow in his dad's footsteps."

Bea gave me an appreciative nod, like she was impressed at how accurate I could be without saying anything about vampires.

Taylor chewed on her lip for a moment, tugged thoughtfully on her *hijab*, and then came to the conclusion: "Man, I hate that family shit."

I laughed a little. "Yeah, me too."

"The musical is going to be way awkward," Bea noted solemnly, as we made our way to first period.

Except, even updated to some kind of rock opera, *My Fair Lady* was *so* not my kind of production. What kind of part was there for a gangly, pasty girl with different-colored eyes?

"I'm not even sure I'm going to try out," I said, though my gut clenched at the mere thought. I'd never missed a show.

"What?" Bea couldn't have sounded more offended. "Ana Parker, you are going to the ball! No boy is going to keep you from the audition!"

"Yes," Taylor agreed, taking up the cause with enthusiasm. "The show must go on!"

"Besides," Bea said, quite seriously, when we'd come to my classroom, "you know you're the best singer of any of us"— which meant a lot coming from Queen Bea, who always considered herself a diva and the best of everything theatrical.

"Wow, Bea. You mean it?"

She flipped a wave of her dyed black and pink hair over her shoulder and said, "Of course. Besides, you can't let down Stassen High just because some stupid boy hasn't the sense to hold on to a good thing. Us theater freaks have to band together, you know."

I smiled at her. "Great pep talk, BB. Can you give it to me again the day before auditions?"

"Silly goose, auditions *are* tonight!"

That news threw a wrench into the rest of my day.

I hadn't planned on concentrating terribly hard during classes, since I'd expected to wallow over the breakup for at least a few days, but now my mind raced. What should I sing? Should I really go? Had Mom washed my lucky audition shirt?

The good news was I didn't think about Nik at all; the bad news was that I was so distracted that I missed Mr. Feirria's explanation of a really critical function in precalculus, and I completely botched a pop quiz in biology.

But by lunch I'd figured out that I was going to sing the "Wouldn't It Be Loverly" song, since I mostly knew the words already. I hated musical tryouts, actually. I thought of myself more as an actor than a singer. I tended to get stage fright when asked to sing, especially solo.

I was chewing on my sandwich, and my thoughts, when Bea pulled up the chair. "Hey," she said with a sympathetic pat on my shoulder.

Suddenly, looking up into her big, brown, pity-filled eyes, all my Nik emotions came rushing back. Bread and cheese stuck in my throat. "Hey," I managed to choke in return.

"He said it was your idea," she said without preamble.

My milk came out with a *spat*. "You texted Nik already? Damn, Bea! Let the body cool before you pounce!"

Bea laughed like I wasn't seriously pissed. "I thought you'd want to know he's depressed about it."

That was something at least; misery loves company. Still, I shot Bea a warning stare.

She neatly unfolded her bento box. "So—was it? Your idea, that is?"

"I guess I sort of suggested it, but, for the record, I expected him to protest and not agree right away." I leaned closer and dropped my voice. "I meant what I said to Taylor. His dad is pressuring him to, you know . . ."

"Ah," she said, but I could tell she wasn't as horrified by the prospect as I. I suspected that Bea and Nik shared a similar attitude about vampires. Bea, at least, had contact with only one—well, half a one: me. And we'd agreed not to really discuss that stuff. "I suppose it's star-crossed-lover stuff, you and him."

Her reference to *Romeo and Juliet* only further served to depress me. I munched dejectedly on my cheddar cheese sandwich. Finally, I asked what I'd wanted to all along, "Did he say anything else?"

"Not really," she said in a way that made me think perhaps he had. I glanced up at her, trying to read her expression. She seemed unaccountably fascinated by the contents of her box, and wouldn't look up at me. Then, I saw it: the hint of a blush! That cheat!

"You have a date or something, don't you?"

She blushed harder, and looked around nervously at everything but me. "It's not a date. He's not ready for that."

"But you're going out."

"Just to talk," she said. Finally, her eyes met mine, with an expression that begged forgiveness. "He said the breakup was your idea, Ana. I thought it would be okay with you."

"Bullshit!" I snapped. "And it's a break, not a break*up*."

"What? He said things were over with you."

I couldn't believe this. Shoving the remains of my sandwich into my bag with trembling hands, I got up. "Look, I don't even care," I lied. What I meant was I couldn't deal right now. My head hurt. My own best friend! Less than twenty-four hours later! "Okay, well, when you see him, say hi for me, will you?" I all but yelled, and stormed off.

"It's not like that, Ana. I swear," I heard her say, but I didn't even turn around.

Could this day get worse?

* * *

During study hall, I slunk off to the back of the library again. This time, I sat on the floor in the dusty poetry section, my legs splayed out in front of me. Randomly pulling books off the shelf, I flipped through pages until I found one that spoke to what I was feeling. The poem was several thousand years old, from someone named Sappho, but it pretty much summed up everything:

"To Eros," it was called, the god of love. The only line was, "You burn me."

The words inspired me to pull out my phone. Though the signal was weak, I was able to get enough bars to send an angry text to Nikolai. It wasn't nearly as succinct or cutting as Sappho, but I thought it held a certain poetry of its own: "Going out with B already? You suck!"

What else was there to say? I sent it, stabbed the Off button, and slammed the phone closed.

It wasn't difficult to avoid Bea most of the day. We didn't have any classes in common until drama, last period.

Seeing her standing with Taylor at her locker made my lips purse into a thin line of pure hate. To think that at the beginning of the day she was cheerleading me, trying to talk up tryouts, and by noon, she'd utterly betrayed me! I was so angry. I stomped right past the two of them without even a backward glance.

Mr. Martinez's eyebrows quirked upward to see me come into the room without my usual entourage, but I ignored him too. I went to my seat, opened my book, and put my nose into it, like I lived to study *My Fair Lady*.

I looked up only when I heard Taylor say, "No, I don't think so. Even if he is a rock star, friends should come first."

Catching my gaze, Taylor gave me an "I'm with you" smile.

Ugh. I didn't want it to come to the whole friends-choosing-sides-in-the-divorce thing. It made me depressed and pissed off all at the same time. Damn Nik's vampire-hunting family, and double-damn Bea for being such a flirt that she couldn't leave well enough alone.

I refused to look at either of them. Instead, I concentrated on being a good student. I filled my notebook with salient bits about the Industrial Age in England, and doodled broken hearts and cartoonish pictures of Bea with Xs for eyes and a halo of daggers around her head. Jinny tapped my shoulder. I thought about acting like I hadn't felt it, but it wasn't Jinny's fight, so it didn't seem right to snub her. Just as I twisted in my seat to retrieve the missive, Mr. Martinez swooped in between us and snatched it up.

"Perhaps I should read this out loud if it's important enough to disrupt class time for, eh?"

Across the room, Bea made a gasping sound. Then, I felt magic tickling the air, like the cloying scent of lilies.

Mr. Martinez unfolded the note. I half expected it to burst into flames in his hands, but instead he adjusted the round glasses on his nose and frowned. "Code? You people are getting very clever. Ms. Parker," he said to me. "You can retrieve your highly classified secret missive after class, understood?"

"Muh," I said, because embarrassment had choked out any articulate response.

Bea let out a breath of relief that released the tingle of magic in the air. My nose stopped itching. We shared a glance and a conspiratorial smile flicked across her lips, like we were still friends. I sharpened my expression to remind her we weren't.

The bonus was that when the bell finally rang, I had an excuse to hang around while Bea and everyone else filed out. Mr. Martinez had placed the note on the corner of his desk. He was putting files into his briefcase when I stopped to pick it up. "You are coming to tryouts tonight, aren't you, Ana?"

Taylor loitered near the door, clearly waiting for a chance to talk. I nodded for her to wait up just a second. "Yeah, I guess," I said.

Mr. Martinez feigned horror. He placed a long-boned hand on his slender chest. "You guess? Surely you can muster more excitement. Thanks to Ingress, this should be the social event of the season."

"Yippee."

He frowned at my sarcasm, and seemed ready to ask me more.

"I have to go. Don't want to miss my bus," I said.

"See you tonight?"

"Yeah," I agreed. That was, if Mom had washed my lucky shirt and I had decided I could face seeing Nik for the entire run of the show.

"I can't believe Bea," Taylor said as soon as we'd rounded the corner from Bea's locker. She shot a glance over her shoulder, as if she worried that Bea could somehow hear anything over all the clamor of students at the end of the day. "You only broke up with Nik last night."

"It was supposed to be a break, not a breakup," I kept insisting, though clearly I was the only one who thought so.

"Oh, breaks never work," Taylor told me, unhelpfully. "Unless you really talk about what it means, you know, lay some ground rules. Did you do that? Did you decide if it was going to be monogamous or how long it should last?"

"No," I said miserably.

"Trust me, boys need clear rules."

Taylor exclusively dated the nerd-gamer set, which was particularly fond of rules, especially if they involved hit-point charts, but I could see her point.

"I don't really understand how Bea can horn in; I thought you said that this was about Nikolai's family. They wanted him to date inside the gene pool, right? Bea's last name is 'Braith-waite.' She's not Russian or Romany, is she?" Taylor continued. We stopped at her locker. It was weird not to have Bea there. The end-of-the-day debriefing had been such a long-standing tradition.

"She's a witch," I said, even though I probably shouldn't. Taylor knew that much, though she thought we were the garden-variety Wiccan types. "They're in the same coven."

Where most girls had pinups of the latest teen heartthrobs, Taylor had character sheets from favorite role-playing campaigns and screen shots from the online game she obsessed over.

"Oh," Taylor said, giving me a confused look. "I thought you were a witch too."

"I failed my graduation test," I admitted. "I'm kind of on the auxiliary team now."

Taylor had been around, though on the outside, when all that had gone down earlier this school year. Her thin eyebrows knit together. "That distinction matters?"

"Oh, yeah," I said, especially since I failed the Initiation be-cause I was half vampire, and oh, an entire troop of vampires showed up and crashed the show and declared me their princess. "A lot."

"No offense," she said, "but religions can be really stupid, especially when it comes to stuff like this."

"I hear ya, sister," I said with a soft smile.

I pressed my cheek against the window of the bus and watched the trees roll by. The rain had made the leaves pop, and everything was covered in a haze of green. The sidewalks and road had been stained a darker gray, but light reflected off every wet surface.

My phone trilled with a received text. I hadn't remembered switching the phone on, and the bus driver shot me a dark scowl. Dragging my backpack into my lap, I dug through everything until I found my phone.

When I saw it was from Nik, I almost didn't open it. I mean, did I really want to read a hostile reply to my angry note? Oh! That reminded me—I still had the note from Bea.

Gee, which horror to open first?

I could guess what Bea's note contained. She probably wanted forgiveness and to make excuses. I so wasn't in the mood for that, so I flipped open the cell. To my surprise, Nik's text read: "Forget B. I need 2 see u 2 nite."

"What's changed?" I wrote back.

Two seconds later, he replied, "Everything."

"After auditions?" I asked, not quite believing I was agreeing to this, considering how mad and hurt I was.

"OK."

Suddenly, I had a date with Nikolai again. WTF?

Chapter Four

I was changing into my lucky audition clothes when I came across Bea's note wadded up in the pocket of my jeans. My first impulse was to toss it in the garbage, but I was going to see her in less than an hour. Sitting down on the bed, I carefully unfolded the scrap of lined notebook paper. My fingers buzzed with the residual magic that had transformed it into unreadable code for Mr. Martinez. In Bea's loopy, expansive cursive I read: "I know you think I'm a slut." No wonder she didn't want this read out loud! I continued reading. "But I have no chance with Nikolai. No one does. He's so into you, it's sad. He'd do anything for you."

Which would have been awesome if she'd left it there, but that wouldn't be Bea—she had to add, "P.S. Doesn't mean I can't be a shoulder for him to cry on. You can't blame a girl for trying."

Actually, I could.

Plus, the little smiley face she drew after the last line ticked me off. Somehow it managed to look smug. I ripped the note into shreds.

I mean, I supposed I could take the higher ground. Nik was taking me out tonight to talk about how everything had changed, so I'd kind of won the bigger argument. Still. It didn't change the fact that Bea was unapologetically trying to steal him from me.

Maybe Taylor was right. There should be detailed rules for situations like this. Boys were available for pouncing, but only after an appropriate time of mourning. Two weeks, maybe. Previous girlfriend gets dibs on changes of heart within twenty-four hours.

I snorted a laugh at the thought. Mom called for me to get going if I wanted a ride back to school.

Mom had some horrible New Age album playing in the MINI. A chorus of women was chanting about a boundless, protective goddess that I doubted ever existed. I reached for the Stop button. "How can you listen to this crap, Mom?"

"It's empowering. You wouldn't know—you've grown up with all the advantages my generation of feminists fought for."

Switching to a Lady Gaga song, I rolled my eyes. "School's out, Ma. No lectures, please."

Mom adjusted her glasses before taking her eyes away from the road for a moment to frown at me. "Maybe you wouldn't be so—" She flattened her lips rather than choosing an adjective, and then continued. "If you could experience a bit of magic now and again. You should join one of my women's groups."

"Magic? You're calling your little separatist meetings magic now?"

"Ana," she scolded. "You of all people should know that

there's more than one kind of magic. So theirs isn't the capital-letter kind. It still has a place."

I couldn't imagine it would be satisfying to sit around a circle of mundane women wishing really hard when I knew that Bea could just point her finger and "zap" reality to any shape she wanted. "I don't think it's my thing, Mom."

"You shouldn't judge before you try it."

Oh no, she used the *tone*. Mom had already made up her mind. I was going, like it or not. "Uh," I said. "I might have rehearsals, remember?"

"Do you really think there's a part for you in *My Fair Lady*?"

That was it, then—even my own mother thought I was too weird to play Eliza Doolittle.

As if noticing my crushed expression, Mom quickly added, "Honestly, I don't know what that Mr. Martinez is thinking. Surely, there are plays with better roles for women. And the theme of that thing—that a woman will transform herself into some rich, white man's ideal for love—it's offensive."

I could see the letter she would be writing to the PTA or school board already. "He's making the music edgy," I pointed out. "Maybe he's going to play up the ironic."

"I can only hope so."

I was shocked by the number of cars in the parking lot. It looked like everyone in the entire school was going to be trying out. I shook my head. Mom was right. There was no way I was going to get a part in this play.

After I'd waved good-bye to Mom and headed into school, I felt a tug on my sleeve. I turned, expecting Bea, but instead saw a kid I didn't know. Her heart-shaped face was pale, and she had dark rings under her wide, un-makeup-enhanced eyes. The hair was the giveaway. She was one of the honor guards—an Igor. "What do you want?" I said, pulling my lucky shirt from her grasp.

"A message from the prince," she said, her voice wispy with that weird awe they all seemed to have for vampires.

"No time," I told her, hurrying my steps. "Anyway, tell Dad I'm not sorry about that betrothal thing. This whole arranged-marriage stuff is weird. It should be abolished or something; this is the twenty-first century, you know."

The girl's lip quivered like she wanted to say more, but luckily I spotted Taylor talking to Lane. I shouted a hello to them, and the Igor did what Igors do—she faded into the crowd, so as not to be seen by regular people.

Taylor waved frantically at me, pointing to something that looked like a raffle ticket in her hand. "Numbers!" she was saying when I got close enough. "Just to get into the auditorium! I'm so screwed. What are the odds of a black Eliza?"

"I'm telling you, Taylor," Lane said, as if this was an argument they'd had already. "It totally could work. Instead of East End, you're a Somali immigrant, see—"

"I *am* a Somali immigrant," she pointed out. "Or at least my family is."

"Exactly," he said. "And I, as Professor Higgins—"

"Assimilates her into upper-class white culture?" I was beginning to see Mom's point. "Are you sure Martinez is going to go there? Do you know how pissed off people will be?"

"Isn't that kind of what the play is saying anyway? Give up your accent and pass as noble class?" Lane asked. I thought he'd made an interesting choice for an audition outfit. He wore a black vest over a bright, white T-shirt. I was surprised at the muscles he sported. They weren't huge guns or anything, but I didn't remember his arms being so defined before. His hair was almost working too. It looked like he might have tried to tame it with some gel or something.

Like me, Taylor had a specific outfit she always wore. Her *hijab* was canary yellow, and she wore a similarly bright red, long-sleeved silk shirt.

She pointed at my shirt. "Mime stripes!"

It was true. My lucky audition shirt did resemble those black and white striped shirts that mimes wore in movies and on TV. I'd never actually seen a mime anywhere else, so I had no idea if that was just some kind of weird Hollywood thing or what. The truth was, it was really kind of silly looking, but I landed the role of Medea wearing this hideous thing . . . and again got cast as one of the sisters in *The Madwoman of Chaillot*. That kind of clinched it. It was my lucky shirt.

Plus, it was one of the few shirts I owned that hugged my figure and showed off what few attributes I had topside, as it were. Even though skintight, muffin-top-revealing clothes were the rage, I tended toward things that fit loose and comfy. I think my audition shirt had the element of surprise.

Lane seemed to be checking me out too. "I think it's nice," he said in a way that made heat rise to my cheeks. But, in typical Lane fashion, he added drily, "For Marcel Marceau."

Taylor snickered behind her hand, and I just shook my head and tried to hide my initial reaction to his attention with a snarky, "Touché."

"You'd better go get a number," Taylor reminded me. "Or you won't get out of here until after midnight."

It took me a while to find out where the line ended. Wouldn't you know it? There was Matthew Thompson wearing his letter jacket and dragging his knuckles. "Check you," he said loudly. "You forgot the face paint!"

"And I suppose you think the jock wear is going to make you look professorial?"

He looked down at his clothes as if he suddenly remembered what he was wearing. "You think I should have worn one of those tweed jackets with the elbow patches?"

I tried to picture Thompson in that getup and laughed— again, a bit unkindly, but, seriously, could you see him dolled up like that? Ape Professor!

"What's so funny?" He actually sounded hurt, which was rich, since he'd basically greeted me with an insult.

"Nothing," I said, and because it seemed like we might be stuck in this line for a while, I said, "Big crowd, huh?"

"Massive," he agreed.

Kind of like Thompson, himself. He really was built like the linebacker he was. I had to crane my neck to talk to his thick chest. "What are you going to sing?"

"'On the Street Where You Live,'" he said without a second's hesitation. "How about you?"

My mouth was too busy hanging open to reply. "You . . . you know the songs?"

He tapped his pocket meaningfully and smiled slyly. "Are you kidding? I downloaded them all after the assembly."

My head spun with the idea of the entire football team

cheerfully listening to *show tunes* on their iPods. The natural order had been violated. Next the seas would turn bloodred.

Thompson's face broke into a wolfish smile. "Unless you want to do 'Rain in Spain' together? A duet!" The line moved forward, and I lurched along dumbfounded, as Thompson continued. "Maybe we could get in faster if we were together. Dude, let's do it."

"I don't know if I know the tune—," I stammered.

Thompson whipped out his iPod. Before I even knew what was happening, he'd put one bud in his ear and the other in mine. "It couldn't be simpler," he explained to my bulging, incredulous eyes. His fingers scanned through his playlist quickly. "We're going to totally rock."

Rex Harrison started singing in my ear. Beside me, Thompson was smiling and humming along. When it was over, he asked expectantly, "Easy, right? Are you up for it?"

We were still connected by the string of wire, so I finally said what had been on my mind since the moment he started talking to me: "I thought you hated my guts."

His face contorted through a myriad of emotions I couldn't fathom. Finally, he settled on a frown. He pulled the bud from my ear with a pop. "Just don't lick me onstage, okay?"

"Uh," I said, not knowing how else to respond.

There was that broad smile again, and he nudged me with his elbow. "You're onto me, aren't you?"

What? That he secretly liked me all this time? "Well, I—"

"I don't have any theater cred," he said before I could embarrass myself by guessing the totally wrong thing. "If we do a duet, it's kind of like you're saying you vouch for me."

"But . . ."

"You owe me."

The licking incident was pretty infamous, and then there was Bea's unpopularity spell. Of course, I pretty much figured him for the guy who'd defaced my locker with a "witch bitch," and he had kind of threatened to punch me out, so I wasn't convinced the slate wasn't already even.

We'd gotten to the front of the line. The assistant director, Todd, looked up at Thompson and handed him a ticket with the number one hundred on it. "What song?" he asked, his voice a dramatic combination of bored and long-suffering.

Before I could protest, Thompson jerked his thumb at me and said, "Ana Parker and I are doing 'Rain in Spain' as a duet."

Todd leaned on his elbow to peer around Thompson's massive body to give me the "Seriously?" eyebrow raise. I shrugged. "I guess so."

"I'll put you both down." As I left, following Thompson like a stunned sheep, Todd's eyes tracked me with the "Well, well, what's going on here?" curious smile. Great, now the rumor mill would be churning.

Taylor looked ready to run away when I came back to stand next to her with Thompson. Lane's nose wrinkled like I'd brought along something dead and rotten. I thought I heard Thompson grunt something that sounded like "fag."

"You know this isn't football practice, right, Thompson?" Lane sneered.

"Ana and I are going to sing a duet," he said calmly. You would have thought he'd suggested genocide by the reaction of my friends.

"Are you insane?" Taylor sputtered into my face. Lane turned pale as a sheet, and asked me, "You . . . and *him*? Does he even sing?"

"Catholic choir," Thompson said, puffing out his chest proudly.

This only served to horrify Lane more. "An altar boy and a witch—this I have to see. What number are you?" Thompson held up our ticket. Lane checked his own. "Not too far apart. I'm totally staying."

"Altar boys aren't the same thing . . . ," Thompson started to explain at the same moment I felt the need to clarify, "I'm not actually a witch like Bea. . . ."

He waved us both off. "Whatever. This is the most awesome odd-couple combination since Bono and Pavarotti." Then he pulled out his phone and started texting. I heard answering bleeps within seconds.

"Please tell me you did not just inform the entire class . . . ," I started, but Lane's smirk confirmed it—as did the sound of cell phones beeping throughout the room.

Perhaps I could just curl up and die now, and avoid the rush. My only hope was that, compared with Thompson's, my voice would sound spectacular.

Turned out, Thompson had been hiding his light under a bushel. The guy could sing. I mean, really *sing*. He didn't exactly stand out on the acting part of the audition, but cue the piano for that boy, and wow, did he shine.

We harmonized surprisingly well too. I found myself getting lost in the fun of it, and we did a little impromptu dance around the stage. He led me in a waltz that surprised me with its grace, but also tenderness. Who was this guy? The Thompson I knew had none of this class.

I was breathless at the end. When there was no reaction from the packed house, I thought maybe I'd imagined our awesomeness. Then, someone whooped. Probably one of Thompson's football buddies, but it broke the stunned silence, and suddenly the auditorium erupted in applause.

Thompson held my hand, and together, we bowed. Then, he scooped me up like a prince rescuing a princess and hauled me bodily offstage. Pressed against his chest, I could feel his heart pounding, just like mine. Once we were behind the curtain, he set me down. "You were incredible," he breathed in my ear.

"Uh, you too."

He clung to me, as if uncertain if he should let go. Once again, I found myself reconsidering everything I knew about him. Cheerleaders liked to swoon over Thompson's classically chiseled features, the dimples that appeared when he smiled, and that slight curl to his dark brown hair, but to me, his personality obscured any of that.

Until this moment.

As I watched him breathing hard, his face flushed with the heady excitement/embarrassment of public performance, his face seemed fresh and new. Eyes glistened, searching mine for something. In fact, Thompson seemed to be staring at me as if he'd never really seen me before either. His face was still close enough to kiss. I might have considered it too, had I not heard a cough from the wings.

The spell between us broken, Thompson let go of me like his hands were on fire. We both jumped back two paces. Before I could say anything, Thompson muttered, "See you around, I guess," and disappeared backstage, heading toward the exit near the greenroom.

I turned to see Nikolai leaning against the curtain pull.

He was shrouded in darkness, and for a moment, his casual pose could have passed for the languid grace of a vampire. His leather jacket appeared silky in the half-light. If he'd been the one to interrupt us, the only indication was the slight crease between his eyebrows. "Are you ready?" he whispered because someone new had taken the stage. When I looked confused, he added, "Our date? I've got something I need to tell you. I think it's a game changer."

"Did you see us sing? Thompson is good," I said quietly when Nikolai came up to take my arm. I couldn't focus on what Nik had said; I was still trying to process what had just happened onstage. "He's an altar boy or something."

Nikolai laughed. "I highly doubt that."

"Did you hear him? I can't get over it. He can carry a tune, and not just in a bucket. Ha." I know I sounded stupid, but the audition had done that to me—stupefied me.

Nikolai pushed the exit door open, and the overhead fluorescent light in the hallway made me squint. It was always so surreal to come out from the magical, hushed blackness of backstage into the ugly, carpeted, mundane school. The row of age-muted, fire engine red lockers seemed shabby compared with the polished gleam of the wood floorboards of the stage.

I blinked, trying to reground myself in reality. It was hard, considering my brain was stuck in a time warp, reliving the last twenty minutes over and over. "He's going to get a part," I said. "I mean, there's just no doubt. I think he surprised everyone."

"So did you," Nikolai said quietly.

"You heard it? You did, didn't you? Was it as good as I think it was? I mean, it was crazy! Right?"

"It was." Nikolai stopped walking and grabbed me lightly by the shoulders. He swung me around to face him. I blinked into his amber eyes. I found myself comparing the moment and the men. I could feel Nikolai's strength in his grip, but it hummed under the surface like a hidden danger—not the WYSIWYG way of Thompson, who wore his physical prowess like his letter jacket for everyone to see. "This is important, Ana. Can you focus on us for a moment?"

I shook myself out, as if trying to brush everything away. Nik released me, watching with those intense, fraught eyes. We stood near the gym's double doors. Around the corner, I could hear the dwindling noise of those remaining souls waiting for their audition. "Sorry," I explained. "It's been a really weird day. You didn't help, by the way. What's with letting Bea ask you out on a date?"

He shrugged guiltily. "She's always liked me, you know."

"Oh, I *know*," I stressed.

He waved off this thread of conversation impatiently. "Look, it was your idea to take a break."

"You agreed awfully quickly," I snapped. The audition broke something loose in me and everything I'd been holding back came spilling out. "Admit it: you've been waiting for an excuse to dump me."

"What are you talking about?"

"Come on, are you saying you don't notice all the hot groupies?"

His eyes slid away. "Of course I do, but what does that have to do with us?"

"You're kidding me, right? It has everything to do with us."

He shook his head, like I was talking nonsense. He sneered, "They're mundane."

Bea wasn't, which I suppose made her fair game. But was that really what he was trying to suggest? "So what're you saying? You only date people from the coven now?"

"And vampires." He smiled.

Was he serious? I couldn't tell, except that his whole scornful expression regarding nonmagical people seemed genuine. "That's a small gene pool," I commented.

He looked like he had some kind of response, but his words were lost in a loud squeal. We'd come to the end of the corridor and Bea spotted us from across the room. She shouted, and pretty soon everyone who was still hanging around the theater came rushing toward us. "OMG, were you awesome or what?" shrieked Taylor. "Best ever!" agreed Lane. Bea, meanwhile, caught sight of Nikolai and her smile faded. She gave a possessive sidelong glance at him, and said a bit poutily, "Nice enough, I guess."

People I hardly knew came up to tell me how epic Thompson and I had been. Everyone kept repeating the same thought I had, "I had no idea Thompson could sing like that, did you?"

We all agreed Thompson had played the dark horse. Everyone had a theory. I got caught up in the swirl of speculation. Suddenly, I realized I'd been talking a while. When I turned to ask Nik if he wanted to get going, I discovered he was nowhere in sight. I skimmed the crowd for his familiar leather. In a panicked moment, I thought he might have just gotten bored and left. Then, over by the first row of lockers, I spied him and Bea with their heads together.

My fangs clicked into place with a painful shift in my jaw.

I covered my mouth. I hadn't intended for them to come out, but the sudden flare of jealousy I felt must have brought them down.

Despite the intensity of their conversation, Nikolai must have sensed my transformation, because he glanced up. The overhead light glinted in his eye. Something about his intense, hooded expression made me take a step back. I nearly knocked Lane over.

"Sorry," I mumbled around the teeth and my hand.

"Are you okay?" Lane asked, frowning deeply. "You look really pale all of a sudden."

The last thing I needed was for everyone to see me in full-on vampire mode. What if my eyes changed? How would I explain that? The whole school thought I was weird enough after the licking incident. "Got to go," I said, and pushed my way deeper into the crowd toward the door.

Behind me, I heard Nikolai shouting for me to wait.

Vampires can move pretty fast when motivated. I was out the door and into the cool kiss of the night in the blink of an eye.

I stood on the sidewalk in front of the school's main doors. With the moonlight on my cheek, I felt light and buoyant. Vampire senses on high, my feet itched to run—to become part of the night. When I heard the doors swing open behind me, I gave in to the impulse. The pavement flew underfoot. I moved easily. In fact, a wild, wide smile danced on my face. I started singing, "I could have danced all night. . . ."

By the time I finished the chorus, I was coming around the block of my house, ten miles away. I skidded to a stop. I hadn't even broken a sweat. I laughed with the joy of it. If only I could do this in the daylight! Think of how small my carbon footprint would be!

I was still laughing breathlessly when my hypervamped

awareness caught the impression of movement out of the corner of my eye. I swiveled my head, like an animal tracking a scent. Out of the shadowy tangle of hedges, a tall, pale figure materialized briefly. Ghostly skin flashed and then disappeared.

Someone was stalking through the bushes around my house.

I had no doubt it was a vampire. But what kind? Was s/he friendly?

Vampires could move stealthily when they needed to too. Kicking off my shoes, I tiptoed along the sidewalk. The pavement felt cool and damp with evening dew. My socks snagged slightly on the roughness, which sounded loud to my ears. I had to assume that the intruder was as supersensitive to noise as I was, so I was about to slip them off when my cell phone bleeped.

The clamor might as well have been a cannon going off.

Whoever had been sneaking around dashed through the underbrush with an explosion of speed and leaves.

"Crap," I muttered, especially since the guilty flight of the prowler indicated that the vampire in question was probably not of the friendly variety. Elias, for instance, wouldn't have run off.

When the phone rang again, I scrambled to retrieve it from my pocket. Irritated, I flipped it open without even checking caller ID. "What?" I hissed.

"Still feeling vampy, eh?" It was Nikolai. There was something in his tone I wasn't sure I liked. Was it threatening or . . . did he sound turned on?

"You sure call me a lot for a guy I broke up with."

There was a moment of stunned silence. I'd scored a hit, though I wasn't proud of that. I needed to learn to curb my impulse to blurt out the first thing on my mind when I was upset.

Nikolai cleared his throat finally. "Yeah, well, I was going to tell you how I fixed that, but I guess you don't care. Oh, and I'm no longer an apprentice hunter."

"You . . . ? What?" But I was talking into dead air. He'd hung up.

Chapter Five

stared at the neon green "call ended" message on the screen, and tried to catch my breath. What had he just said? He was no longer an apprentice? Did he mean he quit or did he graduate? But . . . but there was only one way to become a full-fledged hunter!

My finger jabbed the redial button. It rang through to voice mail. He must have turned off his phone. That Nik was a much better drama queen than I was just made me angrier. "If you mean what I think you do, we are so over. For good."

My heart hammered in my ear. The air was cool enough that my breath misted in sharp puffs. Perhaps the interloper had come to warn me of Nik's new hunter status. But if the vampires knew, why wouldn't Elias have come himself?

Unless he couldn't. Because . . . because he was . . .

Oh no! Nikolai couldn't have, could he?

I struggled to remember exactly what Nik had said when he'd arranged our date. Something about a "game changer"?

I had to find out if Elias was okay.

"Come back!" I shouted into the neighbor's shrubs. I frantically dashed through into the "naturalized" landscape, my stocking feet squishing wetly in moss and fern. "Come back!"

But the vampire—friend or foe—was long gone.

How was I going to find out if Elias was okay? I vaulted the fence between the yards in a bound worthy of a superhero. Rather than take the time to go up the stairs, I scrambled over the porch railing. It wobbled, threatening to give way under my weight. Instead, the wood gave a loud groan of protest. I pulled at the door, surprised to find it locked.

Had Mom gone to bed?

Stretching up on my toes, I peeped through the door windows. Everything looked dark. But that could just mean that she was in the back office/craft room upstairs.

I dug out my keys. My thought was that I'd leave the sock "welcome" in the window for Elias. And then . . .

Wait, I guess.

Hmmm, that plan sounded pretty frustrating, actually. But what else could I do? Even though I'd been the vampire princess for a couple of months now, I didn't go into the underground unescorted very often. St. Paul was riddled with natural sandstone caves, abandoned rail tunnels, bootleggers' caves, and sewers. It would be pretty easy to get lost down there. According to Elias, one of the main jobs of the Igors, besides watching over me, was to keep the urban spelunkers from invading vampire lairs.

Oh! The Igors! They could get a message back to Elias or someone who might know if he was okay.

Now that I needed one, where were they? Oh, that's right. I

ditched them. Maybe some were hanging around anyway, doing their creepy stalker thing. Before going in, I took a look around. With my fangs still out, all life around me was illuminated. There were tons of squirrels, a raccoon family, and Mr. Becker's mangy cat. No people of any variety.

Crap. That meant I was back to plan A: waiting.

With a sigh, I went into the house. I didn't particularly try to be quiet. After all, Mom was a pretty heavy sleeper. She knew that when I had auditions, I came home late, so it wasn't like she was going to be waiting up to lecture me. Besides, I had more on my mind than worrying about Mom.

What would I do if Nikolai had killed Elias? It was hard to even formulate that thought. I'd seen Nik fight a number of times, so I knew he was capable of violence. But it was one thing to protect yourself and another to kill somebody.

But did he really think of vampires as somebody? There was all that talk about sending them back to where they belonged, too.

He just couldn't have. No, not Nikolai. The guy whose lips I'd kissed—the guy who laughed at my stupid jokes and read manga and played guitar. I mean, that person was decent, nice. Not a killer.

Maybe he was trying to tell me he quit. He was awfully mad when I'd made that snide comment about how he called all the time. Maybe he'd decided to throw it all away—for me.

My socks squished on the hardwood floor, and I tossed the sneakers I'd been carrying onto the rug next to the coat-tree. I toed off my damp stockings, and wadded them into a ball. Looking around for a place to put them, I found none, so I jammed them into the pockets of my jeans.

Upstairs was dark. Mom must have gone to bed, after all.

Mindful of waking her, I waited until I shut the door to turn on the light.

When I turned around, I had to swallow a scream of surprise. Elias sat on my bed.

"How did you get past the wards . . . ?" I started to ask, but then I just threw myself at him and wrapped my arms around him. I squeezed as tightly as I could, just to make sure he was really there. "I'm so glad you're okay! I thought you were dead!"

"Well, technically, I'm kind of neither alive nor—"

"Hush," I said, and laid my head on his shoulder. Elias put his arms around me with a light chuckle.

"What's brought all this on?" he asked after the shaking in my shoulders had stopped, and my fangs retreated. "Why did you think I'd been injured?"

I sat back so that my back rested against the bedpost. With my legs stretched out, my bare feet nearly touched his thigh. "Nikolai told me he's no longer an apprentice."

Elias frowned. In the harsh overhead light, his face looked drawn, almost sickly. He ran a hand through the short hairs at the back of his neck. "I have waited here some time for you. Could more have happened?"

"More?" I poked him with my toe. "Yeah, what's with the threshold-crossing thing? I didn't think you could do that."

He gave an unconcerned lift of his shoulder. "My prince's blood has been spilled inside this house. No spell can keep a pledged knight of the realm out."

Good to know. So the house was vulnerable to any of the "good guy" vampires, and, probably, specifically Dad's Praetorian Guard. "Okay," I murmured a bit unhappily. "So what's going on?"

"The talisman has resurfaced."

My mouth hung open. "You mean *the* talisman? The one that can enslave us?"

"The very one."

"Where is it? Who has it?"

Elias's mouth twitched. "The Minnesota Historical Society by way of the Smithsonian. It was spotted by one of our spies on the inside. It's listed as 'Snake-headed goddess figurine,' but it is as I remember it."

"Are you serious? The talisman is at the History Center?" Like a lot of St. Paul kids, I visited the History Center on a field trip in elementary school. The only thing I really remembered about it was a big grain elevator that we could run around inside, pretending to be wheat or corn or something like that. "I can't believe it!"

"The Smithsonian traveling exhibit opens tomorrow."

"What are you going to do?"

Elias glanced at me. His eyes seemed tired, heavy. "Your father wants to do nothing. There's no way of knowing if the witches know it is the one. Our memories are as sharp as the first day we were brought over. The witches are human. They grow old and die. Those witches we fought in the secret war who are still alive are in their dotage. There is a chance it may pass undetected. Our prince, your father, is afraid that if we make a move—attempt to steal it—we will have done the hard work for them. They will simply take it from us once it's in our possession."

I supposed that made a kind of sense. But Elias wouldn't have been waiting in my room in the dark just to tell me they weren't going to do anything about it. "You disagree?"

"I think if we have spies, they have spies. If nothing else, their spies watch ours. If they don't already know, they will soon. I want to move before we all become slaves and no longer have any will of our own."

I'd never seen Elias like this. He faced my desk, his feet on the floor. He held his hands between his legs, and the knuckles were white with tension. He seemed ready to burst. "What's stopping you?"

His storm gray eyes were ice hard when he turned: "Your father's orders."

Now I understood. Elias had broken my mother's wards, risked potentially having to face Mom and her full-on magic, and sat in the dark all night while I was singing it up with Thompson, because he wanted me to grant him some kind of royal permission to go against my dad.

"Uh, I don't know about this," I admitted, pulling my legs up to hug them. It was one thing to tell some random vampire chick that it was okay for her to run off with the boy she loved, and another thing to start a rift between my dad and his trusted personal guardian.

Elias bowed his head like he was utterly defeated. "Inaction is the fool's strategy. Action is the traitor's. What am I to do, Princess?"

I tucked my chin up against my knees. Elias seemed to be searching my face for a clue, but I had none. My room seemed too small for this conversation. Hugging myself tighter, I asked, "If you stole the talisman, could you keep it safe?"

His head snapped up. "Your father asked me the same thing. Only when he asked, it was no simple question, but an accusation."

I didn't understand. "An accusation?"

Color dotted the high arches of his cheekbones. He stared at his clenched hands. In a low voice, he said, "Yes. All those years ago, when we rebelled, it was I that stole the talisman. I lost it as well."

My mind stumbled over the magnitude of this revelation. "Are you saying that you're the person responsible for freeing the vampires? Like, some kind of undead Abe Lincoln?"

Despite the seriousness of our conversation, Elias laughed. "More like Spartacus," he corrected, and then his smile faded. "Perhaps my freedom too shall be short-lived."

I didn't know how to respond to that. I didn't know many details about what the vampires called the secret wars, other than it was a bloody rebellion that ended with the talisman no longer in witch possession. I had no idea Elias had played such a key role. "Why aren't you the prince? I mean, you were the hero of the secret war, right?"

"Your father was the architect of the plan; I was only the foot soldier who carried out his orders. And . . . ultimately, I showed poor judgment. I trusted the wrong person, and the talisman slipped away into the mundane world and was lost to us."

That didn't sound so horrible to me. The vampires had still won their freedom. "Everyone makes mistakes." I shrugged.

"Mine could result in enslavement of an entire people."

I gave him a reassuring pat on the leg.

But he seemed to take my sympathy the wrong way. Stiffening, he gazed out the window as if tracking something. "I should go."

"But what are you going to do about the talisman?"

As he pulled open the window, he sounded angry. "My duty is, apparently, to do nothing at all."

Halfway out, he paused. He caught my eyes and held them. Should I say something? It didn't seem right, him shackled like this. What if Dad was wrong? What if the talisman ended up back in the hands of someone willing to use it to bind us again? Then it would be more than duty that bound him; he'd be some-one's slave. I couldn't cope with that thought.

"You should do it," I said, my voice shaking. "Make sure no one gets the talisman."

His eyes flashed. With a brisk nod, he disappeared into the night.

lay awake for hours wondering if I'd made the right decision, and trying to imagine how furious my father would be when he found out what I'd done. I didn't know him very well, despite the blood relation, but I couldn't think of a scenario where he'd be happy that I'd turned his trusted personal guard against him.

Yet, at the same time, the more I thought about the talisman being out there, unguarded and available for the other side to snatch up and use against us, the happier I was that I'd sent Elias to get it. After all, I'd just finished reading a chapter about the horrors of slavery. I sure as hell didn't want to live it firsthand. Okay, so Elias was apparently the same guy that lost the artifact, but in his defense, it wasn't like it had instantly fallen into the wrong hands. The talisman had stayed buried this whole time.

Though how secret was it if the Smithsonian had it?

I supposed it was like hiding in plain sight, except with museum-quality security to back you up.

Huh.

Suddenly, I could see my dad's point of view.

I flipped over in the sheets again, pounding my pillow with my fists in an effort to get comfortable. But suddenly, the bed-sheets felt too restricting and the mattress unyielding. A car passed down the street, its engine straining and thumping bass blasting on the stereo.

The break-in was bound to make the news, and unless Elias was smart enough to steal some other random items, everyone would wonder what was so damn special about— What was it he'd called it? "Snake-headed goddess figurine." Even the dimmest bulbs in the True Witch community would be able to put two and two together.

Crap.

I sat up, wondering if there was some way to recall Elias from his mission. Surely, he wouldn't go out right this minute and break into the museum, would he? Maybe I could talk this over with him tomorrow, let him convince me that he knew what he was doing and that this wouldn't be a total disaster.

Dad was going to kill me—and, hopefully, not literally.

The only silver lining was that I wouldn't have to worry about dear Papa showing up at school tomorrow, even with the sewer access Khan had used. Apparently, you got more sensitive to light the older you were, and Dad was mighty old. If he was going to kill me—either literally *or* figuratively—he'd have to wait until nighttime.

Cold comfort, honestly.

To distract myself from the thoughts zipping round and round in my head, I fumbled for my iPod. It was still set to loop "Teardrops," which only made me remember all the awful with Nikolai earlier tonight. Why was I so stupid? Always blurting out the first thing that came into my head? I'd messed it up with Nik by saying something without thinking, and now I might have FUBARed vampire freedom forever.

Awesome.

After setting the player to random shuffle, I plopped back down on the bed. I stared at the shadow patterns the pine boughs made on the ceiling and concentrated on listening to the lyrics of the songs as they played.

Somehow I must have fallen asleep, because I woke up far too early, startled by the silence of an empty house.

My bedside clock showed an ungodly hour that began with a six. The tree outside my window, which was usually home to vampire knights, now seemed to be bursting with birds determined to wake me at dawn.

Despite all that, my brain much more keenly registered the absence of my mother's presence. There were no dishes clinking in the kitchen, no muffled sighs of getting dressed, no weather radio in the bathroom murmuring about forecasted highs—nothing I'd come to associate with morning routines.

Had she left already?

Or had she never come home last night?

My mom had been a single parent my whole life, even though I found out belatedly that she was actually married to my vampire dad this whole time. I knew she was lonely sometimes. We both sighed after Chace Crawford and Justin Bieber—okay, that last one was all me, and only sophomore year—but we both teared up over the same romantic comedies where the guy went back for the girl just in the nick of time. I remember asking her, when I was young, if she ever hoped to be *that* heroine one day, and if I'd ever, you know, be that precocious kid who brought the two love interests together.

Sadly, my professorial mom always saw those kinds of questions as "teachable moments," and gave impromptu lectures about the antifeminist message Hollywood perpetuated, all the while, I should add, wiping away the sentimental tears. In all my sixteen-plus years she had never, ever brought home a boyfriend.

Maybe she'd spent the night with someone last night.

Perhaps when I got downstairs and fumbled around in the pantry for something for breakfast, I'd find a note explaining that she'd finally found the love of her life, some perfectly sensitive yet just-enough-alpha man who respected her feminism and her empowerment and was totally hot.

Or, more likely, she just stayed over when one of her women's ritual groups ran late.

Knowing I had the house to myself, I changed the radio station in the bathroom to Cities 97 and turned the volume up. I ran a hot bath—our house was so old that we had no showers, only one of those huge, claw-foot tubs. Having only a bathtub sucked when all I needed was a quick hair wash, but I'd grown up with it and had learned to luxuriate in a long soak. Besides, thanks to the birds and the weirdness of a noiseless house, I was up early enough to take time to do all my morning primping unhurried.

As I sang along to Matchbox Twenty, I remembered my duet with Thompson last night and the strange moment of closeness afterward, backstage. He must have gotten swept up in the magic of theater, because he'd seemed almost tender.

Was there another side of Matthew Thompson I didn't know?

I remembered that he'd totally bought the story I circulated after the licking incident in gym, wherein I hadn't so much stuck my tongue on his skin as kissed him due to an unrequited crush. I figured he preferred the implied flattery of that scenario. But maybe . . .

I mean, what if he secretly liked me? He'd been acting so hurt when I'd been cruel about his interest in theater, and Thompson was just enough of an idiot to think that the kindergarten approach of tossing rocks and pulling hair was the way to a girl's heart.

Then again, maybe I was just the easiest path to getting into the season's hottest show. Dipping my head under the water, I sighed.

Like I needed more boy trouble. On top of everything else.

I listened intently at the news break at the top of the hour. A brown bear had been spotted in some golf course in the suburbs, apparently, but no mention of a break-in at the History Center. Maybe luck was on my side and Elias hadn't done anything yet. I'd have to try to talk to one of the Igors at school today and get them to pass on a message to him, tell him we should wait. Or at least talk about it more.

But I still wasn't sure that was the right thing to do.

If being a princess meant making these kinds of decisions, I didn't like it much.

After I washed my hair and shaved, I was ready to hop out of the tub. I scrubbed my body all over with the cheerful yellow towels my mom had impulsively bought at Macy's. I put on my makeup and then wasted some time trying to induce some volume with that hair-dryer flip method, which I never quite understood. Back in my room, I set upon the arduous task of choosing what to wear. Some days I wished we were a uniform school so there wasn't this pressure. At least today, I could be prepared for the gossip storm. I mean, it was probably self-centered to assume my performance with Thompson would be the topic du jour, but I could always dress for success, as they say. I wasn't one of the school fashionistas, since I tended toward Goth monochromatic clothes and comfortable shoes. But I had a few sparkly bits I could add for flair.

Once again, I ate breakfast alone—just me and a big box of Cap'n Crunch. At least with the sun streaming in the big bay window, the house didn't seem quite so hollow. Halfheartedly I checked the usual spots for a note, but didn't find one. It was sort of strange that she hadn't even bothered to leave a voice mail on my cell or call the landline's answering machine, though that boded well for the spontaneous-love-affair theory.

You go, Mom. I smiled to myself as I shouldered my backpack and headed off to the bus stop.

If Mom had been home, she would have nagged me to wear a coat. Since I hadn't listened to the weather station, I was unprepared for the chill in the air. It wasn't entirely uncomfortable, since I'd worn a long-sleeve button-down shirt over my sparkly halter top, but the breeze was crisp and nipped at my cheeks.

Crocuses, with their bulbous yellow and lavender petals, huddled near the fence line of our property. The rain had coaxed the delicate bells of Siberian squill to open in a scattering of icy blue throughout the lawn. I could see buds thickening on the lilacs, and everywhere green shoots colored the tips of tree branches. Though the leaves hadn't fully opened, maples busily dropped their helicopter seeds, like alien snow showers, as I walked underneath.

I turned my head, hoping to see an Igor trailing behind. Wouldn't you know? No one. I sighed. I hoped Elias was okay, wherever he was.

After digging in my pockets and uncovering an unspent five-dollar bill—bonus!—I decided to detour to my favorite coffee shop for a mocha. The drink would not only keep my hands warm but also take the edge off the late night and far-too-early waking. Many of the houses I passed were massive mansions built at the turn of the last century. My eyes lit on jutting dormers, graceful towers, and wraparound porches. A cat blinked at me from a bay window and, noticing my attention, cleaned her paw, uninterested.

I turned onto Grand Avenue. Even at this hour, traffic moved in a steady stream under arching branches of oak and maple. I walked under the broad awning of a family-owned hardware store and past the inviting window display of spices at Penzeys. Here, the boulevard had fewer old, towering trees, and more of those scrubby ginkgoes, planted to withstand salt and exhaust. A few cottonwoods towered over the one- and two-story brick businesses.

Pulling out my phone, I caught up on the news. Taylor had left three texts, two of them about how surprised she was at Thompson's singing ability and asking why I'd taken off so quickly last night. Apparently, a whole bunch of the usual theater types had met up at a fast-food joint that was open late to talk. There was a lot of speculation about who'd get cast, and I got so wrapped up scrolling through it that I nearly stumbled off the curb.

After I'd waited for the light to change and made my way safely across the intersection, I went back to my phone. A lot of people had sent messages saying how cool the duet had been, though Lane suggested that Thompson wasn't a very believable Professor Higgins. He was more the Pygmalion in need of class. Despite my warming feelings toward Thompson, that one made me chuckle a bit. I returned a smiley face and an LOL.

I sort of secretly hoped for a text from Nikolai, but must have burned that bridge right to the ground. I did tell him we were off for good. There really wasn't much point in trying to go back on that.

My coffee shop was in a mall. An unimaginative two-story brick building, it took up a quarter of the block. The largest, most prominent features were a faux-French restaurant that advertized "les hamburgers" in neon above the door to the outdoor patio, and a Birkenstock shoe store. I walked in through the glass doors near the restaurant and made my way up a short polished wood hallway to an atrium. A mother and her toddler sat underneath a skylight on a bench around a large stone fountain. I smiled at them as I passed.

The interior of the coffee shop was dark in comparison with the airy, spacious hall. *A vampire would totally dig this dim, cavelike atmosphere,* I thought. I ordered my drink from a perky brunette.

While I waited for her to make it, I flipped open my phone. I wanted to write to Nikolai, but I didn't know what to say. Maybe I could just apologize for being rude and tell him I was interested in what he'd tried to say last night. That seemed good. I'd just opened a text message when the barista called my drink. When I checked the overhead clock, I realized with surprise how late it had gotten all of a sudden. Nik would have to wait. In fact, I should double-time it to the bus stop. Luckily, it was less than a block and a half away.

I stowed my phone, and quickly put a cover on the drink. As fast I as could without spilling, I made my way to where the school bus would pick me up. When I rounded the corner, I was grateful to see the grungy skateboarder that shared my stop still waiting—his board tucked casually under one arm.

He gave me the nod. You know, the barely perceptible head bob that said, "I acknowledge your presence so as not to be rude, but I am far too cool to converse with you."

I gave him one back.

Turning to watch the street, I sipped my mocha. I didn't expect to be required to do any other interaction, so I was surprised when he said, "Hey, you're Ana Parker, right?" Before I could even agree that I was, he said, "You date Nikolai Kirov from Ingress, don't you? You wouldn't happen to know how I could score tickets to the show at the Turf Club?"

"We broke up," I said, though I wouldn't have had any advice for skater boy even if we hadn't. The Turf Club was a seedy bar in the Midway neighborhood, and not a typical all-ages venue. Despite his attitude and edgy fashion, I didn't think any bouncer would mistake skater boy for eighteen or older. He was gangly in that way of guys his age, and had an unfortunate eruption of pimples across his cheek.

"Oh, hey, sorry to hear that," he said genuinely. "He seemed pretty cool at the assembly, but you know, musicians are always trouble." He shook his head and flashed me a knowing smile. "Artists, eh?"

"Yeah, I guess," I said, and I couldn't help but grin back. "You dated a musician?"

"Double whammy," he explained, shaking his bangs from in front of his eyes with the memory, "drummer *and* sculptor. Super diva and moody as all get-out. And in the end, I was always second to that bitch, the muse."

Okay, so he'd sort of lost me there at the end, but I found myself sort of fascinated. We'd stood together at this bus stop for years, and I could remember only one other conversation of this length in all that time. "How long ago was this?"

"A couple months ago," he said. I don't think I'd made any expression, but he reacted as though I had. "Yeah, yeah, I should be over it by now, I know, but artists . . . they have this way of getting under your skin, don't you think? It's that avant-garde lifestyle, maybe. But I'm still hung up over him."

Him? This scary, grungy guy was gay? Cool. I nodded sympathetically. "Yeah," I said. "I get that."

We shared a smile of understanding that lasted until the bus pulled up with the warm hiss of brakes and the smell of diesel. I made a friendly motion to let him go first, but with the arrival of the bus, his face hardened. He gave me the "Loser!" snarl as he pushed past me.

I stared after him for a second, shocked at the change. I guess we could commiserate about boyfriends at the stop, but once at some semblance of school, clique boundaries couldn't be transgressed.

Whatever, I thought with a shrug, and stepped up into the bus.

The driver frowned at my mocha, but I defiantly cupped my hand over the cover and made my way to an open seat. When the bus didn't start up immediately, I thought for sure he'd make a scene and make me dump my drink somewhere. Although where I'd do that, I didn't know. Apparently, neither did he, because the bus started up with a frustrated groan.

Settling in, I surreptitiously sipped my mocha and tried to wake up. I blinked sleepily and allowed the strobe of sun and trees to mesmerize me. A soft tap on my shoulder broke my reverie. "Ana? Ana Parker?"

I swiveled on the slick plastic seat to see who wanted to know. It wasn't anyone I immediately recognized. He had the nervous/eager expression of a freshman, and a tween pop-star-inspired bowl cut that nearly obscured his eyes. "Uh, yeah?"

"I was at auditions last night," he said. "You were super. I'm sure you'll get a part."

His gushing both embarrassed and flattered me. A blush rose, tingling my cheeks. "Oh. Thanks," I murmured.

The kid seemed inordinately pleased at any kind of response. He nodded enthusiastically, but then his expression twisted into a frown. "Man, it was hard to go on after you guys. I totally flubbed—I was so nervous."

"Sorry," I said somewhat distractedly, remembering everything that had happened afterward. Had Elias stolen the artifact yet? Was it still safe? How cranky was my dad?

The freshman must have noticed my nervousness, because he bobbed his head apologetically. "You must have a lot on your mind, huh?"

"You have no idea," I told him with a smile I hoped softened any unintentional rudeness on my part. Did he look like the type to watch the morning news before school? Or to follow a local station's Twitter feed? I decided to ask, anyway. "Uh, you didn't happen to hear anything about the History Center this morning, did you?"

"The what?"

Yeah, I should have predicted that response. "Never mind," I said, and turned back to face the front. I was grateful to see we were turning in front of the school so I didn't have to explain my sudden interest in some dorky museum.

The weirdest thing I saw all day was Thompson holding court with a bunch of theater types at lunch.

Like a king, he sat in the center of the long foldout table. Lane and some of the other people I knew, even some of the out-of-my-league seniors, crowded around him. They hung on every one of Thompson's utterances. He waved for me to join him when I passed by with my tray of cafeteria food—another thing moms were good for, nagging me to pack a sack lunch— but I couldn't violate my pact with Bea.

Since first grade, we'd vowed to always eat together so neither of us would have to be the lone class weirdo. Even when we were fighting, we sat together. Our being the only True-Witches-in-training for so long isolated me to the point that I didn't really have a lot of good friends. So Bea and I were kind of stuck together, no matter what.

Besides, I was glad for the excuse. Given how embarrassed I was with the attention of one freshman on the bus, I didn't think I could handle the adoration from people I considered colleagues.

So I shook my head at his questioning eyes, and jerked my chin in the direction of my usual table. Bea looked surprised when I set my tray down opposite from her. But if anyone had the skinny on what was up with Nikolai and his hunter status, it would be her.

"You sure took off fast last night," she said brightly, as if pretending we weren't fighting would get her off the hook. "You missed some fun."

I leaned in slightly and lowered my voice, ignoring her attempt at small talk. "Did Nik kill somebody? Or did he quit? He told me he's no longer an apprentice."

Bea's dark eyebrows shot up. "He's exaggerating," she sniffed. "He *thinks* he's graduated, but it's not official."

"I don't get it," I said. "Did he just wound someone or something? How is there a gray area in hunting?"

Bea glanced around behind her. She spotted one of my grungy honor guard—or maybe just one of the skanky kids, it was impossible to tell—at a nearby table. "I'm not really sure. Have you talked to him about this?"

At least I'd forgotten my lunch on pizza day. They even had pepperoni, my favorite. I picked up the slice and bit into it, thoughtfully, grateful Bea didn't have a quick answer. There was hope Nik hadn't completely gone to the dark side yet. "Kind of. We ended up having a fight, so I don't really know what this game changer of his is."

"He's got some crazy plan, all right," Bea said. "I didn't understand much about it either."

I stared at her pointedly. It seemed to me that she knew more than she was saying.

She did another quick survey for eavesdroppers. I couldn't help but check too. "Okay," she said, leaning across the table. "The only thing I know for sure is that it's illegal."

"More illegal than murder?"

Bea's lips flattened into a thin line, and I realized I'd blurted my true feelings out again. She clucked her tongue dismissively. "Look, Ana, it's not like he'd get arrested for staking some demon nobody knows exists. No, I mean something really serious."

Okay, that pissed me off. I stood up, my whole body shaking. "*I* know Elias exists. It's serious to me."

I guess I must have shouted that last bit, because a hush fell over the cafeteria. Bea's eyes darted around wildly. She put up her hands as if in surrender. I could see her heartbeat pulsing against her collarbone. The smell of her fear, like something sour and tangy, hung in the air between us. I could even hear the rasp of her breath, and her whispered words sounded too loud against my sensitive eardrums. "Hey, it's okay. Relax."

Relax? I felt the opposite of agitated; I was cold and certain and utterly deadly.

Oh. My eyes had changed.

The entire lunchroom was staring at me too. Fortunately, Bea and I always took a table closest to the main hall. I faced away from the majority of the crowd. In my heightened state, I sensed the growing discomfort.

I ignored them. Focusing my rage at Bea, I said firmly, "Why does everyone forget that I'm half demon? Vampires are my people."

"So are witches," Bea snapped. Her voice was steady, but my amped awareness caught the nervous sweat that prickled her skin. "But that's not convenient, is it? Especially when you're so busy playing 'pity the poor victim.'"

My jaw popped with the speed with which my fangs descended. I had to clench my fists to keep myself from launching across the table at Bea. I was so intent on controlling my reaction that the approach of the lunchroom monitor nearly took me by surprise. I barely had time to avert my eyes and keep my mouth shut. "Is everything okay here?" she asked.

Holding back the urge to say no, I stared sullenly at a shiny white pair of women's Nikes. I knew instantly it was Ms. Knutson, the women's tennis coach and freshman-English teacher. To her question, I shrugged. Bea made some excuse I didn't hear, though I felt the thrum of her magic hit my solar plexus like the beat of a big bass drum.

"Well, all right, then," was Ms. Knutson's dreamy, disconnected response. She walked off without further ado. As Bea's spell permeated the cafeteria, the murmur of normal conversation slowly returned to the room.

"You told me once that you didn't want to take sides—vampire versus witch—but you have," Bea said. "Look at yourself, Ana. You're one of them. A hundred percent."

It was impossible to deny her accusation with my cat-slit eyes and fangs hanging out everywhere, but my shoulders stiffened anyway. "It's not like I have a choice."

"I think you do," she said, crumpling her paper bag and standing up. "I think you like being a vampire with your superpowers and tragic history. You'd rather push all of us away, even Nikolai, than face the truth."

The sting of her accusation caused my resolve to crumble. My fangs slid back into their hiding place. Still, I wasn't ready to back down entirely. "You talk tough, but it's not like the coven accepts me. What am I supposed to do, stand by and ignore all the threats against my people?"

"'Your people,' O wise and powerful Princess Ana? See what I mean?"

"Actually, I don't. It's not like vampires are out hunting witches on a regular basis."

Bea laughed, but it had a hard edge. "Wow. You really are completely out of it, aren't you? Why do you think they're called vampires and not just demons?" I had no immediate answer, except a frown. So, very slowly, as if explaining to a small child, she said, "Because they drink blood."

Oh, and here I thought she was going to actually tell me something I didn't already know. Though I hadn't tasted much outside of the one lick of Thompson's cheek, Elias told me about that. I put my hands on my hip, and I could feel the sharp edges dulling as my eyes returned to normal. "Duh, Bea."

"Witch blood," she said meaningfully.

I sat back down, feeling deflated. She hesitated, but joined me after a moment. The cheese on my pizza had congealed. I poked at it with one finger. It no longer looked appetizing. "If you're trying to make a point, girlfriend, I'm not getting it."

"Do you remember that zombie spell your mom put on you last semester?"

How could I forget? Mom had decided she couldn't trust me to stay away from the vampire initiation rite, so she'd bespelled me into a sleepy haze. "What does that have to do with anything?"

"Remember how strong you got after you bit me?"

Though it had been Bea's idea, I still felt a little guilty about munching on my sometimes best friend. She happened to catch my gaze, and I flinched under her scrutiny. I pretended interest in the mess on my plate. "The blood kick-started my vampire powers. You thought it might help break the spell and it did. So?"

"So did the same thing happen with Thompson?"

"Well, no, but I only got a taste," I said, feeling more and more uncomfortable about this conversation. Just because I knew vampires drank blood didn't mean I liked the idea.

"Have you drunk anyone else's blood?"

"Um." I looked away. I had, but it had been Elias's. It was why we were engaged. It had also made me feel extra strong and had given my magic a serious boost.

"Okay, gross," Bea said when I didn't elaborate. But after a moment of consideration, she flipped her hair back. "Was it . . . human?"

"Was what human?"

"The blood you drank."

"No," I said.

"Proves my point," she said with a flourish.

The first bell rang, but I stayed in my seat. Everyone who hadn't already done so took their trays to the conveyor belt. "What point was that again, Bea?"

She stood up, her paper lunch bag still crumpled in her fist. "You should ask one of 'your people' about this sacred hunt of theirs sometime. You'll see that I'm right." With that, she walked away, leaving me sitting alone at our table.

Great, now my head was really spinning. So not only did I have the talisman resurfacing, the breaking and entering I ordered Elias to do, and Nikolai's game-changing something mysteriously illegal, but now I also had my BFF's conspiracy theory to contend with.

And I'd forgotten to read today's history chapters.

Because that's just how it always goes, we had a pop quiz in history. I'm a pretty good guesser, so there was some hope for a C, but this day was shaping into a real humdinger, as my mom would say.

Where the hell was Mom, anyway?

Add that to my growing list of migraine-producing problems: an AWOL mom.

Worse, my honor guard was becoming much more obtrusive. One of them followed me into the bathroom between periods. Taylor even noticed them when we gathered at Bea's locker before drama. "Have you noticed those creepy kids dogging you, Ana? There's one now."

We turned to look where she pointed just in time to see a stringy-haired mop disappear behind a row of lockers.

Bea and I shared a look. I didn't like to lie, especially to Taylor, but I didn't know how to explain them. "Uh, I guess I have a fan club."

Okay, it wasn't the exact truth, but they were into me—maybe not for my audition, but in my role as vampire princess.

Taylor crinkled her nose. Today her *hijab* was a print of one of Escher's black-and-white puzzles where birds faded into fish. It was really cool. I was about to ask her where she found the fabric when she said, "You don't actually talk to those people, do you? They're so weird. And smelly."

I felt a growl of protest building in my throat. Before my lips curled into a snarl, Bea took my hand and squeezed. I smelled the calming scent of woodsmoke. I got the hint. So I bit back the urge to explain to Taylor that as stinky as those kids might be, they were only looking after my interests. "Yeah, I guess," I said, letting go of Bea's hand.

As we headed into class, I caught Bea's eye and gave her a quick frown to let her know I didn't appreciate being the focus of her spell. She just shrugged and made a gesture with two fingers by her mouth.

Did she really think I'd drop my fangs that quickly?

The changes certainly had come up fast at lunch. Was Bea right? Had I become more vampire than witch? That was no good because what little magic I had came from harnessing the tension between the two parts of myself.

Mr. Martinez announced that the callback list would be posted tomorrow morning in the usual place, with the cast list on Monday. My stomach shivered slightly as it always did at the prospect of getting or not getting a part. Mr. Martinez also recognized that anyone who wasn't exhausted from the late night last night was too distracted to learn anything, so he wheeled in the TV and put on some black-and-white movie starring Katharine Hepburn and Cary Grant.

The movie was actually kind of interesting, so I let myself be distracted by it. For one hour, I didn't think about auditions, vampires, talismans, AWOL moms, or crazy ex-boyfriends.

Too bad I knew it wouldn't last.

The last thing I expected was for Thompson to be waiting for me after class. He was so tall that his head cleared the top of the row of lockers. As usual, he wore his letter jacket, a white T-shirt, and jeans. Once again, I was struck by the juxtaposition. How could a guy whose entire wardrobe consisted of one costume possibly be interested in theater?

"Why, if it isn't Eliza Doolittle," he said with the worst attempt at a British accent I'd ever heard.

"Oh, God, Thompson, stop!" Bea said with a laugh that we all joined.

His eyebrows drew together, making him look even more like a caveman than usual. "Lane said it was pretty good."

"Lane lied to you," I said. "He's trying to make sure you don't get the part."

"Whoa. Tricky," he said with an appreciative chuckle. It was strange how easily he slid in between Bea and Taylor to walk next to me as we threaded our way down the busy hallway. It should have felt odd, the three of us outcasts accepting this behemoth lumbering alongside me, close enough to brush fingertips, as one of our own.

People nodded a greeting to Thompson, and then gaped openly at the company he was keeping. I wasn't sure if he was helping our popularity or hurting his own. But he seemed content to just walk along with us, not saying anything.

I was fairly certain this was one of the seven signs of the apocalypse.

"Hey, Bea," Thompson said, turning to look at where she trailed a bit behind. "I just wanted to tell you I saw your audition. I think you have a good chance," he said, his dimpled smile taking in all of us. "Honestly, I don't know how Mr. Martinez is going to choose between the three of you."

It was such obvious flattery I was almost more embarrassed

to find myself blushing. So I covered by doing the usual theater talk. "Taylor has the best range, but Bea's the most professional. You've had voice lessons, haven't you, Bea?"

"Um, yeah," she said with uncustomary modesty, "through extension classes at the U."

"My dad won't pay for that," Taylor noted.

"My mom either," I offered. "She doesn't think theater is a viable profession, but it's good on the college application, I guess, so she tolerates my interest."

Everyone commiserated about that attitude.

"My mom thinks only fags do plays," Thompson said. "Actually, most of my friends think that too."

Okay, he just won the "Who had it worst?" contest, hands down. None of us had anything helpful to say. I was mostly still reeling from the fact that Thompson actually used the word "fags" unironically, instead of "gay guys."

Taylor was the first to regain her composure. "I thought I saw half the soccer team at tryouts."

"Yeah, but most of them were too chicken to actually sing. And you didn't just sing—you danced too. You're like *super* fag," she teased, then snorted. "Except no one could deny the chemistry between those two."

I caught Thompson looking at me the same time I glanced up to check his reaction.

"Yeah, that's the spark," Taylor said.

Looking away quickly, I blushed furiously. I was so busy not looking at Thompson that I almost ran into someone.

Bea and Taylor laughed. "Wow, you're totally smitten," Bea said.

"As if," Thompson snorted. "It's just theater magic."

"Yeah," I agreed, but I was glad we were at my locker and I could busy myself with getting the books I needed for tonight. It didn't help that I could feel the heat of Thompson's body standing behind me. Normally, we went on to Taylor's locker, but I had to bail. The last thing I needed was to add "weird crush on Thompson" to my list of crap I had to deal with. So when I had everything together, I checked my cell. "Oh, man, I'm going to miss my bus. I've got to go. See you guys later."

I took off before anyone could argue.

"She runs away a lot," I heard Thompson say as I slid ahead of a group of freshmen carrying band instruments.

He was right. Yet, staying was just confusing and embarrassing given that Thompson didn't seem to feel the same way about me. Anyway, I wanted to get home to check the news—as weird as that sounded.

When I turned the corner, I unconsciously scanned the street for a sign of Mom's blue MINI. I only realized I was doing it because my heart skipped a beat when I mistook the neighbor's similarly colored little car for hers. But it was too big. The wrong shape. There were no goddess bumper stickers covering the back. The moment my brain registered my error in perception, I felt this horrible tingling sensation in my gut.

Mom still wasn't home.

My pace quickened. I dialed her cell and got the same message I'd been getting. It picked up so fast that I knew she didn't have it turned on. "Call me," I told it. "You're probably running late, but I'm getting worried."

I tried her office and got voice mail.

"Damn it," I said, and hung up.

The mulberry tree near the porch hadn't leafed out yet. Twisted and gnarled, its trunk reminded me far too much of a creepy skeleton. I hurried past. My shoes clunked hollowly on the wood planks. Should I really be this worried? Who would even know where she might be?

As I got the mail from the box and fished out my house key, I tried to remember the names of people she worked with. The problem was that Mom wasn't tenured. She taught at a dozen different colleges as an adjunct. Plus, she ran about a million women's spirituality groups, not only through the colleges, but also with local New Age centers and bookstores.

The fact that she was constantly busy had always been a plus before. It worked well with my theater schedule. But Mom liked to be home before me—something about "latchkey kids" and her generation. Anyway, she never took a class that would interfere with that.

Setting the mail in its usual place on the radiator, I flicked on the front-hall light. "Hello, empty house," I said.

I didn't even get much of an echo for a reply.

Kicking my shoes off onto the rag rug in front of the coat-tree, I headed up to my room. I was probably being stupid. After all, it had only been one day—maybe less. She'd driven me to tryouts last night. It was possible I was wrong about her not being here when I came home. Perhaps she'd just taken off ridiculously early this morning. If I tried hard enough, I could convince myself that it could have been the sound of the door slamming or her car driving off that woke me in the first place.

A predawn ritual with one of her crazy women's groups was definitely a possibility.

As for tonight, Mom was running late, that was all. We'd have dinner as usual. The hitch in my breath was only from climbing all the stairs so fast. It was stupid to be worried about her. She was a grown woman and the Queen of Witches, for crying out loud. She was fine.

In my room, I fired up my laptop. There wasn't much to do but wait, anyway. I might as well check the news. I googled "Minnesota Historical Society" and got a lot of noise. There were a few articles about the Smithsonian exhibit, but no headlines screaming about theft.

I surfed the local stations. The TV people all featured the same story about a bunch of drunk idiots who drove off the River Road, crashed down a sixty-foot wooded cliff to take a dive in the Mississippi, and lived to tell about it. Radio and newspaper covered all the international and national stuff, and whatever the governor was doing this week.

Giving up, I streamed the local radio station and was surprised to hear Nikolai's voice. On Fridays they did a feature about the local club scene, and Ingress was in the studio. I turned up the volume.

The host asked Nik about the school play and their other upcoming shows. I listened intently for a while, impressed by how sophisticated and urbane he sounded. They played a live version of one of the songs I'd heard a dozen times, which was neat to hear, if only because it sounded somehow fresh, but then it was time for a commercial break. Digging through my backpack, I pulled out some homework I thought I could do half-heartedly while listening in.

I was skimming the history chapters I'd forgotten yesterday when the DJ asked, "So, now to the really important question: do you have a girlfriend, Nik? Are you spoken for?"

I froze.

There was an almost imperceptible pause. He cleared his throat. "I'm actually quite heartbroken at the moment."

Stevie made some joke then about how Nik's lovelorn state was great for the creative juices, and the conversation meandered back to safer topics like songwriting and the music business.

Closing my book, I stared at the computer screen as if trying to see Nikolai's face through the airwaves. It wasn't that I doubted his sincerity—not entirely, anyway. He'd been clearly trying to get back with me. And as Bea pointed out at lunch, I did have a tendency lately to let my vampire side out every time he made an overture, which served only to push him away further.

I cupped my chin in my hands, and scowled at the laptop.

Was Bea right? Did I favor vampires?

My prickly defense of the honor guard had triggered that first fight between me and Nik, and then Elias, and then my fangs. . . .

Shit.

I was saved from further self-recriminations by the sound of someone downstairs. "Mom!" I shouted, as I jumped up to peer down the open staircase. "Finally! Where have you been, young woman?"

Only it wasn't Mom. From my vantage point from the railing, I could see a figure standing next to the coat-tree. He was shutting the door behind him, quietly. I was about to run back to my room to dial 911 when he turned and I saw his face clearly.

It was Dad.

Chapter Seven

Oh crap. I was in more trouble than I thought. My dad had tried to come in the house once before. Mom had wrapped him in a magical spiderweb cocoon and kicked him, literally, to the curb. Things must be pretty serious if he was willing to just waltz in like he owned the place.

Man, our wards sucked.

And I should really start locking the door. Anyone could wander in.

"Amelia?" he called for my mother, and then for me, "Anastasija?"

"You must know Mom's not home, Ramses," I said, coming down the stairs. Vampires were vulnerable to witch magic, and my dad had always held a healthy respect for Mom's abilities. But I had no idea what he thought of me. We almost never spoke, which was another reason why his visit was so extraordinary. I'd gotten the sense that he generally approved of the way I handled myself during the big showdown last fall between the witches and vampires, but there had been no coronation or any other public recognition that I was his heir since. Maybe this princess stuff was all just a figurehead position, since he was, well, immortal. It wasn't like I would ever sit on the throne.

So I tried to sound tough, as I asked, "What I want to know is, did you kidnap her?"

Dad and I shared the same straight, jet-black hair. He wore his slightly longer than I did, and tied it back at the nape of his neck. Somehow, despite all the time he spent underground, it shone silkily in the half-light. Vampire magic—or damn good conditioner.

"I couldn't hold Amelia captive even if I wanted to," he said lightly. My dad's voice had the trace of a foreign accent, though I couldn't tell you which one. "Besides, it seems you're the one playing political games, not me."

It always surprised me that Dad wasn't taller. He commanded a lot of presence, as we say in theater, so when I came up to stand beside him, I was shocked to notice that he wasn't that much taller than me. He did have this fabulously regal, hawklike nose, which made up for a lot. I was just as grateful not to have inherited that, but it made him look kingly.

"Elias came to me," I said, deciding that it was best just to confess. I was terrible at court intrigue, despite what Dad might be implying. "I just gave him an excuse to do what he already wanted to do."

"Oh?" Dad's eyebrows drew together. His eyes were the color of my left one, a startling ice blue. Though his shone with an intense brightness; I doubted mine ever did.

"Yeah," I said, feeling kind of stupid arguing in the front hall. I should offer him a seat in the parlor or something to be polite, but that would kind of ruin the moment. "He would have gone against your orders anyway. He's got something to prove about the talisman."

"Elias went after the talisman?"

"Um, that's not why you're here?" My voice broke.

"No," he said coldly. "Though I'm glad to be apprised of my knight's intended treachery."

Cripes. *Way to drop Elias in it, Ana.*

"Why don't you invite me into your parlor? It seems we have some things to talk about."

Mom had gotten really mad at me the last time I officially invited Dad in. So instead of actually saying the words, I gestured in the direction of the unused formal sitting room. My dad dipped his head in a nod and confidently walked into the dark room and found a seat on the sofa. At least, I assume that was what he did. Without using my vampire eyes, I could only guess from the sound of the squeaking springs. Fumbling around for a few minutes, I found the faux-Tiffany lamps and switched them on.

"Don't be too mad at Elias. He was awfully torn up about it," I said, settling myself into a large overstuffed chair that smelled faintly of dust and pipe smoke. "Anyway, I don't think he did anything against you. There's been nothing on the news about a break-in."

"And yet, my spy inside the History Center tells me otherwise."

"Wait—what do you mean? It's gone?" Dad nodded at my question. "You mean Elias did it? He stole the talisman?"

"Someone did," he said, leaning back. His arm stretched across the doily-covered back, and he crossed his legs. I had to admire Dad's air of command; it was quite studied. "At this point, it seems I must hope that my trusted knight has gone rogue."

I chewed my lip. "Yeah, I guess so."

What would happen if it wasn't in Elias's possession? If a witch had it, they could enslave all the vampires again. Possibly even me. That would totally screw up my plans for the spring play, to say the least.

Dad seemed to be studying my reaction. His lips twitched before he said, "This is why spontaneous engagements are such a bad idea."

Was he talking about Khan or me and Elias? "Why is that again?"

"Because people make foolish decisions for love."

I stared at him, and he glared back with a challenge in his eye, as though he knew I'd take his comment personally. But . . . I thought he approved of me and Elias. Had he changed his mind? I frowned at him for a long time. One thing was certain: I wasn't very good at this kind of political cat-and-mouse conversation style. "Are you implying something about me?" I finally asked.

He looked startled, but recovered his composure quickly. "As a matter of fact, I am. Especially in light of recent developments, I feel Constantine is beneath the attention of royal blood." I opened my mouth to tell him exactly what I thought of that, but he held up a hand and talked over my protests. "However, the reason I am here is because I suspected Amelia had the talisman. I'd hoped to try to bargain for our freedom. But instead you accuse me of kidnapping her. Should I assume the worst?"

"I haven't seen Mom since last night," I admitted, my voice shakier than I intended. It distressed me that I'd lost track of the time, and now it was well past supper. I cleared my throat. "But, well, you know, maybe she's got a new boyfriend or something."

I was hoping Dad would have some insight into Mom's whereabouts, but he snorted, like he had as much trouble imagining a boyfriend as I did. "Amelia would never leave you alone for so long. Especially not for a *man*."

Well, I guess Dad knew Mom pretty well after all.

"Perhaps she's holding council with those irritating Elders of yours," he said, "deciding what to do with the talisman."

"You don't think Elias has it?"

"Elias, as you said, wants to prove his ability to hang on to the talisman this time. If he had it, I'm sure he'd let me know."

"Maybe he thinks it's safer if you don't."

Dad's eyes narrowed dangerously. His posture stiffened. Leaning forward, he rested his elbows on his knees. Thin fingers pointed at me like arrows. "Be certain before you hurl accusations, little princess."

Man, Dad was touchy. Or nervous. Maybe he didn't trust himself to hold on to the talisman either. Still, it wouldn't do to ruffle his feathers any more than I already had. "Um, okay."

Silence stretched, and I found myself noticing the tangled cobwebs clinging in the folds of the velvet curtains, smudges on the leaded-glass window, and the smell of old books. After staring at me for a long time, Dad visibly relaxed. "You will do something for me," he said.

"I will?"

"Yes. You will be my spy here. Amelia knows something, I'm certain. It's far too convenient that she's missing at the same time as the talisman. You will report her comings and goings to Elias."

"Uh," I started, but he lifted a hand again.

"It's decided," he said with a flourish. Standing up, he swept out of the room. "I will expect word of anything suspicious or strange."

Strange? My mom was always strange. "I don't think I can do this," I said, but he was already at the door, letting himself out. I scrambled to my feet. "Dad!"

He stopped midstride. I'd forgotten that I'd never called him anything other than Ramses out loud. "What is it, my child?"

"I can't spy on my own mother," I said from where I hugged the archway. "It's not cool."

The look he gave me was patronizing. "You'll do fine. You already speak to Elias on a regular basis. Just let him know if you think Amelia has the talisman. You would tell him that anyway, wouldn't you?"

He had me there.

I nodded. "All right," I said. "I suppose."

"Then I have your word," he said. "Oh and please stop making marital decisions for vampire families you know nothing about. You've caused the family quite a lot of trouble. I should make you handle the Southern prince who no longer has a wife," he added, and swept his royal self out the door.

I poured myself a bowl of cereal and took it back into the parlor to eat. It was such a grand room. Kind of a shame we never used it. Against one wall was an upright piano I had vague memories of taking lessons on. The rest of the room was filled with a half dozen bookshelves piled with the kinds of things regular people read—mysteries, nonfiction, philosophy, cookbooks. I imagined

Grandma and Grandpa spent a lot of time in this room. I wondered sometimes if Mom avoided rearranging things to preserve their memories or because she wanted to leave them locked in one place and forget them.

My own recollections were based more on yellowed photographs than actual impressions. Had they been alive to meet Dad? What did they think of the whole vampire/witch union? Did they approve?

I should remember to ask Mom sometime.

Sitting in my grandfather's chair, I munched Cap'n Crunch. Through rippled glass, I watched clouds pass in front of the full moon.

Full moon!

Relief washed over me. Of course! Mom was at the covenstead, celebrating esbat!

It was still unusual that she hadn't left me a message, but she probably ran late at work and forgot. I'd gotten myself worked up over nothing! And worse, the fact that I'd had no idea tonight was full moon meant Bea was right. I'd completely abandoned my witch side. What kind of witch didn't even follow the phases of the moon?

When I finished my cereal, I switched off the lights in the parlor and put the bowl in the kitchen. On the wall near the sink Mom had a trivet with a pentacle in the center of it. My fingers brushed the five-pointed star shape, allowing me to sense the residual magic with which Mom had invested it. Under my hand, the cast iron felt warm, and the scent of loamy dirt tickled my nose briefly.

Back in my room, I discovered the station on my laptop playing an old 10,000 Maniacs song, and my phone complaining about a low battery. I found my charger, and when I plugged it in, I decided to text Nikolai. I told him I heard his interview, and I wished him a happy esbat. While I was thinking of it, I sent Bea the same, only I asked her if she'd heard Nik on the radio.

Then, before Bea could even respond, I added that she was probably right about me. I'd been a terrible witch lately. Well, to be fair, I was kind of pouting. Since I didn't pass my Initiation, I wasn't allowed in the Inner Circle, where Real Magic was practiced. But it wasn't like I didn't know the Goddess was real insofar as magic worked. Heck, even the vampires worshipped the Goddess in their own way. Ah well, I could at least pray like I used to.

My altar had been gathering dust. I used to be so proud of its simple, elegant design, even though it wasn't much more than trinkets gathered on the top of a bookshelf. Grabbing an old T-shirt from my dirty-clothes pile at the bottom of my armoire, I polished everything. I replaced the statuette of the Egyptian cat goddess, Bast, and the snake-headed Nile goddess figurine.

Snake-headed. Weird.

I held the goddess in my hand for a moment. Wasn't that what the infamous talisman was supposed to look like too? The image of the sleek female figure with her arms upraised was ubiquitous in both the Wiccan and True Witch communities. You could find versions of it everywhere—coven logos, Web sites, and even T-shirts. I think I'd ordered this one from some New Age store in Madison. No, Mom had given it to me as a solstice present.

Had nonwitches recognized the power of this symbol unconsciously? Or had they seen it held up by witches to control vampires in the past and tried to copy it?

Either way, I no longer wanted this symbol of vampire slavery on my altar. I dropped it into my desk drawer. It landed at the bottom with a thunk. Great. Now I didn't even have my familiar goddess to look to for guidance. I felt weirdly adrift.

My phone trilled. Bea sent me a smiley face and said she was glad I'd "come around."

I asked her if her dad had given her a Nile goddess for her altar. Bea's dad was one of the coven's Elders. Though witchcraft traveled matrilineally through the bloodlines, Bea's mom had, like me, failed the Initiation. Anyway, I was curious if we were all encouraged to have this same icon. Like Elias had said the other day, we might forget what it meant, but vampires would always remember. But I kept that last part to myself.

Bea wrote back that of course he had. Why did I ask?

In my room I could find a dozen or more likenesses of the Nile goddess. Mom had even sewn one into the quilt on my bed. Wow. It was such a slap in the vampire face. Like saying, "We could own you again, see?" I determined to get rid of every one of them. Why hadn't Elias said anything?

"Just curious," I returned.

Then she told me she'd heard Nik on the radio too. What did I think of it?

It seemed to me like she was fishing to see if I'd heard him say he was heartbroken. So I replied, "Cool songs."

Just then, Nik texted. I opened it with some trepidation. All it said was, "It's true."

What was I supposed to say to that? My first impulse was to type, "Oh, really?" But, you know, there were too many ways to take that, and I didn't want to always be the one to start off belligerently.

In the meantime, Bea prodded me with, "Did u hear what he said?"

I answered that I did. I knew she wanted more than that, so I added, "Don't know how 2 feel."

Reopening Nik's message, I stared at the words. I decided not to make it too easy for him, so I typed, "What's true?"

"Miss u."

By chance, the radio played "Teardrops on My Guitar." "Miss u 2," I keyed. I almost pressed Send, but decided to remind him, "Complicated."

I waited, but there was no response. I turned my phone off and laid it facedown on my desk. I laid my head down next. Emotions roiled in my gut, sitting uneasily with my sugary dinner. The breeze coming in from my window was cool, inviting.

Stuffing my phone in my pocket, but not turning it on yet, I grabbed a sweater and my keys. On a piece of paper from the printer tray, I scribbled, "E. Find me," and then taped it to my window. Then I positioned the sock signal, even though I doubted he'd see it. He had things on his mind, and it wasn't our usual "date" night.

On another piece of paper I wrote, "Mom—out for a walk," and left that one on the kitchen table near the bowl into which Mom always dropped her pocket change. I made sure to lock the door behind me.

Bea might be right about the vampire thing, but I couldn't help but feel better out under the stars, fresh air in my lungs. Not for the first time, I wondered why vampires were such nature freaks. If they weren't even from this earth, why did they have such an affinity for all things outdoors?

It was baffling.

Even though it was Friday night, the streets were empty. A common joke about St. Paul was that it rolled its streets up after five. Most people assumed that was because St. Paul was naturally more sedate and grown-up than its twin, Minneapolis. I knew the truth. Vampires.

Unlike Minneapolis, St. Paul was built on porous sandstone, and the ground beneath my feet was riddled with caves—man-made and natural—and most of them were occupied by creatures of the night. My people.

My responsibility.

No matter what Bea said, the truth of the matter was that I was their princess. Okay, when I put it that way, it seemed kind of silly. I mean, so far I'd issued exactly two orders and apparently both of them had been wrong.

And it was probably just as big a mistake to agree to spy on Mom. But if Dad was right and Elias didn't have the talisman and witches decided to enslave everyone again, then I really did need to warn everyone.

But at least there wasn't much I could do about that right now. When Mom came home tonight, I could see if I could get some information from her without giving too much away—practice my acting skills.

Old-fashioned streetlamps cast pools of soft yellow light on the boulevard. Not a lot of people had mowed yet, and the grass was dotted with heart-shaped leaves of woodland violets and brazen, leggy dandelion stalks.

Cars lined the street. TV screens flickered bluish white. Voices and canned laughter drifted through open windows. I walked alone, like a trespasser, down the street. I shoved my hands into the pockets of my jeans, and my fingers curled around the lump of my phone.

I'd come out here to think about Nikolai; I needed to make a decision about how I felt about him, about us. There was no doubt in my mind that I liked being his girlfriend. The concerts were cool. I enjoyed hanging out backstage and even with the band while they practiced. The groupies were a nuisance and made me horribly insecure. But if being in a popular band was the only problem between me and Nik, I could find a way to deal.

The real issue was that Nikolai was training—or had finished training—to kill vampires. Honestly, the distinction didn't matter all that much. Okay, so I could push the thought to the back of my mind when he was only an apprentice, but it was always there.

I walked along a retaining wall made of stone, letting my hand trail along its rough surface.

Could I date someone who hunted vampires? It would be different if vampires were actually as inhuman as Bea and Nikolai kept telling me they were. So, they came from hell and Bea was convinced they supped on witch blood, but that wasn't what I saw. Elias was a nice guy. He brought me flowers and sat in the tree outside my window and listened to my woes.

Granted, I'd been kept at arm's length from a lot of what went on underground. The one time Elias and I crashed the scene down there, it had creeped me out a little. Vampires didn't always wear clothes and I'd seen a lot more nakedness than I wanted to. The whole thing was animalistic and unsettlingly alien.

There was a lot I didn't know.

Had I been kept in the dark on purpose?

Dad could have brought me into the fold after the big show-down last fall when I inadvertently became betrothed to Elias, but he didn't. It was ironic, really, that he was all bent out of shape over this Khan woman when it wasn't as if anyone had taken the time to give me a vampire culture 101 course. How was I supposed to know arranged marriages were the norm? How was I supposed to know *anything* about being a vampire princess?

Maybe they didn't want me to know because they knew there would be things I'd object to.

A dog barked from behind a wooden fence. I hurried past its territory.

But if I knew all the vampires' secrets, would it make a dif-ference in my relationship with Nik? Let's say vampires *were* one hundred percent evil. I was still half one. Even if I somehow helped Nikolai take out every last vampire on earth, wouldn't he eventually look at me and wonder? Even if he didn't, wouldn't his dad or the other True Witches put pressure on us?

I rubbed the space between my eyes. Now I was *over*think-ing things.

The dog barked again. Someone was following me. I stopped and turned. "Elias?"

Chapter Eight

The sidewalk was empty. I checked the trees. No sign of anyone. Yet I still had the sense I was not alone.

"Who's there?" My voice sounded small, the empty sky swallowing the impact of my question. But I stood my ground and continued to scan the street.

A raccoon scuttled out from under a car. Scurrying across the street, it slipped into a rain gutter.

"Oh, okay. Now I feel stupid," I said.

Though I never entirely shook the sensation of being watched, I made it home without incident. I didn't really have an answer to the Nik question, but I also couldn't see how we could work things out either.

Elias waited for me on the front porch. I sat down on the swing next to him. His long legs stretched out to cross at the ankles elegantly, but otherwise his posture was slouched. He was dressed in his usual basic black, though this time he had shoes—engineer boots, no less. I tapped the toe of his boot with the tip of my Converse.

"I think I got you in trouble," I admitted quietly. "With Dad."

He lifted an eyebrow, and sighed. "I failed. I was too late. The talisman is gone."

"Someone else has it?" A shiver flitted across my skin. My voice dropped to a whisper. "Um, us . . . I mean, the witches?"

Elias's head bowed in defeat. "It's uncertain, but likely."

"Wow." I hadn't meant to say that, exactly, but it was the only thing that came out.

"I was pleased to find your note," he said, the strain of trying to sound cheerful evident in his voice. "I wanted to see you. We should celebrate the end of the world."

"Oh, Elias—," I started, but he cut me off.

"The time for pity is past. Tonight is about freedom, and enjoying it while it lasts. Come with me? Some of us are gathering at Lilydale."

If Mom was out at the covenstead celebrating the full moon, she wouldn't be home until late anyway. Besides, it was Friday night. "Sure, why not?"

Elias had brought his car, which was a big black hybrid. I never thought of vampires driving around, so it felt strange to buckle into the passenger seat. Once, when I'd asked him about it, he explained that no one rode horses anymore, so what alternative did he have? Most of the public transportation services cut off sometime after midnight, when his day was just getting started. Still, it was so odd to see him behind the wheel of something so modern, I asked, "Do you even have a license?"

"Yes, but it's forged."

"Um, eek?"

"The DMV hours are not vampire-friendly."

I guessed not much was, like banks or even car dealerships. "Do I want to know how you got this?" I ran my hands along the shiny dashboard. It still smelled new.

"Igors are good for a lot of things," he said simply, pushing the ignition button. Of course, I still didn't know if he meant for buying cars or for stealing them. I didn't ask for clarification. The engine hummed quietly to life. Patting the steering wheel, he said, "I'll miss driving. Perhaps my new master—" He stopped, his grip tightening.

What to say to that? I looked out through the window as we rolled down the street I'd just walked. Still, his comment got me thinking. "How does the talisman work? I mean, there's only one. So how do you get, well, assigned masters?"

"That's actually a good question. I suppose we'll return to the family line," he said with a shrug. When I looked confused, he explained. "Whenever a witch wanted a new servant, the Council of Elders gave permission for the talisman to be brought out of its hiding place. You see, we're bonded to whoever is holding the talisman when we're brought over. Then, like any valued piece of property, we are inherited down the family tree."

No wonder witches kept such careful track of lineage. "What if there are no children or none of them become witches?"

Elias gave me a sidelong glance. "That's why hunters were invented. They tracked down and destroyed all rogue demons." He said nothing, letting that information settle in for a moment. "There were always stories, legends, really, of people who'd stayed free, and attacked witches from hideouts deep in ancient forests or along forbidding mountain ranges."

"Like Robin Hood?"

"More like Dracula or Carmilla." He laughed.

"Oh," I said quietly, absently playing with a loose thread on my sweater. So Bea was right about this too. Vampires did go after witches, or at least their folk heroes did. "Is that what the hunt is about? Killing witches?"

Elias turned down Summit toward John Ireland Boulevard. Spotlights made the cathedral's stone walls glow brightly, and it appeared almost surreally crisp against the night.

"Ah," Elias said. "Someone has been speaking out of turn."

"But is it true?"

"Yes." I must have looked stricken, because he added, "Keep in mind, my lady, though we were no longer oppressed by our masters, we were still a hidden, unaccounted-for people. If we fed on mortal men, we would surely be discovered. Only witches would keep our secret, lest they risk exposing their own."

Did Bea have to be so damn right about everything? My mouth twisted into a grimace. "Plus it must be satisfying to sink your teeth into people who used to order you around."

We turned past the Historical Society; its flat, impenetrable stone facade made it look like a fortress of knowledge. It must have taken powerful magic to get inside there. Elias didn't speak until we turned again, this time onto 35E heading south.

"It was, at first," he admitted. "But one hunt will satisfy us for many years—a generation, in fact. Time passed; hated masters died of old age. There was no one left to take revenge on, and their children were innocent of their mothers' crimes."

"And you killed them anyway."

"It was decided, for our survival, that we must."

"Decided? You mean by Dad?"

Elias's eyes stayed focused on the road. But even without his acknowledgment I knew the answer. The vampires weren't a democracy. "Pull off," I said. "I want to get out."

He shook his head. "If you had completed the hunt with us, you'd understand. It is how it has always been."

When I turned sixteen, Dad had shown up and tried to convince me to do their sacred hunt instead of the witches' Initiation. I wasn't able to do either, so I stayed something in between, neither witch nor vampire.

"You didn't . . . that night? I mean, I didn't hear—no one died, right?"

"No, when it was clear you wouldn't join us, the prince called it off." Elias hadn't moved the car toward the exit. In fact, he switched to the middle lane. "We'd waited a long time for you to mature. The hunger grows." He snorted a dark chuckle. "At least our bondage will come with a high price."

"What does that mean?" I looked out at the cars rushing past, feeling trapped.

"It means, my dear lady, that once again the witches will have to provide for us, as they did in the past. I wonder if anyone remembers the dark gift, the devil's deal."

He sounded so sinister, not at all like the gentle courtier I'd grown to like. "I really want to go home now," I said, my hand groping uselessly at the car handle. Lights whooshed past, dizzying strobes. "You need to let me out."

"It was the weakest ones, you know." He didn't seem to have heard me. "Those who couldn't pass their Initiation that they sacrificed."

"Wait—what are you saying? Are you saying that the witches used to feed you one of their own?"

He took his eyes from the road long enough to give me a hard stare. He nodded. "Yes, Anastasija, that's exactly what I'm saying."

It had to be a lie. I shook my head violently. "No way would people put up with that."

"Protesters were easy to silence with us under their command," he said grimly. The sound of the tires changed as we crossed onto a wide bridge spanning the Mississippi.

I looked out at the expanse of water, a strip of moonlight rippling across the blackness. Beside me, I heard Elias let out a soft sigh. I jumped when his hand briefly patted my thigh. He pulled it away quickly, guiltily.

"I didn't mean to frighten you. I understand that it's hard to believe," he said, as if reading my mind. "But unless our new masters decide to let us all die of hunger, you'll see. The bargain will be struck once again, and a sacrifice will be made."

This was awful. My stomach clenched. Bea was so right, but yet so wrong about everything. I didn't know whom to be more disgusted by. For the first time since I turned sixteen and found out about everything, I was really, really grateful that I hadn't chosen a side, because the truth was, both sucked.

That wasn't fair, I supposed, but I was frustrated by this whole hunt situation. "Can't you survive on human blood? I mean, when I tasted Thompson . . ." I stopped. It was too weird to admit how delicious the experience had been.

Elias smiled sadly. "Human blood is like chocolate or junk food. It tastes great, but there's simply not enough nutrition to sustain a healthy life. Vampires who have gone rogue often subsist on human blood at the cost of their sanity."

"Oh." I chewed on my lip for some time, before offering up

another suggestion, "What about taking just a little from a witch and, you know, not killing?"

"Do you think in all the millennia that witches and vampires have existed, no one has tried that?" He kept his tone sympathetic, but I could sense his frustration building. Elias shook his head as if trying to let something go. "Forget it for now, Ana. Now it's time to dance one last dance of freedom."

Elias pulled off the highway onto a residential street. Houses slid by and we were in the park almost instantly. A small sidewalk ran along a narrow strip of manicured grass. The cliff's edge was marked by a tangle of trees. Where the curb curved inward, he maneuvered the car into a parking spot. The streetlights were set farther apart than the ones I was used to in the city, somehow making the night deeper. As I stepped out and closed the car door, I could see stars through the clouds.

I hugged myself from the cold and the heavy knot in my gut.

Elias came around and put his arms on my shoulders. Though I cringed away, he gave me a reassuring squeeze before letting me go. "None of this will matter soon enough, my princess," he said. "What will happen with the hunt will no longer be in our control."

I blinked. "You mean, you think it will happen to me too?"

When he offered a hand, I took it this time. He led me down the sidewalk, away from the car. "It's hard to say. There were, of course, witch children born to vampires, and vampire offspring born to witches, but . . . few were allowed to survive, at least of the former variety."

"I don't understand the difference."

We passed under one of the long-neck streetlights. "I suppose there really isn't one, only a matter of perspective. If you're born in the master's house, different rules apply."

"Gross," I said with a *tsk* of my tongue.

Elias laughed. "That's a word for it."

I could hear the strains of music. In the distance, someone played the fiddle. The tune was light and airy. Drums picked out a dancing rhythm. Elias flashed me a playful smile and pulled me along faster. I followed as we ran down the sidewalk past a chain-link fence that looked over a steep drop. On the other side, the grassy area widened. Elias guided me off the pavement to a narrow opening in the woods. I would have thought it was little more than a deer trail, except for the crunch of gravel underfoot.

We went only a short distance before the path twisted and became steep. My steps skidded, but Elias didn't slow. "I'm going to fall," I protested.

"You're a vampire princess, Anastasija Parker," he reminded me. "You could fly down this hill if you chose. Stop holding me back. I want to dance."

He let go of my hand. I grabbed for him and almost ended up on my ass. Bounding ahead of me, he disappeared out of sight into the darkness. "Wait!" I shouted. I didn't know this park at all. I didn't want to be lost.

"No, Ana. Fly!"

I didn't have to dig very deeply to find my inner vampire. She seemed closer to the surface than ever before. In a second, the landscape brightened, pulsing with energy. Every obstacle became visible, and I saw Elias just at the fork in the trail. He flashed a knowing, fangy grin as he dashed to the left.

The downward momentum that I'd been fighting against

now became my ally. In a burst of speed, I caught up with him. I could have run past, but I didn't know where we were headed. The music was much louder now. I smelled the swampy scent of river nearby. A bat skimmed over my head.

"Echo Cave," Elias shouted against the wind of our speed.

The path evened out, and I could see tall reeds along the riverbank. We'd come to the bottom of the valley. Sandstone cliffs rose like a wall, and I could see the mouth of a cave. Vampires had camped out in front of the boarded-up entrance. A row of drummers leaned against the concrete pylons, and the fiddler stood under the lip of the entrance, taking advantage of the natural acoustics. Bats streamed in and out over their heads.

People danced free-form to the music. Men and women, all the indeterminate age of vampires, leaped and turned in the absolute darkness of the night. The city lights were far beyond, and no campfire or torches blazed.

Elias took my hands, and spun me out into the center of it all. "Come," he said. "Let us be free."

The drums pounded an infectious beat. The music was unlike anything I'd ever heard before, though it seemed some strange amalgam of an Irish jig and a powerful West African tempo. My body didn't care. The music swept me in. It was easy to forget about all the crazy I'd just learned, and lose myself in the rhythm.

I danced.

At school formals, I was very self-conscious and awkward. But here, under the stars with the wild all around, I moved without a thought of how I might look to others. Though dozens of bodies spun and wove in the clearing with inhuman grace, I felt alone—just Elias and me, hidden together under a protective blanket of darkness.

He circled me, twisting and turning with the music, our bodies tantalizingly close, but never quite touching. My heart thumped in time to the song. My skin flushed.

In his element, his features softened. His body retained its predatory sharpness and angles, but dancing soothed something in him. Taut lines on his face disappeared, replaced by an elation I'd never seen before. Noticing my attention, he pulled me close, wrapping his arms around my waist.

Our dancing slowed to a gentle sway. We were an island of stillness in the center of a pulsing crowd. Reaching up, I clasped my hands around his neck. His eyes searched mine. Apparently finding what he was looking for, he leaned down, drawing me even closer.

Our lips met.

The kiss was over in a moment, but the giddy sensation of it lingered, spreading deep inside me, all the way to my toes. We'd stopped moving entirely. His neck bent again, but this time his lips brushed my ears. Somehow over the music, I heard him whisper, "If fate takes me away from you, my lady, know this: being your betrothed was my greatest honor."

Expertly, he spun me away from him, back into the dance. Energized by the kiss and his words, I rejoined the frenzy with a whoop. He returned my wild smile, and the music took us again.

Chapter Nine

One by one in the hours before dawn, vampires disappeared into the warrens of Echo Cave. The music wound down, leaving Elias and me holding hands on the banks of the river solemnly watching as the instruments were packed away.

I'd been out all night. Mom was going to kill me.

"We should get you home," Elias said, reluctantly. The moon hung low on the horizon. Though it was still dark, the light had a different quality to it. I felt certain deep in my bones that sunrise was imminent.

"What about you? Will you be okay?"

We started up the path that led back to the car. The muscles in my legs felt the strain of the sharp incline, not to mention the long night. "I'm not expecting a traffic jam." He smiled. "I can get you home quickly, but I may have to leave my car in your neighborhood."

I knew from past experience that Elias had a hidey-hole not

far from my house. My shoulders relaxed somewhat, but I did my best to keep up with the brisk pace Elias set.

We hadn't spoken about the kiss. I held his hand firmly as we made our way up the slope, reveling in our nearness. Exhaustion began to insinuate itself into every pore. By the time we reached the car, I had only enough energy to slump into the seat and tip my head back against the rest. I closed my eyes to the gritty heaviness. The soft sounds of the car and empty road soon lulled me to sleep.

Like a fairy-tale prince, Elias woke me with a kiss. Though the pressure on my skin was featherlight, his heat raced through me. I blinked, instantly awake.

"It's time for good-bye," he said, pulling away.

I sat up and sucked in a deep breath. "I hope not forever."

"Me too, dear princess," he said, turning away, avoiding the concern I was sure etched my face. "Me too."

Though I wanted to linger, I knew he had to get underground before the sun rose. I pulled myself up out of the car with effort. My feet dragged from tiredness, but also with reluctance to break the spell of the incredible night we'd shared. I wanted to say something hopeful like "See you soon" or "Let's do this again," but it all seemed inadequate. The next time I saw Elias, he could be someone's slave. I could be too, but I didn't want to think about that. I wondered how the talisman would change him. How completely would he be enthralled? Would he know me? Or would he simply be unable to speak freely?

I must have looked stricken, standing stock-still on the curb with the open car door still gripped in my hand, because Elias mustered a soft smile. "I'll think of you, always."

The sky had begun to lighten, changing from black to deep blue. Elias reached across the seat and gently pulled the door from my grasp and closed it with an awful, final-sounding latch. The car engine thrummed to life. He hesitated only a moment longer before driving off.

I stayed on the boulevard, unmoving. His car retreated into the distance, finally moving out of sight. Numbly, I stumbled into the house. Sadness and fatigue overwhelmed me and I dragged myself upstairs to collapse onto my bed, too tired to even cry.

I woke up to the sensation of my pocket vibrating. The numbers on the alarm clock told me that I'd gotten only a couple of hours' of sleep; it was nine a.m. I tried to roll over and go back to sleep, but there was a buzzing at my hip again.

Through the fog of drowsiness, my brain finally registered the fact that my phone was ringing. Clumsy fingers dug it from my pocket and put it to my ear. "Mmmr?" It was supposed to be "Hello" but my mouth wasn't working properly yet.

"Oh my God! Oh my God! We're on the callback list! All of us! Even Thompson!"

"Bea?"

"I've been standing outside of school since six a.m. waiting for Martinez to post the list. A whole bunch of us were camped out, actually; it was kind of cool. I texted you, like, six times. Where have you been?"

"Dance." I could hardly keep my eyes open, much less formulate coherent responses. I had a vague memory of having switched off my phone to go for a walk, but I couldn't remember when I turned it back on. I must have done it out of habit before going facedown on the sheets.

"You went to a dance? Was this at some other school? Well, it doesn't matter," she said before I could do more than grunt. "I called to give you fair warning, girl. You'd better start practicing something phenomenal, because I'm going to kick your ass and take the lead."

"Mmm, okay. Good luck," I said without thinking.

"Ah, no fair! The curse!"

It was a well-known theater superstition that you never wished another actor good luck on a show. Instead, you were supposed to trick fate by inviting calamity instead. I quickly apologized. "No, I'm sorry. I mean break a leg."

"Too late! Ah! Oh!" Bea reminded me of the cartoon character of Lucy after Snoopy had just given her a doggy kiss, shouting about disinfectant and other paranoia. It all seemed far too loud to my weary ears.

"Hanging up now," I told her, and I did so.

I drifted back to sleep without even remembering to ask when callbacks started.

A wild beat invaded my dreams. Vampires, in various states of undress, undulated and rippled, finally melting into a squirming pile of fleshy snakes. The sun was rising and I was yelling for them to go underground, but they were all on fire, bright, hot light pouring everywhere.

I woke up sweaty, with the afternoon streaming in the window. Squinting, I sat up, shaking the remnants of the strange dream from my mind. I picked up the alarm clock and held it close to my eyes, willing the number to make sense. Was it really nearly three?

My teeth felt slimy. I shuffled my way to the bathroom, but stopped when I passed the door to my mom's bedroom. The bed was made; it looked as though it hadn't been slept in.

"Mom?" I called, and then again, louder, with an edge of panic, *"Mom?"*

I thought I heard a faint reply. The voice had come from outside. Even though I rarely entered Mom's sanctum sanctorum without permission, I scooted across the floor in my stocking feet to look out her window to the backyard. To my extreme relief, Mom was standing on the grass with her hands on her hips looking up. She had on the wide-brimmed straw hat and bright yellow galoshes she wore for gardening. Seeing me, Mom put a hand over her eyes to shield them from the sun. "Finally up?"

"Um, yeah," I said, waiting anxiously to see if she'd mention what time I'd come home. But then again, maybe she'd come in after me. I hadn't seen her MINI when Elias dropped me off, had I?

"I'll come in. We should have a little lunch."

I smiled. Even though Parkers weren't native Minnesotans, Mom meant "a little lunch" in the way people used that phrase around here, which meant a big spread. My stomach gave an anticipatory growl. "I'm starving."

"I'll make bacon."

In a half hour, I sat down to the promised bacon, scrambled eggs with cream cheese (my favorite), fresh strawberries, orange juice, and a good, strong black tea (Mom wasn't a coffee drinker). Once I'd devoured as much as my stomach could hold, I felt almost human again. Mom said very little while I stuffed my face, and I wondered what she knew. Did she know I'd been out all night with Elias? Could she tell that Dad had been here, past the wards? And that he'd asked me to spy on her, to find out what she knew about the talisman?

At the thought of the talisman, I swallowed wrong, nearly choking on the orange juice.

"Are you all right, Ana?" Mom had finished her brunch—or maybe it was lunner, lunch/dinner, given the hour. She sat watching me, the large, round glasses perched on her nose making her look like an owl.

"Fine," I said much too defensively. Clearing my throat, I covered my mouth with a napkin as I tried to compose myself. "So, uh, how was esbat?"

Mom seemed surprised by the question. "Oh, the same as usual, I suppose."

Was it me, or did she sound unconvincing? "You sure left early the other morning."

"You certainly came in late last night."

Damn. Checkmate.

Mom smirked like she knew she won that round, so I said with a casual shrug, "Yeah, Elias and the vampires were celebrating. They asked me to join them." I squinted a little as I waited for her response. I figured I'd get a chewing out, given how much Mom hated Elias and the vampires.

When no rant was forthcoming, I hazarded a glance at Mom's face. Her brows were knit together, but she seemed less mad than curious. "Celebrating? Really? What exactly?"

"The end of the world as they know it." I'd meant that to come out more sly, but a note of sadness crept in.

She might have had a response, but my phone trilled. It was a text from Taylor. "U coming? Starts in ten."

"Oh crap!" I jumped up, wishing I'd had time to take a bath or at least comb my hair. "I've got to go. Callbacks are starting!"

"You got a callback for the musical? That's lovely, dear." Mom was getting up, and gathering her purse and keys. "I'll give you a ride and we can continue this interesting conversation."

So I was stuck with Mom, which was a good/bad thing. She was certainly acting suspicious. Normal Mom would have given me an earful for staying out with Elias, but it turned out I wasn't so good at weaseling information out of people. I hoped that didn't mean my acting abilities were slipping, especially with a second audition looming.

When I headed for the front, Mom waved me to the back door. I discovered she'd parked the MINI in the alley. We had a mostly abandoned carriage house with a barely there paved space behind it, but she'd never used it once we got the fancy MINI. She always said that even as small as the MINI was, she feared people would hit it or steal it. As I waited in the alley for her to back it out, my eyes lit on the windows of the top floor of the carriage house. The curtain moved.

Was someone up there?

"Do we have a guest?" I asked as I buckled in. Sometimes when visiting witches came to town, Mom put them up there, since it was private and had all the amenities of a small guesthouse.

"No. Why do you ask?"

"I thought I saw someone in the carriage house," I said.

"I'm sure you were just imagining it," she said, which made me instantly suspicious. Because Mom refused to rent to mundanes—we couldn't have them accidentally seeing us practice True Witchcraft, after all!—she periodically worried about squatters. No, rephrase that—she was unbelievably *paranoid* about squatters.

For her to dismiss my concern so quickly could mean only one thing.

Now the real question became, who was it? And why didn't Mom want me to know they were staying there? Could it be that the person who had the talisman was right in my own backyard?

My stomach tightened.

"Now, what's this about the end of the world?" Mom was saying as we turned out onto the street. "You know that whole Mayan calendar thing is a hoax, right?"

"Elias is worried about his freedom," I said boldly. I thought maybe if I told a bit of the truth, she might give something more away. "He seems to think it might go away."

"Why would he think that?" Her voice was all professorial, as if she was fishing for a specific answer.

Damn. She was good at this cat-and-spy thing. I shrugged and averted my eyes by looking out the window. Even though I clearly needed the practice, I didn't think I could lie convincingly right now. "Because . . ." Should I tell her what I knew? "I don't know."

We rolled through the residential streets, Mom slowing at every intersection. "So, he didn't tell you?"

Was she about to reveal that she had the talisman? I tried to keep the interest out of my voice. "Tell me what?"

"Why he thought he was going to lose his freedom."

I let out the breath I didn't realize I'd been holding. "Oh. No, he didn't."

Mom frowned at the windshield. "Well, that's not very helpful."

"No, it isn't," I agreed.

This time the number of people loitering around the atrium in front of the main theater doors seemed much more typical. It was empty expect for Taylor and Lane, who stood over by the lockers, their heads bent together over a script page. Seeing me come in, Taylor looked relieved. "You made it!"

"Mr. Martinez has only just started," Lane agreed. They scurried over to me. "We should probably go in. He's going to lock the doors in a couple of minutes."

It was standard practice to keep the riffraff and stragglers out, but it made me hurry to think I'd almost defaulted on a possible role.

We pulled the doors open quietly. Inside, the houselights had been dimmed. A single circle of light gleamed center stage. The three of us shared a glance. This wasn't the informal system we were used to. Mr. Martinez had pulled out all the stops; it was hard enough to do callbacks, but to have to do it in a spotlight? That was harsh.

Mr. Martinez had taken the stage. We dashed to the first set of open seats. I could see the frizzy curl of Bea's hair a few rows up. She'd positioned herself next to Todd, the assistant director. It was the suck-up spot, but it was also a dangerous gamble. If Todd found you too helpful, you could end up as another directorial assistant running gofer errands, and not in the show at all.

Mr. Martinez cleared his throat and the soft murmuring in the house dropped to dead silence. Because there were newbies to theater present, he explained how callbacks worked. Everyone would have a chance to perform something small. But when that was over, you needed to hang around. You might be asked back to the stage just to stand next to someone or say a line or two.

"Now it's time to get started," he said. Tipping his glasses up onto his head, he scanned the names on his clipboard. You could almost hear the collective breath being held. With a dramatic flourish, he scanned the room. "Ana Parker? Matthew Thompson?"

Oh God. First.

I took the script sheet Lane handed me, adrenaline spiking, as I made my way up the aisle to the stage. Thompson bounded up the other side, confident and smiling. I wanted to shake my head and tell him to wipe that grin off his face. Being first was the worst! You didn't have a chance to assess everyone else's performance, figure out the nuances they'd missed, and really do it right. Now we'd be the ones everyone else was riffing on and improving on.

Great.

Ah well, actually getting into this play was a pipe dream, anyway. I mean, I had two different-colored eyes. Eliza Doolittle and Ana Parker could not be more different. I had a better chance at being Mary Magdalene in *Jesus Christ Superstar* than getting this role.

By the time I stood next to Thompson, I'd talked myself out of about six other plays as well, and my shoulders dropped. Besides, my lucky shirt was in the hamper. In fact, I was still wearing my clothes from last night.

Thompson gave me a broad wink. I smiled back, but I was thinking what an unlikely pair we were. Neither of us was going to get a part. I might as well relax and have fun.

From the darkened house, Mr. Martinez told us where to start. Thompson wasn't a polished actor by any stretch of the imagination, but he didn't stumble over any words. In fact, there was a kind of raw sincerity to the way he spoke the lines that was sort of endearing. The scene Mr. Martinez had picked was one where Eliza and Professor Higgins are kind of flirty, but sort of not getting along too. It was easy for the two of us; in a way, that was already our relationship in real life.

He asked Thompson to stay onstage and sing a solo, which, to no one's surprise this time, he totally nailed. Music, this boy could do.

I went back to my seat as directed. Taylor and Lane gave me the usual murmurs of encouragement, but I found myself feeling distant, removed. What if the talisman was activated today, like Elias feared? How would it happen? Would the vampires get returned to their masters one by one, or would it be some kind of instantaneous thing? Would it affect me at all? Would I just get up and walk away, compelled by some outside force?

Lane elbowed me in the ribs. At my confused look, he pointed to the stage. Had I been called? I pointed to my chest, and he nodded. I hurried back up the aisle. When I got there, I noticed I'd forgotten my script. Mr. Martinez sighed at my empty hands. "Could someone please loan Ana a script?"

Bea handed hers to Todd, who gave it to me. For the next ten minutes I read the same lines over and over with a number of different boys. First, there was Malcolm, one of the few black guys in our theater clique. I thought he might actually make a good lead; he was certainly arrogant enough to play Professor Higgins. Next up was Lane, who, IMHO, totally overacted. Some guy I didn't know followed. He was pretty good except he flubbed a laugh line, and then Thompson was called again.

When he caught my eye, Thompson gave me a look that made me blush. It was sort of a secret smile, only just in his eyes, and it made me feel like he wanted more than just this part. I actually stammered the opening line that I'd just repeated a zillion times!

Thompson started speaking, and that simple, natural way he had with the lines drew me in. In a moment, the scene was over, and I was left staring up at Thompson again. "Thanks," he whispered. "You always make that easier."

Funny, I'd been thinking the same about him.

Now it was Thompson's turn to stand up and read against the others. From my seat, I watched Bea flirt outrageously, Taylor look a bit frightened, and some of the other girls fall flat. While I watched the parade—and it definitely was, as there were far more girls than boys—I got a funny feeling at the back of my neck. My hairs stood on end.

I shivered.

Was it starting? Had someone activated the talisman?

As if expecting to see the goddess figure floating threateningly in the air, I glanced over my shoulder. Behind me sat a vampire. Okay, I couldn't be certain that was what he was, but the boy—man, really—had an unearthly beauty. His skin was porcelain smooth, and he had deep, silky auburn hair.

"Do I know you?" I asked quietly.

He just shook his head and flashed a feral grin that glinted menacingly in the darkness. Mr. Martinez called Malcolm up to replace Thompson, and when I returned my attention to the vampire, he was gone.

It was like he'd disappeared. I couldn't see a trace of him anywhere in the theater. Scanning the rafters, I almost missed being called up to read against Malcolm.

Our reading went okay—actually, in some ways I had a similar chemistry with Malcolm that I did with Thompson. Malcolm kind of irritated me, but he could be cute when he wasn't being so full of himself. He didn't make me flush or stammer, however. That, apparently, was a skill reserved for Thompson.

As I went back to my seat, I passed Bea. She looked up from whatever she was helping Todd with to give me a jealous sneer. I smiled back, trying to convey that she shouldn't worry.

You could never tell with directors, after all. Sometimes it was very meaningful if you got a lot of stage time during callbacks. Other times, all it meant was that he'd already decided the leads and was having trouble filling the lower spots. Even though I'd been up against a lot of different guys, I was sure Mr. Martinez was just ruling me out for all the other roles. Seriously, Bea made such a better Eliza.

I wished I could tell her so. But she'd just think I was being patronizing.

After another half hour or so, Mr. Martinez thanked everyone for coming. He said his shtick about how everyone had done very well, and what a tough decision he had facing him—blah, blah. We all knew he'd already made up his mind, but he wasn't going to tell anyone until the cast list went up on Monday.

The doors opened, and after the intense contrasts of the theater, even the fluorescents in the atrium seemed subdued and dull. It didn't help that outside, the sky had clouded and a misty rain had begun to fall.

"Are you going to hang around this time, Ana?" Lane asked. "I thought a bunch of us might hit Chipotle for dinner and trash talk."

It sounded good to me, honestly. I could use something normal for a change. I called Mom and let her know my plans and made sure she was cool about it. "Oh, yes," she said, sounding strangely relieved. "Take your time. I'll make something for myself here."

With your mysterious guest, I thought but didn't say.

I should try to sneak out a little early and see if I could catch them together. "I might be out late," I said.

"Fine," she replied cheerfully, which was strange too. Usually if I was open-ended about when I thought I'd be home, she'd take the opportunity to give me a curfew. Or, given my late night, say something about needing to be responsible and get enough sleep.

Something was definitely up with her.

My back itched again, as if someone was watching me. I spun around, half expecting to see that red-haired vampire, but it was Thompson. Malcolm was talking to him by the stage doors, but Thompson's eyes were locked on me. I felt that heat rising again, and I managed to say good-bye to Mom without stammering too much.

"I invited Thompson," Lane said, his voice almost a mischievous purr. "I hope that's okay with you."

"Why wouldn't it be?"

"Chemistry," he said meaningfully.

"More like hormones," Bea added as she came up to us.

I shrugged them off, and pointed to my temple, making the crazy twirl of my finger. "It's all in your imagination." Of course, Thompson chose that moment to come up beside me, and so I choked a bit on the last word.

Everyone laughed.

"What's so funny?" he wanted to know.

"Nothing, darling," Bea said, taking Thompson's arm, although he hadn't offered it. "We just love watching Ana get all gaga over you."

As she swept him out the door, he craned his neck to look back at me. I tried to avoid his curious glance, but I think Thompson noticed my I'm-so-busted expression. How was I going to make it through a whole dinner with him?

I noticed Taylor looking glum, so, to distract myself, I tugged her sleeve. "What's wrong?"

"I really wanted to be in this show."

"What makes you think you won't be?"

"Come on, he hardly called on me," she said, suddenly angry. "Anyway, I'm the only girl in a *hijab*. I'm never going to get a lead."

I understood how she felt, sort of. My eyes had kept me from a lot of the good roles too. So I told her my theory about stage time and callbacks, and that made her brighten a little.

Lane, who I was now pretty sure had a crush on her, reminded her of his idea about how she could be the perfect Eliza. "Besides," he said, "the only way it wouldn't be racist is if he cast Malcolm as the good professor. You saw how he had Malcolm read with everyone. I think for sure he's going to get the part."

I frowned at Thompson's broad shoulders. Despite the light rain, we'd decided to walk.

Lane saw where I was looking and said, "No way. I've got him pegged as Freddy. You heard him sing 'On the Street Where You Live.' He's perfect for something light, but there's no gravitas, you know. Not for Higgins."

I wanted to dismiss Lane's predictions, but for past shows, he'd proven remarkably accurate at guessing Mr. Martinez's taste. And given that we were going rock-opera-y with the music, making the story about something as relevant as the Somali immigrant community finding a way to fit in to "high" society had some merit.

Rain soaked the cotton of my shirt and clung to my shoulders heavily. The drops pitter-pattered as they fell through the canopy of leaves. The smell of wet reminded me of the river, and the kiss Elias and I had shared.

He'd be sleeping now. Younger vampires could stand being out on overcast days, but it was a struggle for Elias.

The conversation continued to buzz around the topic of the play.

I listened halfheartedly, my eyes scanning the street for any sign of the red-haired vampire. Had he been sent to watch over me? That seemed likely, but was he one of the good guys or one of the loyal servants who worked for witches? I kind of doubted Mom had sent him. After all, it wasn't like she didn't know where I was or what I'd be up to. She'd driven me here herself.

He seemed kind of spooky to be one of Elias's knights, though. They tended to at least *try* to be courtly and deferential around me.

As tired as I was, I wondered if maybe I'd imagined him.

The restaurant wasn't too crowded for a Saturday evening, and after getting our food, we managed to find a spot that fit all of us. I ended up squashed in a booth between Lane and Bea. Thompson sat directly across from me.

Taylor looked around helplessly for a moment before determining there was no other option, and put her tray down beside Thompson. "I'm not going to bite," he said.

She seemed unconvinced, especially since he seemed to be inspecting her food choices.

"Are you a vegetarian or something?" he asked.

Taylor looked at me for help. So I explained, "She's Muslim, Thompson. She can't eat meat that's not halal."

"Seriously?"

"Don't be such a bigot," Lane admonished. "It's almost exactly like keeping kosher, which I could do, but it's a hassle."

"You're Jewish?" a bunch of us asked at once.

Lane rolled his eyes, "Yes, yes, Lane Davis, just like Sammy *Davis* Jr. And, let's see, Bea and Ana are witches, and Malcolm is an atheist."

"Secular humanist," he corrected around a mouthful of burrito.

"And you're Catholic, right?" Lane continued, ignoring Malcolm. Thompson nodded. "So that's everyone."

Thompson raised his hands as if in surrender. "Okay, okay, I was just curious." We all went back to our food momentarily, and then, after a thoughtful chew, Thompson asked, "Wait, Sammy Davis Jr. was Jewish?"

We all laughed, the brief tension broken.

I wondered what would happen if Thompson really did get a part in the play. He was so different from the rest of us. Most of the theater people were politically and socially liberal, academic, and, well, a bit odd.

Thompson sort of defined the norm at our school. He was a straight-C student whose only hope for college involved a sports scholarship. I didn't know that for certain, of course. Let's just say I'd never seen his name on the honor roll, and his picture was all over the trophy case.

I shook my head. After all, he wasn't really one of us yet. If he got a part, then we'd have to see if we could transform the jock into the theater geek.

I ate my burrito, letting the familiar banter distract me. I kept a close eye on the clock in the restaurant. My plan was still to get home and surprise Mom at whatever she was up to.

Finishing, I crumpled up the tinfoil. Lane was in the middle of regaling Thompson with a story the rest of us had heard a hundred times, about the time he fell from the catwalk in the middle of opening night of *Macbeth*. Of course, then he had to explain how "that Scottish play" is always cursed. When he was done, I motioned for him to let me out.

"Going already?" Thompson asked.

"Um, I have some . . . stuff I have to do."

"Can I give you a lift?"

I must be the only sixteen-year-old without a license, and everyone at school seemed to know it. "It's okay. I can walk; it's just a bit of a hike."

"If you're sure." The disappointment was obvious on Thompson's face.

"Aw, give the boy a break," Malcolm said. "He couldn't be more obvious!"

Pretty soon everyone was encouraging me to let Thompson take me home. I gave up with a sigh. "All right, all right. I'd love a ride home, Thompson."

"Matthew," he said. "My first name is Matthew."

"Oh, uh, right. Sorry, Matthew," I said, but I was afraid he'd always be "Thompson" in my head. The problem was that all his buddies called one another by their last names and, of course, it was written on their jerseys.

"It's okay," he said, standing up to follow me out the door. "Everybody calls me Thompson. I just sort of wanted to hear you say my name."

That was *awfully* sweet. What was going on here? It was one thing when we were pretending to be other people onstage, and something else entirely in real life.

He grabbed the door for me and held it open.

I heard someone back at our table whoop. I couldn't believe Thompson had a cheering section. It wasn't like I could date him. We were in different social circles. His buddies would mock him mercilessly. The cheerleaders would murder me in my sleep.

"Ignore them," he said as I passed under his arm. For a second I thought he meant the homicidal cheerleaders, but he jerked his square jaw in the direction of where Lane was flashing us the thumbs-up. "They've never seen a gentleman before."

"They've never seen *you* be a gentleman, you mean," I said before I could censor it. "Oh, sorry. I tend to forget we're in détente."

The rain had mostly stopped, but everything was covered in a wet sheen. Car tires hissed through puddles as they passed. "Actually, that's why I wanted to talk to you."

"To be insulted?"

I'd meant it as a joke, but he shook his head seriously. "Everyone else has been treating me like . . ." He groped for an appropriate metaphor for a moment, then gave up with a shrug of his massive shoulders. "I don't know. Not you, though. You're still the same."

With all the talk about chemistry and hormones, I felt exactly the opposite. I thought I'd been acting the strangest around Thompson. "You think so?"

He hunched his shoulders again. His hands were shoved into the pockets of his jacket. "I trust you to tell me the truth."

"About what?"

"The play. Do you think I really have a chance?"

Though the sidewalk had already dried in places, the clouds remained thick and gloomy. As I considered my answer, I watched a crow soar lazily through the gray sky. "You have a phenomenal voice," I said. "There's always more spots for boys, and a lot fewer boys who try out. I'd be surprised if you didn't get in. Everyone would."

"I've never done anything like this before," he admitted. His eyes watched his shuffling feet.

I nodded, tucking a stray strand of hair behind my ear. Theater could be scary when you weren't used to it, all that standing up in front of people and the massive opportunities for embarrassment. But that was the exciting part too, like when you had to ad-lib your way through a missed cue or a misplaced prop. Nothing was quite like the kick of the audience's response—a laugh or applause.

"What's so funny?" he asked, suddenly angry. "Man, you really are an evil witch."

"Wait—what did I do?"

"Here I'm trying to talk to you, you know, seriously, and you've been laughing at me."

I hadn't realized I'd been smiling. "Oh, hey, listen, it wasn't like that. I was thinking of something else."

"Oh. I see." For some reason my explanation made him madder. "You really haven't changed, Parker. I don't know what I was thinking. Walk home for all I care," he spat. He stalked back in the direction of the restaurant.

I had no idea what had just happened exactly, but at least our relationship was back to normal. Thompson hated me. All was right in the universe.

About a block from home, I noticed someone on my trail. The sun remained obscured by a blanket of storm clouds, so I had no idea if the person who followed me was human or vampire. But in St. Paul, there's just not a lot of foot traffic, so I noticed my shadow once I turned off Lexington and headed onto side streets.

Whoever it was stayed about a block and a half behind me. I kept twisting to see if I recognized any of the person's features, hoping against hope it was just Thompson acting all stalkerish or Elias checking up on me.

The only thing I could really make out at this distance was a dark leather jacket, like a biker might wear. I was pretty sure it was a guy. Turning again, I saw him pass under a streetlamp just as it flicked on. Was that reddish hair?

Crap.

Picking up my pace, I randomly turned a corner. The neighborhood near my high school was a mix of houses and apartment buildings. Even though many of the single-family homes dated from the same period as mine, they seemed shabbier and neglected. A chain-link fence surrounded a yard that was more dirt than grass. A filthy pink plastic tricycle lay tipped on its side, abandoned.

I hazarded a glance behind. Had he gained on me?

I started to run.

At the corner, I turned again. But I instantly regretted my choice. A bunch of guys leaned against a sports car smoking. The stereo blasted something in Spanish. It was too late to change course if I wanted to outdistance my pursuer. "Hey, sweetheart," one of the men teased as I raced toward them. He wore a basketball jersey that showed off toned, muscular arms and a dragon tattoo. Black hair was shaved to little more than stubble. "What's your hurry?"

"There's a guy following me," I said honestly, my breath coming in puffs. I pointed just as red-haired vamp turned the corner and kept running.

Jersey pushed off the hood of the car, and shouted, "Yo, what you doing, scaring the lady?"

Being verbally accosted seemed to stump the vampire. He slowed, as if assessing his chances against the four guys, who now stood a bit taller and began to close ranks behind me.

As I made the corner, I apologized to the Goddess for thinking ill of anyone, especially when I heard someone shout, "Hey, I'm talking to you." Red-haired vampire had been quite effectively slowed down. I had a good chance of losing him, thanks to my would-be champions.

I was fairly certain I made it home alone. When I got to my block, I set out for the alley. Even though our house was in the middle of the block, I could see the nose of Mom's MINI sticking out from its parking space. I crept along the alleyway to our carriage house. Finally, some luck! A window was open, and I could hear voices coming from inside.

I pressed myself to the wall. Virginia creeper climbed much of the brick, and its wide leaves had begun to unfurl, providing extra cover. Droplets from the brief shower collected in the nooks and crannies of the vine, and now and again random drips snaked down my neckline.

Holding my breath, I listened.

"But we don't know what would happen. It's dangerous to assume in this case. What if we unleash something we can't control?" It was my mother's haughty Witch Queen tone; I'd recognize it anywhere.

"We can't do nothing. We've been doing nothing for generations and the vampire problem hasn't solved itself." This was a man's voice, thick with an Eastern European accent. He sounded tired, like they'd had this argument a dozen times already.

It was hard to distinguish the words over the chatter of birds and nearby traffic sounds, so I closed my eyes and concentrated.

"Let's be honest—their very existence is our fault. Every death from the hunt is our responsibility. We should take them back under our control. Then we can decide what's to be done." I had no idea who said this. It sounded like a woman, but it wasn't Mom.

"You make it sound like that's an easy option." Mom sighed.

"It could be," the woman said, "if you would just agree with the rest of us."

"Hush," the man said suddenly. "There's a vampire near. I can sense it."

When I opened my eyes in surprise at his words, I realized my mistake. Everything had the sharp focus I'd come to associate with my heightened senses. In my desperation to overhear, I must have gone a bit vampy.

Crap!

I pressed myself against the wall, but my sharp ears detected the sound of footfalls on the stairs. Someone was coming down! Running would expose me, I was sure. Frantically, I looked around for a place to hide.

The door creaked open. In a minute, I'd be discovered.

When a raindrop hit my head, I knew what to do. Surrendering completely to my inner vampire, I climbed the ropy stems toward the roof. That strange ability that made the forest glow with an inner light guided my hands and feet to sections that could support my weight. By the time the door clicked back on its hinges, I'd hauled myself onto the roof.

Unfortunately, thanks to the slant of the roof, I was still exposed. I clambered quickly across the shingles to crouch behind the chimney. Then I felt it, a spike of magic that sizzled across my skin like lightning, making the hairs on my arms stand up.

An energy blade!

The man circling the carriage house searching for me must be Nikolai's dad, the vampire hunter.

"Check the roof," he said. "They tend to go up."

"There he is!" Mom shouted, and I ducked, half expecting to feel the pierce of a psychic missile through my shoulder blades. "At the end of the alley."

Carefully, I peeped around the chimney. Sure enough, there, near the sidewalk, was the red-haired vampire who'd stalked me from school. Mom and the other woman started toward him. Nikolai's dad lagged behind, and without warning he turned back to look me directly in the eye.

I cringed and quickly huddled behind the chimney. Had he recognized me? Nikolai had never brought me back to "meet the parents," and since Nik's dad wasn't a witch, I never saw him at the coven gatherings. I wouldn't have recognized him at all if it weren't for the familiar sensation of the blade.

The worst part was there wasn't really anyplace for me to go. The closest thing I could jump to was a power line, and though my vampire form seemed light and swift, I didn't think I could zip along it like a squirrel. I might make the neighbor's garage roof if I took a run at it, but I didn't have the same experience Elias did at midair acrobatics. Then his words came back to me:

You could fly, if you wanted to.

Could I really?

I guess I'd have to try. From the shouts, it sounded like one of the women was hot on the heels of my unlucky stalker. Where was Nikolai's father? I stood up to see. He'd made only a perfunctory step in the direction of the other vampire and, instead, was watching me. When our gazes met, he motioned for me to come down with a crook of his finger.

Though there was something similar about the shape of his eyes, I could see very little resemblance between Nik and his father. His dad's frame was stocky and square. A shock of blond brush stood up on the top of his head. In his hand, I could see the glimmer of a long, curved ghost blade.

He pointed downward again.

Like I was just going to surrender myself? What a cocky bastard!

I'd show him.

Pivoting on my heels, I took off at a run for the edge. I'd forgotten about the rain, however, and my Converses began to slip. Soon, I was hurtling uncontrollably down the slope.

I had all the momentum, but none of the trajectory. It probably didn't help matters that I flapped my arms uselessly and squawked like a chicken when I found myself airborne. I hit the other roof just long enough to know that under other circumstances I might have made it. My fingers frantically pawed for purchase, feeling the drainpipe slip from my grasp.

Then I fell.

The only good thing about my misaimed jump was that my bounce off the roof sent me careening into the neighbor's buckthorn hedges and not flat, splat, on the pavement. Though the snapping branches scraped and clawed my skin, they also slowed my descent. Even so, the impact knocked all the air from my lungs.

Stunned and feeling half dead, I lay in a flattened tulip bed, waiting for Mr. Kirov to come and finish the job.

I heard my mother's voice: "Was there another one, Ivan?" When she said his name, it sounded more like "Evan."

"I thought so, but a vampire would have made that jump. It was just an Igor. It landed over there somewhere."

"Shouldn't we make sure he's all right?"

"If it's still alive, the vampires will take care of it," he said, and then added ominously, "One way or another."

Wow, he was *cold*. Yet, I had to bite my tongue to fight the urge to croak out an inappropriate Monty Python reference, "Hello? Not dead yet!" Instead, I decided my best defense was just to lie perfectly still. As it happened, that was about all my body could manage.

"I told you they know something about all this," Mom said.

"And I told you my opinion."

"Yes, well, your plan seems to boil down to 'kill them, kill them all,' Ivan. That hasn't worked out very well so far."

"It would with the talisman."

I'd been ready to snicker at Mom's evil-overlord rant, but Mr. Kirov's words froze my throat dry. Was that how they planned to deal with their "vampire problem"? Bind everyone's will and then slaughter every last one?

That was too horrible. No way would my mom go for that. Right, Mom? Mom?

But she had no reply.

Chapter Ten

The mud under the crushed tulips had seeped into my jeans by the time I felt ready to move. My entire body ached, though I didn't think I'd broken anything beyond my shattered pride and about a zillion stems of our neighbor's prized flowers. "A vampire would have made that jump," I repeated in Mr. Kirov's snotty tone.

And they never even came to check on me!

Seriously, what kind of soulless monsters left a kid for dead—or vampire food? Apparently my mom and her cronies, that's who, because they went back to their League of Evil conference in the carriage house without a backward glance. I pulled myself upright with some effort. My knees wobbled and my back felt like a huge mass of bruises. With scraped fingers, I picked branch bits and tulip shreds from my hair.

I had to find Elias.

This was too important to wait for him to wander by and

happen to notice socks sticking out of my window. I had to go underground.

Though my mom and her pals clearly couldn't have cared less about whether I lived, I took care to walk around the far side of the neighbor's garage so as not to be easily spotted. Mr. Kirov might change his mind about letting me live if he knew I planned to report back to the vampire prince. I did not want to deal with Nikolai's dad again. I was so mad at him, I might bite him. Making things up with Nik would be really hard if I sucked his dad's blood. Even if he totally deserved it.

I limped down the alley, and when I reached the sidewalk, I wondered what became of my luckless red-haired stalker. Had Mom chased him off with magic? Did he get away?

I'd have to worry about him later. My biggest problem right now was figuring out the best way to get to the vampire underground. Once, Elias had taken me down a manhole. From there we'd walked along an abandoned railroad tunnel to some natural cave formation and the remains of an underground river. There was no way I could navigate through all that again.

However, I remembered that the rail tunnel eventually opened up in the train yard in Lowertown. Maybe I *could* find my way back there.

I headed to the nearest bus stop that would take me into downtown. Underneath the T sign was a concrete bench. Even though the wooden-slat seat was dotted with moisture, I sank down onto it gratefully. As I waited for the bus, I made an inventory of my injuries. Scraped knee, check. Banged elbow, check. Sore ribs. Scratched arms and fingers. Aching back. Check, check, check, and check.

I was inspecting individual cuts when the bus pulled to

a stop in front of me, warm air escaping from the door as it swished open. After digging the fare from my pocket and dropping it in the slot, I took the first seat available. Hardly anyone was riding on a Saturday evening. There was a black woman in nursing scrubs reading a paperback novel next to the window, and an old white guy with Gandalf eyebrows and a shapeless green parka in the back.

It was a short, progressively downhill ride. St. Paul was built along a river valley, and nowhere was it more evident than as you traveled *down*town. The angle of the descent could be seen in the slant of the skyscrapers' foundations. Skyway pedestrian walks connected one building's second floor to the next's third.

I got off near the Radisson Hotel on Kellogg. Pointing my nose toward Lowertown, I continued along the sidewalk, my knees feeling the sharp decline in every step. What little nightlife St. Paul had to offer was here in the insular, hidden depths of the city. The open door of a windowless bar let out the smell of stale beer and the jangle of blues piano.

Continuing downward, I passed modern, cavernous parking garages and stately office buildings with faded advertisements etched in century-old brick.

The street made a curve that angled sharply downward. I followed it under a road that seemed private—or forbidden. A barge blew its foghorn out on the Mississippi, just beyond the bright lights of the Wabasha Bridge. Seagulls wheeled overhead.

Highly industrial buildings gave way to patches of tall grass and garbage. The river's fishy smell competed with the city's diesel scent of urine and homelessness. The traffic noise hushed to a distant whisper. A boxcar, sprayed garish with graffiti, sat alone on a nearby track.

I'd found the train yard, at least.

Shoving my hands in my jeans pockets, I looked both ways down the tracks. I thought maybe I'd emerged near the river, which made sense given the cliffs there. So I turned in that direction. Though the sun had never come out from under the heavy cloud cover, the sky grew darker.

Above, the windows of office buildings glowed faintly in strange square patterns. Pop cans and discarded fast-food cups lay tangled in the tall grasses and wild purple and yellow clover that grew along the tracks. I kicked one of the cans. It made a hollow noise as it skittered across the cracked and crumbling pavement.

Next time I had any money, I was going to buy Elias a cheap cell phone.

After a couple more blocks, I saw the tunnel. It was just as I remembered it. Gang graffiti spattered every surface, even bleeding into the sandstone. The stench of piss was strong enough here that I rubbed my nose. At least no one seemed to be hanging around. I jumped onto the tracks and walked along the ties, stumbling on gravel until I found the right gait to hit wood every time.

The entrance was blocked by boards and chain-link fencing. But there was an area that had been dug by many hands that was just large enough for someone slender to wriggle under. Trying not to think about the additional stains I was getting on my jeans, I pushed myself under. My shirt snagged a bit on the rough underside of the fence, but I managed to pull free without tearing anything—much.

Inside, the cave smelled dank. Broken whiskey bottles and crushed beer cans lined the walls, almost like temple offerings. The ceiling was high, but it took only a few steps before the outside light vanished completely. I was surrounded by dark.

Man, I hoped like hell this was the right place.

Since I'd forgotten a flashlight, I was going to have to get a little vampy in order to see. That seemed like a good idea, regardless. The tunnel kind of screamed "serial-killer hangout" and I could use a boost of strength and speed to my advantage if I ran into anyone.

I rubbed my sore elbow, and Mr. Kirov's snotty assessment of my skills came back to me. Could I help it if I was only half vampire? And maybe jumping rooftops was like any sport—I sucked at it, and, you know, maybe I'd get better with practice.

My fangs dropped, and the tunnel came more clearly into focus. Though with the absence of living things, vamp vision didn't help all that much. In fact, it seemed only to heighten the creepy factor of the place. The moist cold sank deeper into my skin, and my sense of smell sharpened. Now, too, the black maw of the cave seemed that much deeper, and I could discern all the evidence of human traffic—a single shoe, cigarette butts, and crumpled food wrappers strewn along the rails.

Great. I was beginning to think that being half vamp came only with all the disadvantages and none of the cool.

But without it, I surely would have walked right past the narrow fissure in the wall. I smelled the water first, and the warm, animal scent of a bunch of sleeping bats. Squeezing through the crack, I heard the soft trickle of a brook. The walls narrowed and lost their man-made smoothness. Above, I could see the bits of rubble the city had used to fill in the river canyon when they decided to pave over the top of it. I ducked nervously as I picked my way along, though the ceiling had stood for at least a century.

Before long, I met the sentry.

He was stationed at a natural bend, so it was impossible for me to spot him until we stood face-to-face. In his hand he held a long stick; its tip had been sharpened to a nasty point. Lanky hair obscured his eyes, but somehow he recognized me.

"Ana?" he said in surprise, but then remembering protocol said, "Princess Ana, do you approach the kingdom?"

It took me a moment to figure out that the sentry was the same Igor that I'd talked to at the bus stop the day Nik's band played at the assembly. "Hey, uh, you." I felt so stupid. Why hadn't I asked his name before? "Um, I need to talk to my dad. Is he around?"

"The prince is holding court," he said, scratching the mop of his hair nervously. "I'll have to get someone to announce you properly. Can you . . . uh . . . ?" He held out the pointy stick.

I didn't take it. "Oh, you want me to watch the door? What do I do if someone comes?"

"I won't be that long. It should only take a minute."

Of course, if I took over, that was when the barbarian horde would choose to attack. "Can't I just go in?"

He seemed to be considering my ability to fend off marauders too. Finally, he shrugged. "Yeah, I guess." In a more formal tone, he added, "You are free to pass."

"Cool." I smiled. "Thanks, uh—"

"Noah," he said with a slight bow.

"Thanks, Noah."

Did I tell you before about how weird vampires are? Probably the oddest part is all the nudity. And even knowing the vampire tendency toward wandering around au naturel, I was never quite prepared for the shock.

Especially when I saw my dad.

In fact, the sight of Dad in all his glory perched on a stone formation that vaguely resembled a throne was almost enough to make me turn back around and walk home. It was really difficult to stifle the urge to whine, "Dad! Get some clothes on!" because, really, I was the odd one out by not hanging out everywhere.

It was sort of like that dream you have where you show up to school without a shirt, only here I was in real life, surrounded by naked people, with my clothes *on*.

When I got over being scandalized by the multitude of fleshy bits, I heard what Dad was talking about. His voice reverberated with authority in the cave. "What do my scouts report? What news of the talisman?"

Oh! I'd come at the perfect time. I raised my hand. "I've got news," I shouted.

From the horrified looks everyone gave me, this was apparently not the proper way to get the attention of the prince. My dad looked all disapproving until he realized I was the idiot who hadn't received her copy of *Vampire Court Manners for Dummies*.

"Approach the throne, Princess Anastasija Ramses Parker. Speak your piece."

The crowd parted for me to make my way to where Dad sat. There, just in front of his feet, the brook emptied into a dinner plate–sized sinkhole. As I got closer, I could see that the water had hollowed out a larger basin several feet farther down. If a person could squeeze through, it looked like it would probably lead to a huge underground lake complex.

"Cool," I muttered.

Dad cleared his throat.

"Oh, right." Despite my actor training, I felt suddenly nervous talking in front of everyone. That trick of imagining the audience naked was *so* never going to work again. So instead I stared at my dad's uncovered feet. His toes were kind of hairy and the nails needed trimming, but it was much easier to focus on something almost-sort-of normal like that. "Look, I think I have bad news. I'm pretty sure that Mom has the talisman, and Mr. Kirov—uh, the hunter, I mean—wants to use it to kill everybody."

In theater terms, the house erupted. Everybody started shouting. My dad had to stand up—*Oh, don't do that! Look at the toes! Look at the toes!*—and motion for everyone to simmer down.

"Tell us how you came to this conclusion. Spare no detail."

So I told my dad's big toe the whole story; the only part I left out was my embarrassing bounce off the neighbor's garage. Yet, when my dad questioned me further about how I made my escape, I ended up confessing even most of that.

I got a little sympathy chuckle from the audience when I told the details of my crash landing. Even though I wanted to point out it was a lot more painful than funny, I had to admit it made for a good yarn—not unlike Lane's opening-night disaster.

After I was finished, Dad lapsed into a thoughtful silence. Even without looking around, I could tell the whole room waited on their sovereign's opinion. Finally, I heard Dad say, "What's your take, Constantine?"

Constantine? That was Elias's last name. Was Elias here? Did I dare look? Did he have clothes on?

When I looked around, I couldn't see him at first. But everyone in the room was staring in the direction of the far wall. Elias stood on a rock shelf, his arms outstretched. Heavy iron manacles bound his wrists to the wall. He was only half naked— stripped to the waist—which somehow made him seem more vulnerable.

My hand flew to my mouth, hiding a gasp.

"You know my feeling on the matter, Your Highness," Elias said calmly, as if he weren't wrapped up in chains and on display like an animal. "We should attack while there remains any hope of a tactical advantage."

"But if they hold the talisman, how can you fight them? Won't they just, you know, 'zap,' and you're, uh—" I stopped because I was going to say "in chains," which was suddenly awkward. Also, I hadn't meant to say any of it out loud. It just sort of slipped out.

What I really wanted to know was how they could stand to treat Elias like that when they had been slaves themselves only a couple hundred years ago. I also needed to figure out how to get him down from there. I tried to catch Elias's eye, but he stared resolutely forward, holding his anguish proudly in check.

"You see, this is the traitor's problem," Dad said to me, but his words were clearly directed at Elias. "He thinks he knows best for the people, but he doesn't consider the long view, the consequences of rash action."

I bristled. I didn't even notice Dad's nakedness anymore, and glared angrily into his face. Who was he to talk about rash actions? Apparently, he wanted to do nothing—nothing other than casting Elias in chains!

"I didn't say it was wrong. I just wanted to know what the plan was," I shot back defiantly.

Dad's expression hardened. I could see that he wasn't used to one of his subjects mouthing off. Well, I wasn't one of his vampire minions. I was his daughter. If he wanted to throw me in chains, I'd like to see him try.

I planted my feet firmly apart, and stared back. Dad was the first to look away, but in case I'd thought I'd won, he said in a smug sort of tone that implied that he knew best, "Of course you'd defend Constantine. You still consider him your betrothed. But he is in disgrace, and that arrangement has been nullified."

Nullified? Hushed surprise rippled through the court. My jaw hung open. Did my dad just break me and Elias up? "That's not fair. And anyway, I don't agree. No. I don't accept."

"Perhaps you should have considered that when you counseled treason."

"Which you wouldn't know anything about except that I told you," I reminded him. Though shame heated my cheeks at my betrayal of Elias, anger narrowed my eyes. "Just like you wouldn't know anything about Mom's plans if I hadn't hiked all the way down here to your creepy-ass lair to give you this information you're not even going to do anything with. Which is lame. Elias is right—you're kind of a do-nothing. And you know what? I risked my life with the hunter. You owe me." Without looking at him, I pointed in Elias's direction. "Let him go."

All around me, I heard gasps. My dad listened to my rant, his face dotting with color, but he kept his lips pressed thinly together and quirked his eyebrow haughtily. It was clear no one had talked to him like this in centuries. But I was winning. In my peripheral vision, I could see sympathetic eyes turning toward Elias. My dad noticed too.

He tried, however, to act distant, as he said, "Even if I give in to your petty demand, I will not let you court him; do you understand?"

I was so angry, my whole body shook. Words just came tumbling out. "Oh, I understand. I understand you're a jerk, and, betrothed or not, Elias is my friend and he doesn't deserve to be treated that way."

I'd clearly pushed him too far. I could see Dad's fists clench.

"Maybe the two of you would prefer banishment?"

Collectively, the vampires gasped. I had no idea what banishment entailed, but there was no way I was backing down now. Still, I'd caused Elias enough trouble, so I shook my head sadly, and said, "This is such a dumb time to kick out your best knight, but whatever. I'm leaving. Elias can decide for himself what he wants."

"I go with Anastasija."

Elias's declaration caused the court to utter more astonishment. Some people even shouted, "No, you can't!" and "Our best knight! All is lost!"

My dad rose to his feet again. When he raised a hand, there was utter silence. Slowly, his gaze swept the room, lingering on Elias and me. Then he turned his back to us. "Elias Constantine, you are released from service. Anastasija Ramses Parker, you are no longer under our protection." Then he said something very solemn in a language I didn't understand.

Everyone seemed to hold their breath until Dad was done speaking. When it was over, I heard someone sobbing softly. The only other noise was the scrape of the key turning in Elias's manacles.

I watched as he was freed. His arms seemed stiff, and he

flexed his fingers as though to try to return feeling to them. Moving painfully, he came down to stand beside me. Even though Dad's back was turned, Elias sketched a low bow. With a glance at me, he headed for the cave's entrance. I caught up to him and grasped his hand lightly. We walked through the narrow passage and past the surprised sentry, hand in hand.

Only when we got to the train tracks did Elias allow himself to show any sign of how badly he was injured. He sagged against the wall, breathing hard.

"Are you okay?" It was a stupid question, but previously I hadn't noticed the nasty red welts on his back. Seeing them only rekindled the anger I thought I'd spent. "I can't believe he did that to you!"

Elias drew himself up painfully. "I'll be fine in a minute."

"No, you won't, will you?" Given how much my back still ached from my roof acrobatics, I didn't think vampires had super-healing powers. Unless that was one of those things that full vamps did better than half. "You're really hurt. You need—"

"Blood," he supplied.

Okay, I was going to say "help," but I guess that was another answer. I looked around as if hoping to find a spare pint lying on the ties. Next I examined my own wrists. The last time I offered Elias my own blood, we'd ended up betrothed. I guessed there was no chance of that happening again, so I thrust them at him. "This is all my fault. Here," I said. "Use me."

He hesitated. "I need too much."

Remembering biology class, I said, "I'll make more. Just take a little now; you can have the rest later."

"Not here," he insisted. "Let's put more distance between ourselves and the kingdom."

I positioned myself under his armpit, so he could lean on me as we walked. At first, I thought he'd be too proud to accept, but he put an arm around my shoulder with a grateful sigh.

When we got to where the tunnel opened up, I realized another problem. In his current condition Elias would never make it through the narrow gap under the barrier. He must have had the same thought because he rested an arm heavily against the stone wall, and looked up through the gate at the darkly clouded sky.

"Let me sit a minute," he said, already lowering himself to crouch above the loose sand and gravel. Sandburs and other scrubby weeds had established patches among the detritus.

"Maybe I could dig it out more," I suggested, but he put a restraining hand on my elbow when I started toward the passageway.

"Let us make our exchange here, and I'll have the strength to bend the metal aside."

Exchange? Oh. "You will?"

He nodded gravely, but when his eyes found mine, they held a dark twinkle. "Besides, let's just say, I have a little sublimated anger to draw on."

I sat down on the edge of a wooden tie. The flush of my own anger had finally exhausted itself and now I felt empty. I stared down at my hands. Even in the blanketed darkness, my skin glowed pale white. My finely tuned vision could make out the blue veins standing out on my wrist. I supposed I should get this over with. I didn't really relish the idea of being bitten; it hurt. But I had to help Elias. If I hadn't told my dad—

—when I looked up, Elias's gaze was fixated on my wrists as well. His face wore an expression that could only be described as predatory.

I swallowed nervously, and offered my arm.

He didn't seem to notice how much my hands were shaking when he seized my wrist in a surprisingly powerful grip. As his fangs descended, I squeezed my eyes shut.

My eyes snapped open. I didn't feel anything, but the sight of his fangs in my flesh made me shout, and try to jerk away to cradle my arm to my chest protectively. But Elias held firm. Instinctively, I kicked him. My foot connected squarely with his thigh before I could stop myself. He didn't even flinch, though I thought I heard a noise like a growl rumble deep in his throat.

Or maybe it was a passing train.

Yeah, I told myself, that was what it was, because the way Elias hunched over my arm disturbed me profoundly. Did I look like that when I'd licked Thompson's cheek? No wonder he was freaked-out by me.

To distract myself from slurping sounds, I examined the angry marks on Elias's back. Had they actually horsewhipped him? Bile rose in my throat. My hand reached out in sympathy. Before my fingertips could even brush wounded flesh, he recoiled.

The anguish in his cat-slit eyes was impossible to disguise. I couldn't take any more. My arm flew around his neck. Careful of his injuries, I wrapped him in a hug. "I'm sorry," I kept saying, tears sparking in my eyes. "I'm so sorry."

He rested his head against my shoulder. I could sense the exhaustion in his arms as they slowly wrapped around my waist and clung there as I continued to apologize. It was so horrifically ironic, really. I'd thought that by sending him after the talisman, I'd save him from the shackles and lashes of slavery. Instead, I brought it all down on him, hard.

"It was my decision," he mumbled softly. "I chose to disobey."

His word choice set my teeth on edge. "You shouldn't have to 'obey' anyone, Elias. That's what getting the talisman was supposed to be all about, for crying out loud."

His breath caught on the fabric of my shirt. "I'm truly a free agent now."

Untangling myself from our embrace, I searched his face as I asked, "I screwed that up for you too, didn't I? You liked being a knight."

Shutting his eyes for a moment, he seemed to collect his thoughts. "I used to believe we were so superior to those lost souls who couldn't sever their ties to their former masters. But look," he said, raising his hands, palms up, indicating his own ruined body, "how little separates us."

It was impossible to understand what my father had been thinking. I shook my head in bewildered disgust. "Did Ramses really think that would make you more loyal? I mean, since when does torture work?"

"The punishment wasn't entirely for my benefit," Elias said, his voice rough with memory. "It was meant as an example to others."

"Yeah, because you don't want anybody else stepping out of line. My dad, the wicked despot," I said with a sneer. "Shit. Can I just say how sorry I am again?"

Elias laughed lightly. "I think you've expressed enough regret for today. Besides, I meant what I said. I knew what I was doing and, unlike you, I was fully aware of the consequences."

He had a point there. I mean, I knew Dad would be mad if Elias went against orders, but I had no idea he'd have him beaten like a dog for it. I sighed. "It still sucks."

"That it does, my lady. That it does," he agreed with a smile.

A train clacked through the yard. I noted that I'd left a bloody smudge on Elias's neck where my arm had pressed against him. The area where he'd bitten into the muscle of my forearm throbbed, but it had mostly stopped bleeding. I showed it to him. "Oh, um—did you get enough?"

He shook his head. "Not nearly, but the amount I need would easily kill you. It'll do for now."

My stomach tightened at the thought of doing this again, but he was my friend. He'd do it for me; how could I be less willing to help him? I looked at all the garbage and wondered, now that the sun had set, if people would arrive soon. Brushing the sand from the thighs of my jeans, I said, "We should get out of here."

But when I stood up fast, I got a head rush. Elias must have taken more blood than I realized. Woozy, I clutched for purchase and found Elias's shoulder. He winced, and I let go guiltily, stumbling onto my already banged-up knees. I started to laugh. We were a fine pair.

I let myself go face-first into the damp sand. "Or we could just stay."

Elias chuckled at my antics, and I felt him step over me. I was about to tell him that even though he was no longer a knight, it didn't mean he had to stop being a gentleman. But when I looked up, he'd dropped to one knee in front of the fence. He found a good grip on the bottom of the barrier and pushed. It looked so easy, but I could hear the groan of the metal as it bent.

He'd expanded the hole significantly. Before, a person had to shimmy, marine-style, in order to get under. The opening was now wide enough that even someone Elias's size could easily crawl through on hands and knees.

"Wow," I said.

"I don't suppose I should get rid of it entirely," he said, as if bending steel were as easy as crumpling paper. "We wouldn't want the kingdom to have a ready supply of humans, now, would we?"

No, we wouldn't. I felt responsible for enough pain and suffering. I didn't want to add unexplained homeless disappearances on top of everything. "Bea tried to tell me that vampires only eat witches," I said, watching as Elias made his way to the other side.

"'Eat'?"

I ducked under the fence, and accepted Elias's helping hand up. "What else do you do with humans?"

"Touché," he said, with a slight bow of his head. "But who is B. and what does he or she know of the kingdom?"

"Bea's a True Witch. She's been my friend since forever. I can't believe you haven't met," I said. As we started walking toward the lights of downtown, I wondered how many heads would turn at the sight of shirtless Elias. "We need to find you some clothes."

Elias waved off my concern. "I have a stash of clothes at the safe house." He must have noticed my eyebrows jump, because he explained. "I have often been called to move through your world on errands for the kingdom, some of which put me at odds with the local authority. I needed an aboveground home base from which to operate." He cleared his throat slightly, and looked away. "Plus, the advantages of having a place secret from the rest of the guard occurred to me early in my career."

"So you've always kind of been prepared to go rogue?"

He looked a little sheepish. "I would prefer to think of it as careful contingency planning."

"I see," I said, though I was smiling broadly. "You're a dark horse, Elias Constantine. No wonder my dad—," I started, but then I couldn't even bring myself to tease him about what happened. So instead I took his hand and gave it a squeeze. "I'm sorry," I said for the hundredth time.

"I would love to show you my place," he said. He hadn't acknowledged my faux pas, but he didn't let go of my hand either. "It's not far from here. Will you be my guest?"

"I'd be honored."

Elias's house was in Swede Hollow. We walked the expanse of the bridge, past Mound's View Park to a little café surrounded by a huge herb garden. Evening diners sat around patio furniture, sipping lattes and eating organic salads. Elias led me through a thick stand of lilacs, and over a small, wooden walk bridge reminiscent of a Japanese garden. Under lamplight, lavender thyme flowers bloomed among curly parsley and freshly planted basil seedlings.

A few people seemed to notice us; someone muttered something about "kids these days" and "S and M."

I almost turned around to tell that person I'd never hurt Elias that way, but he must have noticed the sudden tension in my body because he pulled me close. He said, "We're almost there. Just one more block."

Once we'd cut through the garden, I could see why this neighborhood would appeal to a vampire. In two blocks the road ended. There was nothing but trees beyond. The park stretched out as far as I could see. But we turned away and up the sidewalk of a crooked little Victorian. The house had a lot of similar features to mine—jutting dormers, a pointy-top tower— but it looked like someone had squished it with Photoshop to half the width, and then let Dr. Seuss do some remodeling.

Elias pushed open the gate of a waist-high wooden fence. That too had seen better days. There were planks missing and the cedar had faded to a brittle gray. After stooping to retrieve a key from under a chubby-cheeked garden gnome, Elias contin- ued around to the back and a rickety staircase.

Every step creaked and moaned, and I thought I could feel it wobble as we made our way to a second-floor deck. Lawn chairs were arranged around a wide plastic sun umbrella. Yeah, this was a good safe house. It was impossible to imagine Elias stretched out on the roof catching some rays. Not to mention the crisp factor.

He saw my expression and smiled. "I don't use that much," he admitted. "Though it has a pretty unobscured view of the sky; I've brought a telescope out here."

When I looked up, I could see only clouds and a hazy smudge of the moon. Elias totally struck me as the telescope sort, but then, what choice did he have, really? "You've never seen the sun."

He'd unlocked the door and held it open. "Not for a long time. The ability to withstand daylight fades the older you get, and I, my lady, am quite old."

"How old are you?"

"I was created when Constantine ruled an empire from Constantinople."

My mind reeled as I tried to comprehend what that must be like. "Dang. That's a lot of dark."

"It is," he said, though he didn't seem nearly as impressed as I was. "Won't you come inside?"

The safe house was no penthouse. Elias flicked on a bright overhead. I squinted in the harsh light after the soft darkness of the evening. I shut my eyes, trying to adjust back to normal human senses.

From what I could tell from a quick survey, Elias's apartment consisted of three rooms. There was a kitchenette directly to my right. Cabinets and a countertop ran the length of the wall, with a sink positioned in the middle under a window. A scuffed, ancient fridge hummed noisily in the corner. The rest of the room opened up into a living area. Elias had a couch pushed up against a bank of windows and a couple of battered recliners across from it.

From the position of the other two rooms, I got the sense that the living room/kitchenette had been fashioned by knocking down a wall between two bedrooms. The other clue was a strip of hardwood where the stained, nubby carpet abruptly ended. It looked like a hallway, without the, well, hall.

My mother raised me to say something nice when first coming into people's homes, but all I managed was, "Wow, look at this place."

"It's not easy to find a landlord willing to rent to someone with no references and no job," he said.

"Yeah, how do you—?" I'd started when the bedroom door

opened, and a pudgy, young Asian guy in plaid pajama bottoms padded into the main room with a yawn.

He rubbed his face sleepily and blinked at the two of us. "Oh, hey, Elias, looks like you're home."

"Ana, this is George."

George and I regarded each other from across the room. He didn't smile or offer his hand. In fact, he seemed kind of annoyed by my presence. "I guess I should go put some clothes on if we have guests," he said finally, and then he turned around and went back into the bedroom.

The bedroom, since the only other door clearly led to a small bathroom.

"George?" George, who didn't seem at all fazed by the fact Elias wandered in not wearing a shirt and had welts across his back. Did my boyfriend have a boyfriend? I asked again, "George?"

Elias scratched his chin. "Ana," he said, sounding a little like a teacher explaining a difficult subject, "keep in mind that it is very complicated for me to operate in the daytime without help."

"So. George helps you."

"Yes."

"So he's like a personal Igor?" It suddenly occurred to me to wonder what Igors got in exchange for all their help, why they were so devoted to vampires.

"I'm going to go change," Elias said. "I'll explain everything when I get back."

"I look forward to it," I said, watching him enter the very same bedroom George had disappeared into. I sat down on the couch and stared at the door. I could hear male voices murmuring heatedly. George, apparently, had some questions for Elias as well.

George came out first. He wore a Hawaiian-print shirt and shorts. "I'm going to the café," he said. "Do you want a soda or anything?"

Oh. I was wondering how Elias and I were going to actually talk. "No, thank you."

"Suit yourself," he said with a sniff. "I should warn you there's not much in the pantry. I suppose Elias might be able to make you a cup of tea or something. Well, you're his guest. I'll let him worry about you."

George seemed to be waiting for some kind of response, so I said, "Okay."

"Okay, well." George stood at the doorway with his hand on the knob. He seemed on the verge of saying something, but shook his head. "Hopefully you'll be gone when I get back."

With that, he left.

If this guy wasn't Elias's boyfriend, he sure acted like he thought he was.

I sat on the couch and pulled absently at a thread that had come loose at the cushion's seam. It seemed like forever until Elias emerged wearing a fresh pair of jeans and a black silk button-down shirt. He'd combed his hair. "Don't you look metrosexual," I said.

"Jealousy doesn't become you, my lady," Elias said, coming to sit down beside me. He perched on the edge of the seat, his back ramrod straight. His posture reminded me that perhaps there was another reason he'd chosen silk, and why he carefully avoided leaning back.

"I'm sorry," I said. "But . . . George? I just wasn't expecting a George. You're not sleeping with George, are you?"

Elias didn't look nearly as shocked by the question as I might have hoped, but he looked me in the eye when he said, "No, I'm not."

I waited for him to elaborate, because, you know, it was pretty obvious *something* was going on with George.

With a resigned sigh, Elias continued. "George likes being bitten."

I decided I didn't really want details, after all, so I put up my hands. "So, he *is* an Igor? He knows what you are?"

"Not exactly. To be perfectly frank, I retain a very loose relationship with George. I'm here only enough to keep this safe house a viable option. We haven't talked about what I am. But he certainly knows how I react when he opens the shades in the morning."

"So you *have* seen the sun."

"'Seeing' would not accurately describe my particular experience."

"Ah," I said, trying very hard not to picture Elias in bed with George. Of course, because I was trying to avoid it, it instantly flashed in my mind. I changed the subject quickly. "What are we going to do about the talisman?"

"My plan remains the same," he said resolutely. "Though I no longer have soldiers at my command, it is critical that the talisman be found. Especially now that we know what they plan to do with it."

"I still can't believe Mom agrees with Mr. Kirov," I said. "Do you think Nikolai knows what his dad is up to?"

"Perhaps you should tell him." At first, I thought Elias was being petulant about my relationship with Nik, but his expression seemed sincere. "Does he hold any sway over his father?"

I thought back to the few times Nikolai talked about his dad. "I don't know," I admitted. "Maybe. But I don't know what good it would do even if he did. I'm not sure Mr. Kirov's mind can be changed. You didn't hear the way he talked about us."

Elias pulled on his lip pensively. "What about you? Could you convince your mother not to use the talisman?"

I didn't think I had any better chance, but I shrugged. "I suppose it's worth a try. What do we do if they're not interested?"

"I go back to plan A."

"What, steal the talisman yourself?" I suppose I sounded pretty incredulous because Elias reddened. I gently put a hand on his thigh. "What I meant was, I want to help."

Elias and I hatched a plan. I'd distract Mom while he searched the house. We'd have to do something about whoever might still be holed up in the carriage house, but we decided to deal with one thing at a time.

The big wrinkle was transportation. Elias's car was still stashed somewhere in my neighborhood. The buses stopped running in a half hour, and honestly, the idea of heading out to carry off our dashing plan on public transportation didn't seem right.

We were still considering our options when George came back.

George's car smelled like moldy French fries. I let Elias take the passenger-side seat. Given the odor, I expected the back to be full of junk, but it was relatively free of debris. I only had to move aside a few library books and a sweatshirt to find the buckle for the seat belt.

Even though he'd agreed to give us a ride, George's reflection scowled at me in the rearview mirror for most of the way. It seemed to take forever to get through downtown. Every time one traffic light changed, we'd only make it halfway up the block before the light turned red again. More infuriatingly, we were the only car on the road. We were stuck at yet another empty cross street waiting for the green, when George asked, "She's one of your . . . people, isn't she?"

"Hmm?" Elias had been staring out the window the entire time, brooding. I'd noticed he hadn't used the shoulder strap; his back must still be hurting. He glanced back at me. "Oh. Yes, Ana is one of us."

Technically, I was only half, but it occurred to me that I was headed off to help Elias steal an artifact that the First Witch made with her own hands. I'd thrown my lot in with the vampires. Clearly.

"It's just that I noticed her arm," George said. "You bit her."

A fairly accurate dental record of Elias's teeth stood out in bluish bruises on my forearm. The mark looked like it should hurt, but I suspected vampires injected something to make the experience of being bitten more tolerable. I wished I had a sleeve to hide it under. Instead, I pressed it to my stomach. "It's not what it looks like," I said. The instant the words came out of my mouth, I realized how guilty they sounded. "I mean, it was a desperate situation."

"Oh, I can only imagine," George said.

"Honestly, I doubt you could," Elias said drily, turning back to gaze out the window.

George's frown seemed on the verge of becoming a pout. "Try me."

"As I've made quite clear in the past, I'd rather not."

Ouch.

I could understand why Elias was putting the guy off, but he didn't have to be quite so mean about it. I leaned forward to stick my head between the two of them. "Hey, George, do you believe in magic?"

The light changed. Though it was obscured by orange construction cones and heavy machinery, I glimpsed the farmers' market as we accelerated through the intersection. The aluminum roof–covered parking lot didn't look like much, but it was a place I'd never forget. The last time I'd been there was for a big showdown between Mom and Dad. I'd been the one doing the biting then, and the results had been quite spectacular, speaking of magic. I still didn't entirely understand how that had worked, and whether I could ever do anything like that again.

George seemed to still be considering his answer as he came to the next stop. "Damn lights," he muttered. "Depends on how you mean that, I guess."

"How about I put it this way: do you believe in vampires?"

Elias made a choking sound and gave me a wide-eyed look as if to ask if I knew what I doing. I didn't really, but I had a kind of working theory, which was that, push come to shove, people would deny magic. Believing in it required too big of a paradigm shift for the average person, especially since to truly accept the kind of magic that made Elias, you had to buy the idea that a Stone Age goddess worshipper bent time and space to draw otherworldly creatures to earth to be her slaves.

Heck, that was hard for me some days.

George looked over at Elias for a long time, as if judging something. I thought for a moment my theory was about to blow up in my face. When the light turned green, George focused his eyes on the road ahead. Quietly, he said, almost as if to himself, "I believe some people *think* they're vampires."

We had George drop us off a couple of blocks from my house. I hopped out of the car and stood on the curb while Elias and George shared a few words in private. Pretending to study the bark of a maple tree, I tried to act like I wasn't deeply curious about what they were talking about. If they stayed in the car any longer, I was afraid I'd accidently go vampy trying to eavesdrop.

At last, Elias got out of the car. He lifted his hand in a wave good-bye as George drove away. "It's a shame," he said, watching his fading taillights. "That was my best safe house."

"Was?"

"I'm afraid it's well and truly compromised," he said. He turned his attention back to me as we started toward my place. "I was in no condition to sense whether a scout followed us, so I must assume one did. Also you planted a seed in George's consciousness that time or another could easily exploit."

"What do you mean?"

"That talk of vampires and magic." He shook his head. "He may consider it more sincerely while I'm away. I have no idea what would be waiting for me if I returned."

Awesome. Something else I'd screwed up for Elias. "I'll bet you're getting really tired of hearing this, but—I'm sorry."

He gave me a gentle, tired smile. We passed under a streetlamp.

The planes of Elias's face were a contrast of silver and black. "Do you think the hunter is the one staying in the carriage house?"

"I suppose if that's where they're hiding the talisman, Mr. Kirov might be guarding it," I said with a shrug. "There was another woman I didn't know, though."

The cloud cover hushed the usual night sounds. Moisture glittered in the halo around the streetlights. Elias ran his hand through his hair; he winced at the movement. "Even on a good day I'd have no hope of defeating a fully trained hunter and a witch of your mother's caliber. If the distraction fails, I'll be forced to run. We'll have to regroup and try again some other night."

I looked down at the dried blood and bruises on my forearm. "Do you want . . . ? I mean, would *more* help?"

"A noble offer and one much appreciated," he said. "But even at half strength, I can easily outrun any mortal."

I didn't want to point out that Mom seemed to enjoy wrapping vampires in cocoons, so I asked something that had been on my mind since I saw the farmers' market on the ride over. "Remember when I bit you that one time?"

"How could I forget?"

Yeah, the world had gone all slo-mo and icy. Then a bunch of vampires fell down. "Um, yeah, well, how come this time when you bit me, nothing like that happened?"

"I'm a vampire, not a witch."

"I'm not a witch either."

"But you are," he said. "You might not have direct access to witch magic, but you can feel it."

I could. I guess I hadn't completely gone to one side or the other, and the thought comforted me a little. "But, so what does that have to do with the explode-y?"

"So, magic is energy for witches. Blood is energy for vampires. Two different kinds of energy, like opposite polarities, if you will. I can only draw on one. You can draw on both."

It made sense. I remember feeling energy rising in me like the internal workings of an electromagnetic generator. A strange analogy, I suppose, but it had occurred to me after reading my science homework. It also made me wonder—if blood equaled energy for vampires, did magic-filled witch blood mean extra-nutritious blood? I supposed that was why vampires were sustained by witch blood for so long, like Elias said.

But before I could ask him about my theory, we got to the point at which we'd agreed to split up. He turned to go, but I grabbed his arm. "Be careful," I said.

His arms slid around my waist. I wanted to do the same, but I was nervous about hurting his back. So I hooked my thumbs into the belt loops of his jeans. Leaning into him, I rested my head against his chest. His lips brushed the top of my head lightly.

Perhaps he could tell that I just wanted to cling there and never let go, because he said, "There's no telling when they will make their move. We must recover the talisman swiftly."

I let him go only so that I could shake a finger at him. "Okay, but I'm serious, Elias. Don't do anything crazy-heroic."

He smiled. "I'll stick to the sane-heroics, then, shall I?"

"Do," I said seriously, though I grinned back.

Placing a hand on his heart, he sketched a bow. "As my lady commands."

I frowned. I still didn't like this kind of servitude talk. He started to turn away, but I said, "How about just—I don't know—do your best? No more orders and obeying, huh?"

He'd turned on vamp speed and made the corner at a gallop. I didn't think he'd heard me. I hoped we got the talisman soon. Thinking about all this slavery stuff was driving me crazy.

Even though it was after one o'clock in the morning, Mom seemed completely unfazed when I walked through the door. She didn't even look at her watch or glance up at the clock above the stove when I came into the kitchen. Even stranger? She was baking brownies.

Mom isn't a terrible cook or anything, but her approach to food tends to be pragmatic. She's very good, even occasionally creative, at basic meals. But dessert? Random baking?

In the middle of the night?

"Are you okay, Mom?"

She tracked my gaze as I looked at the mixer, open egg carton, and brownie-smudged bowl. "What? It's just a box."

Mom had also been on a granola kick lately, so I said, "I didn't even know we had stuff like this around."

Closing the lid of the eggs carton, she shrugged. "I'll start my diet again tomorrow."

"Works for me," I said. I grabbed the bowl from the table and used my finger to lick out the batter. Mom started putting things away as the smell of baking brownies permeated the kitchen. I wondered if Elias had crossed the wards yet. Would she notice the breach in security or had all the vampire comings and goings damped their effectiveness?

I couldn't risk it. I needed to think of something distracting.

"You have a new boyfriend, don't you, Mom?"

She'd bent down to put the vegetable oil back in the cabinet, and my words startled her so much, she banged her head. "What on earth makes you say that?"

"When you gave me a ride to callbacks, I saw the curtain move in the carriage house." I shrugged. "You usually introduce me to all the high-witch muckety-mucks, so I guess I figured you stashed a lover there or something."

I'd calculated that the word "lover" would make her sputter, but she also turned a shade paler.

Just then, I felt it. A low buzz tingled at the base of my neck. Elias had crossed the threshold. Mom stiffened slightly, like maybe she'd noticed too. So I had to think of something outrageous to distract her.

"I think the carriage house is a great place to have sex."

That did it. Mom was completely focused on me now. "What?"

"I'm just saying that if you were going to get it on with your new friend, the carriage house is nice and private."

You'd think parents would be smart enough to know when they're being completely put on. But I've noticed there are two subjects that, no matter how outlandishly you lay it down, they simply must take seriously: drugs and sex. If I wanted to put Mom in a coma, I should have said that I used the carriage house exclusively for entertaining men and smoking crack. It didn't matter that she should know I'd never do anything of the sort or that I could hardly keep the joke out of my voice when I suggested it.

Her face completely drained of color. "Who?"

Okay, this line of questioning was completely unexpected. My smirk faded. "What do you mean, 'who'?"

"Just tell me it isn't the vampire." Then her gaze lit on my arm, the bruises and the dried blood. I quickly tried to cover up, but it was too late. She pointed accusingly at my arm and shouted, "Ah! Go to your room, young lady. You're grounded."

Grounded for having imaginary sex? How unfair was this? "You're the one sneaking around at all hours. How come I'm the one getting grounded?"

"I'm not the one going off"—she choked a bit on the words, but managed—"giving blood. I am on important witch business, not sneaking around."

"Then who's in the carriage house?"

"I thought I told you to go to your room."

The oven beeped. The brownies were done. Mom and I were locked in a stare-down.

You couldn't say I didn't do a good job distracting Mom. I just hoped that when everything was done, it would all be worth it. In fact, I kind of wondered if I should back off a bit, you know, tell her that I didn't even "donate" regularly to Elias, much less anything else she might be imagining. But it irritated me that she automatically assumed the worst. Didn't she trust me more than that?

Neither of us spoke.

The oven beeped once again, sounding more insistent. I hated to see baked goods go bad, so I reached for the door with the oven mitts. "Your brownies are going to burn."

I took them out and set the pan on a burner. With the tip of the mitt, I clicked the timer off. I turned around ready to resume our fight, but found Mom slumped in a chair. She'd set aside her glasses. Her head was cradled in her hands.

"I remember what it was like," Mom said. She didn't look at me, but spoke to her lap. "I still dream about it. But no matter how romantic it all seems at first, the relationship is parasitic. There's no way around that."

Was Mom talking about biting or sex or both? Did I want to know?

Rubbing her face, she put her glasses back on. "The First Witch wanted a way to control them beyond the talisman. So they can't survive without us. They need us for our blood. The rest is an illusion."

I was beginning to think she and Dad must have had a really crappy relationship. And, you know, considering how he treated Elias, I could see the problem. "Dad is a jerk, Mom. Elias isn't like him."

"Your dad wasn't always like he is now. He could be very charming and seductive."

As much as Mom didn't like hearing me say "lover," I could do without "seductive" from her, especially when she was talking about Dad.

"He wrote me poetry, did you know?"

I didn't. In fact, I was surprised to hear about it. Poems seemed awfully sensitive and introspective for Dad. "Do you still have any?"

She shook her head quickly. "I burned it all before you were born."

Since I was still wearing the oven mitt, I picked up the tray of brownies and brought them over to where she sat. I set it down and took the chair on the opposite side of the narrow table. From a crockery bowl we used to store utensils, I fished out a spatula. I carved out a couple of pieces and offered one to

Mom. "I always kind of wondered if you two were still together when I was born."

"The pregnancy was hard on me," Mom said, biting into the chewy chocolate. "Not physically—well, not terribly much harder than I imagine a normal pregnancy is—I mean emotionally. You already sort of feel as though an alien is gestating inside you, and, well, your father is a demon."

That was me, the original demon spawn.

"I didn't get a lot of sympathy from the other witches even though the council had approved of our marriage. And your father's people were . . ."

". . . Creepy?" I supplied when she seemed unable to articulate her thought.

She smiled. "Yeah, kind of creepy. And I was feeling so very protective too. I mean, I sometimes felt like you were something strange taking over my body, but more often I thought of you as a part of me, my baby. I didn't want to see you raised in a cave."

I couldn't even imagine a baby crawling around in the underground lair. How easy would it be for a toddler to fall down that cavernous hole?

Mom nodded at my expression. "But the whole thing was a disaster even before you came along," she admitted. "I wanted to live in a real house, not a cave. I wanted to walk on the beach, in the sunshine, with my husband. Have a backyard barbecue . . ." I sensed she could have continued her litany, but she gave up with a sigh. "I was like you, very nonconformist, and I didn't think I needed all the trappings of normalcy. Until suddenly they were denied me, you know?"

I chewed my brownie. The practical considerations of being married to a vampire had never occurred to me.

Mom laid her hand over mine. "I just don't want to see you end up like me."

"Things aren't so bad," I started. There was more I wanted to say, but I felt a sharp buzzing behind my eyes. Either Elias tripped something big or another vampire just crossed the wards. I winced.

Simultaneously, Mom and I said, "Ow!"

Mom bolted upright. She looked at me. Now was the time to think of another distraction, but the only thing that came out of me was, "What the hell was that?"

"One of your friends?"

Actually, I wondered. Neither Elias nor Dad caused that much of a stir when he crossed the warding line. Something about my blood or spilled blood, I didn't know which—but it made me more and more certain Elias was in trouble.

The sound of glass shattering came from upstairs. It sounded like one of the button jars had toppled in the craft room. Mom dashed up the stairs. I followed behind, feeling her power building like steam in a pressure cooker. As I turned the landing, something in the dining room caught my eye. Elias slid out of the shadows to give me a short wave. Then he slunk into the kitchen, still searching.

I tried to wave in a shooing fashion. He should get out. I wanted to shout for him to run, but I couldn't hesitate too long at the landing or my mother would wonder what I was up to and I'd risk exposing Elias. I hurried up after Mom.

Mom stood in the middle of the hall, her energy crackling around her, staring into the darkened craft room. "Show yourself!" she said in a commanding, witchy-echoey voice.

"Yeah, and stop breaking my stuff!" I added.

Mom elbowed me. I got the hint. I shouldn't mouth off; whatever was in the other room could be dangerous.

The room light flicked on.

Mom and I both jumped back, startled. A very thick Eastern European accent said, "I'll have to replace your jar, Amelia."

"It was *my* jar, Mr. Kirov," I said, stepping out from behind Mom. "And just what are you doing crawling in the window?"

"Hunting vampire," he said. He stepped into the light and looked directly at me. His eyes glinted menacingly as he looked down his long, sharp nose, which was like a wolf's. He chose that moment to unsheathe his psychic blade. Unlike Nikolai's dagger, his manifested as a glimmering, curved scimitar. Heat radiated from it. Even without it touching me, I felt its burning.

I'm sure I turned pale. I faltered.

"There's no vampire in this house, Ivan," Mom said. I felt her take my hand, and my heart swelled when she added, "That isn't welcome."

"Is that so?" Mr. Kirov asked. His eyes locked on mine.

Did he know Elias was snooping around downstairs? Would he bust us? I began to sweat from the heat of his blade.

"I think I know my own wards," Mom said with a haughty lift of her chin. "Do you doubt my magic?"

Mr. Kirov continued to eye me threateningly, but if he knew, he said nothing about Elias.

"I think I know what you're really doing breaking into my house, Ivan," Mom said. "I had a premonition someone would be paying us a visit. That's why I stayed awake, waiting. But you can take your search elsewhere. It's not here. I don't have it."

What "it" was seemed pretty obvious to all of us. So Mom didn't have the talisman, after all, and Mr. Kirov clearly wasn't the one in charge of guarding it or he wouldn't be nosing around our craft room trying to locate it.

"You won't be able to hide it forever. The Elders will eventually see the wisdom of my suggestion, Amelia. Then they will give it to me freely."

"They'll never give it to you. You're not a True Witch."

Mr. Kirov stiffened, and his grip tightened on his mystical sword. Heat flashed outward, and I felt a bolt hit right in the tender spot where Elias had bitten me. I hissed in pain and pulled my arm protectively against my stomach.

My reaction brought a cold, slow smile to Mr. Kirov's face. "Perhaps so, but you're compromised, Amelia. You have vampire sympathies."

Mom's power was at the bursting point. Mr. Kirov didn't seem to sense it, but her energy filled the room like a thick fog. "You need to leave," she told him. "Before I make you."

"The Elders will hear about this," he warned, but he retreated back into the craft room. Glass shards crunched under his boots as he made his way to the window he'd jimmied open.

Forget wards, we needed better security, period.

"The Elders will remember exactly why I'm their queen," Mom said defiantly. "And you'll replace that jar, damn it."

His cold laughter drifted in from the dark maw of the open window.

Mom's power released itself in a violent wind that slammed the window shut and snapped the curtains closed. "Argh," she raged incoherently. "I hate that guy. We should never have agreed to take that bastard in. I mean, I like Illyana and Nikolai, of course, but Ivan! Oooh!"

Nikolai's mother, Illyana, had been made an honorary True

Witch of the coven. She was a magical practitioner who came from a long line of Romany cunning women. Ivan, I imagine, had been a bonus—a vampire hunter from Russia. I don't know; it all happened before I was born.

"Huh, I'll bet Ivan didn't like your marriage to Dad much."

"No, he didn't. If you haven't guessed, we're old rivals."

I shook my head. I didn't know much about Mr. Kirov at all. Nikolai had never brought me home to meet the parents, and his dad wasn't a regular at the outer-circle coven meetings. We didn't interact much. And having met him on the job, as it were, I was just as glad we didn't.

"What you said before," I started, but I wasn't sure where to go. "Anyway, that was cool, about the welcome thing."

Mom smiled and did that annoying Mom gesture of smoothing a lock of my hair over my forehead. "You're my baby, Ana. You always will be. I love you."

Why did parents always have to make things extra-special awkward? "I love you too, Mom."

After clearing up the broken glass, I told Mom I was headed for bed. It had to be nearly three. I yawned as I closed the door. At least this time I didn't yelp when I saw Elias sitting on my bed.

"Did you hear what Mom said?" I asked in a whisper, since I could hear Mom shuffling around in her bedroom. I sat down next to him on my bed.

He nodded. Following my example, he kept his voice low. "Do you know who the Elders are? Where they might be holding it?"

I shook my head. "That's, like, the biggest witch secret ever. Only the Inner Circle knows, and the membership changes all the time."

Elias hung his head. "We are lost."

I kicked my feet against the bed frame. "Not yet, we aren't. Bea's in the Inner Circle. It's high time you met my best friend, Elias. I'll make the arrangements. You can meet her tomorrow night."

He hesitated. "Is delay wise? We must find the talisman now."

"They're not going to enslave everyone tonight," I said, stifling another yawn.

"How can you be so sure?"

"Because they're sleeping. Everyone is sleeping." I couldn't quite keep the whine from my tone as I added, "I should be sleeping."

Elias let out a long, frustrated breath. "All right. I suppose if they decided they wanted to trigger the talisman now, there would be little I could do to stop them. But tomorrow, you'll introduce me to this Bea and we can find them?"

My eyes felt gritty. I flopped back onto the mattress, making the springs squeak. "Yes. I promise."

"One more problem," he said, and the sheepishness in his voice made me open my eyes. "In the morning, I'll need a place to sleep."

"Oh." I pushed myself up on my elbows. "How dark does it need to be? I mean, would under the bed work?" Actually, that sounded really intimate, so I quickly suggested, "Or there's a root cellar in the basement."

"Do you think I could get to the basement without your mother noticing?"

"She's a sound sleeper," I said, though I kept my voice at a whisper. "But after Mr. Kirov's surprise visit, she's going to be hyperaware of the wards. I wouldn't come and go a lot, if I were you."

The prospect didn't appear to thrill him, but he nodded. "As you wish. I'm not in any shape to do much more tonight, even though it is my desperate wish. I may as well stay here in your room until everyone is asleep."

I gathered up my pj's and took them with me to the bathroom. I changed and brushed my teeth. Under the harsh overhead lights, I sat on the toilet seat and inspected my bruised arm. It looked awful. Out of habit I smeared some antibacterial cream over it and found a bandage big enough to cover it. I had to use medical tape to secure it, and when I was done, it looked like I'd had some major surgery or something.

When I got back to my room, I found Elias kicked back at my desk reading *Hikaru no Go*, an old manga series I'd loved in fifth grade. It was only a little strange to notice he didn't need the lamp to read by.

He glanced up briefly when I slid past him to crawl under the sheets, but he returned to the book without comment. I no longer felt the least bit sleepy. In fact, I was acutely aware of the fact that I'd dropped my bra in the hamper along with the rest of the clothes I wore all day. The only thing between me and Elias was my pajama top, a sheet, the quilt, and about a half foot. Okay, when I thought through all the details and added his silk shirt on top, I knew it was stupid. But knowing didn't negate how exposed and naked I felt.

Clasping my hands over my stomach, I stared at the ceiling.

He turned a page.

I twiddled my thumbs.

He shifted his feet, which he had propped up on the windowsill.

"What would you normally be doing right now?" I asked,

rolling onto my side to face him. "I mean, if there wasn't a talisman to hunt down or any of that?"

He rested the book in his lap, a long finger marking his place. "Before or after our exile?"

"Before."

"I would likely be attending the king's court. Perhaps there would be a dance or we would run."

"Run?"

"Sometimes we gather into packs and run as far and as fast as we can. The deeper into the woods and farther from the city, the better."

Remembering the pure joy I experienced the day I'd run home, I could easily imagine joining one of the vampire runs. Like with the dance at Lilydale, bodies would surround me, urging me to quicken my pace, until it was like we were soaring across the landscape.

"That sounds awesome."

Even in the dark, I could sense Elias's smile in his tone. "It is exactly so, full of awe."

I drifted to sleep imagining the ground racing beneath my feet, the stars standing still above, and Elias beside me.

I would have slept the day away, except my bladder woke me up sometime after noon. The sun filled my bedroom, setting dust motes dancing. Oversleeping made me hot and cranky. I pulled myself stiffly from the bed and padded to the bathroom.

A splash of cold water on my face inspired me to take a full bath and wash all of last night's underground adventure from my hair. A lot of soap and a half hour later, I emerged feeling halfway human.

Which I guessed was just about right.

Back in my room, I opened up my armoire and picked out a sturdy pair of jeans and a utilitarian black T-shirt. But the white bandage was too obvious, so I tossed it on the floor and reached for a long-sleeve button-up, also black.

I glanced around for a message from Elias. Finding none, I grabbed my phone from the charger and went in search of something to eat.

The brownies were still on the kitchen table. I ate three while I poured myself a glass of milk. I peered out the pantry window to see if Mom was puttering in the garden. A skinny tabby dashed along the fence line, but otherwise the backyard was empty. I found the note she left on the answering machine.

"Council meeting. Don't worry."

Don't worry? I crumpled the note in my fist. Of course I was worried. They were meeting to talk about the talisman, I was sure. What if they decided to use it while the vampires slept?

My fingers punched in Bea's number. She answered on the second ring. "Hey, Ana-chan. What's up?"

"Where is everyone meeting? I know your dad is an Elder. Tell me. I have to know."

"Why? What's going on?"

Everything was so complicated. I hardly knew where to start. "Can you come over? I've got brownies."

As I sat on the front porch swing with the rapidly disappearing pan of brownies in my lap, I wondered whether I could really trust Bea. She'd been such a bitch about Nikolai, and she clearly had no love for witch-blood-sucking vampires, as she'd called them. But whom else did I have, really? True Witchcraft was a secret. Though, before my failed Initiation, I knew a few of the other witches my age, Bea was the only one who went to my school. We were kind of stuck with each other.

I nibbled on the corner of my sixth brownie and watched the neighbor across the street mow his lawn in perfect rows. Bees hummed in the carpet of deep purple creeping Charlie flowers of our yard, and anxiously buzzed the unopened flowers of the stand of bleeding hearts along the fence.

Yesterday's clouds had dissipated to mere wisps.

I hoped Elias had found a safe place in the basement away from all this sunshine.

Bea's Buick pulled up to the curb. She very carefully cranked up the windows and locked the car before giving me a broad wave.

I scooted over to make room on the swing. Soon the brownies were gone, and she asked, "Are you going to tell me what's going on? Why do you need to see the Elders?"

Despite having all the time that it took for Bea to arrive to consider what to say, I still hadn't quite figured out how to broach the subject. "Do you know about the talisman?"

"Is that the thing that was stolen from the History Center that Mom and Dad have been whispering about?"

I listened very carefully to Bea's words, trying to judge if she was using those formidable acting skills of hers or not. She seemed sincere, so I said, "Yeah. Do you know what it can do?"

She looked me over and concluded, "I'm going to go out on a limb here, but since you're all in a tizzy about it, it has something to do with vampires."

"Tizzy" seemed a bit unfair, but I let it go. "The talisman has the power to turn vampires into slaves."

"Cool," she breathed.

I scowled.

Coughing theatrically into her hand, she said, "I mean, sucks to be you."

Okay, that was not helpful. "I'm serious about this. The Elders have the talisman and I heard Nikolai's dad say that he wants to use it to kill all the vampires. All the vampires, Bea. That means me too."

"Where are you getting all this intel? Who says the Elders have this artifact thing? I heard my dad say a vampire stole it."

A vampire. Elias had said he'd arrived too late. Had he lied to me? Did he actually steal it, and then manage to lose it to a witch again? He was pretty determined to get the talisman, but I would think if he'd fumbled the ball—again!—he'd be completely racked with guilt. "I kind of doubt that."

"Why?"

"Any vampire loyal to my dad would have presented the court with the talisman immediately."

"What about the disloyal ones?"

Of course, Elias had just gotten into a boatload of trouble for being disobedient. But he never denied his treason. I couldn't see him concealing something this major. It wasn't in his nature. "I don't know. I still think that if any vampire had the talisman, there wouldn't be all this panic in the underground, you know?"

Bea shook her head. "I don't know anything about your weird little underground, but I'll take your word for it."

"Thanks," I muttered sarcastically.

The brownie pan sat empty in my lap. Bea twirled a dark curl of her hair around her finger. "You know, I don't think the Elders have the talisman," Bea said. She chewed her bottom lip, as if trying to decide what to say next. She sighed. "Before I came over, Mom told me Dad wanted me to ask you about the talisman, see what I could find out."

Bea was such a better actor than I could ever hope to be. And a better spy. "I thought you didn't know anything about the talisman."

"I don't! Not really. I just know that everybody wants to know where it is. And nobody seems to have it."

"Yeah, that's true enough," I admitted, my fingers absently combing the corners of the pan for chocolaty crumbs. "I thought Mom had it and Mr. Kirov was guarding it, but that turned out to be way wrong. Did you know Nik's dad broke into my house last night?"

"No way! Seriously?"

I recounted the whole story for Bea, especially the parts where I was brave and stood up to him. Okay, so there weren't very many of those, but I also pointed out how scary he was with the Sparkly Scimitar of Doom.

"Wow," she said when I was finished. The sun had come around the house to shine in our eyes. We retreated inside for the shade and a couple of Cokes. I found the bag of potato chips Mom had hidden behind the cartons of whole wheat crackers, and brought out some chip dip from the fridge.

We sat in the kitchen to devour our feast. Bea's laughter filled the room when I told her about Mom's latest diet fad, and after regarding her for a moment I said, "I miss hanging out like this with you."

"Yeah, things have been kind of strained since you went over to the dark side."

"I'm not on the dark side. Besides, you're the one who was all jealous of Nik."

"Listen, sister, I had my sights on him long before you snagged everyone's attention at Initiation Fail," she said, wagging her finger and shimmying her shoulders at me.

This conversation gambit could only lead to a fight I didn't want to have, so I didn't argue. I just chewed another salty chip. I missed Nik more than I wanted to admit, so I didn't look her in the eye when I asked, "Are you talking to him?"

"I wish," she said. "I don't know where he's been. In a creative funk, I suppose, thanks to all that heartbreak."

"When he gets a number one hit, he can thank me," I said.

"I'm sure he will." Bea was starting to sound seriously miffed.

Okay, cross Nik off the subjects to bring up around Bea. "Um, hey, I've got a vampire friend that wants to meet you."

"Eat me? I'm sure."

"No, not eat you; meet you," I repeated impatiently. "His name is Elias, and he's hiding out in the basement right now."

"You have a vampire in the basement? A boy vampire? What does your mom think of that?" I didn't have to say anything. The color in my cheek did. Bea squealed with mischievous delight. "She doesn't know, does she?"

"Do you want to meet him or not?"

"Sure." Bea sat back. Digging her chip into the container, she scooped out the last of the dip. She munched it noisily, and then asked, "Is this why you and Nik broke up? A boy vampire stashed in your basement?"

"Partially," I admitted.

"Then I definitely want to meet him."

We discussed arrangements and settled on a time and place for the introduction. Finding ourselves out of munchies and at loose ends on a Sunday afternoon, we decided to go hang out at the Mall of America.

The Mall of America really was quite big, but not at all very impressive from the outside. I always thought it should rise up out of the prairie of Bloomington like a monolith to consumerism and yet, every time we went there, I found myself disappointed by how squat and square it really was.

Once inside, however, it was like the Tardis—it seemed to stretch in every direction, forever. In fact, I got a little nervous when we strayed from the east side, which was the section I knew best, because I had no bread crumbs to scatter to help me find my way back to Bea's car. Luckily, we'd agreed to meet up with Lane and Taylor at the Starbucks near the entrance to the Nickelodeon amusement park. When I'd texted around to see who of our theater gang might be available, it turned out that they were already here, riding the roller coasters.

"Do you think it's a date?" I asked Bea as we made our way through the curved cobblestone paths of the park. I had to shout to be heard over the splashing of the log ride. Palm trees grew toward the giant atrium's ceiling, surrounded by figs and other tropical plants. "Do you think Lane has a thing for Taylor?"

Bea rolled her eyes. "If you didn't have your head buried in vampire crap all the time, you'd have figured the two of them out long ago."

Possibly becoming a slave hardly constituted "crap," but I didn't correct her so much as make a face.

"When I found out that Lane does that Dungeons and Dragons thing, I knew it was a match made in heaven," Bea said. "He just had to get over his slight crush on you."

Me? I was incredulous. "Lane? But he's always making stupid jokes at my expense."

Bea gave me a look that made me feel like the saddest, most incompetent female on the planet. "Yes, dear, that's one of the signs of geek love. Next is quoting entire skits from Monty Python or *Black Adder* for you."

"Maybe I dodged a bullet," I said with a laugh as we passed by booths of brightly colored plastic trinkets and gaudy stuffed animals.

"Maybe you did, but Taylor is crazy for him."

Now that I knew, it was easy to see that Lane and Taylor were a couple. With beaming smiles and constant attention, she encouraged his long-winded rants about politics and science fiction shows that he loved-slash-hated. He performed all for her, and carried her drinks and did all sorts of other little kind gestures.

It would have made me gag, except it reminded me how much I missed Nikolai.

At least they didn't seem to mind that Bea and I crashed their date. I felt like a third wheel, but not because they didn't make an effort to include me. I kept thinking about Elias and wondering if he was right. What if, right now, while I sat in the corner booth with my friends, one of the Elders activated the talisman?

What would it be like to suddenly lose my will? Once, Mom had put me under a zombie spell and I'd wandered around for almost an entire day at school unable to work up enthusiasm for anything. The enchantment had made me pliant and stupid, which was something like not being able to do what I wanted— though it was really more like not being able to think for myself.

And what if the bloodline I belonged to was Bea's? She was my friend, but she'd also seemed pretty excited by the idea of getting to order a vampire around. As a bonus, she could boss me around night *and* day.

The thought, or maybe the fact that I'd had no real food yet today, made my stomach flip.

"I didn't get much sleep last night," I said, interrupting Lane's reenactment of some great moment in *Buckaroo Banzai*. "I think I'm going to head home." Bea started to get up, but I waved her back to her seat. "I can take the light rail. It goes to a bus stop that will take me home. You should stay. See you later tonight."

"You sure?"

I really wanted time alone to think. And maybe talk to Nik. "Yeah, I'm good."

I sat in the back of the train, listening to the lulling sound of the rails and deleting every message I started to Nik. Thing was, I didn't want to sound desperate. A simple "Thinking of you" was beginning to look like the best option, even though I'd trashed it six or seven times already.

But everything else I wrote ended up sounding needy. Even saying that I missed him felt kind of heavy and intense, and maybe even accusatory, like he should feel the same way and why hadn't he written—did he ever really care or was that all just an act?

See, this was where I always ended up. I needed to stay simple, uncomplicated. I rekeyed "thinking of you" and hesitated so long over Send that I nearly missed my stop.

I pressed the button just as I got off the train. Shoving the phone into my pocket, I tried not to wonder how soon he'd reply.

On the bus, I wished I'd brought my iPod. I couldn't believe I'd left home without it. So, of course, since it languished in my desk drawer, today was the day everybody seemed to be shouting into their cells or sassing one another with their outside voices, as Mom might say. What I wouldn't give for a nice mellow tune from Coldplay or Snow Patrol to drown out all the noise.

I pulled out my phone and stared at the screen. I flipped it open and checked the bars. Despite everyone else on the phone, mine showed only three out of four. But that would be strong enough to get a text—

—if anyone bothered sending one, that was!

Maybe I really should give up on Nik once and for all. He wasn't going to quit vampire hunting, apparently, and I couldn't stop being half vampire if I tried. Maybe it wasn't about Nikolai, anyway. I just missed having somebody to take me bowling or to the movies, and who would put up with *my* stupid stories and opinions.

Somebody who could do that on a Sunday afternoon.

Going dancing that night at Lilydale with Elias was incredible. Running sounded even more intense. But I couldn't really go to the beach or ride the Ferris wheel at the state fair with a vampire who sizzled to ashes in the sun.

Nikolai didn't reply the entire ride home. He hated me. Once home, I sank into my bed and buried my face in my pillow.

My phone woke me up, but it wasn't Nik. Bea was at the front door. I dragged myself out of bed to let her in, wondering why Mom hadn't done so. As I passed the living room, I noticed the grandfather clock read seven o'clock. I'd slept the entire day away. It was night.

Elias would be up soon.

"Where's your mom?" Bea asked as I finally fumbled the locks open to let her in.

"She said something about a council meeting." I shrugged. I was just as grateful; after all, this way Elias had a better chance of getting out of the house without her noticing. In fact, time was ticking. "We should get Elias and get out of here."

"Yeah, where did you want to go?"

My stomach rumbled. "Let's go out to dinner. I'm starving."

"Does the vampire pay?"

"No, I will," I said. "He doesn't have a job."

"Neither do you," Bea pointed out.

Mom, however, always left me money in the cookie jar for those nights when she worked late. "I'm covered."

"Well, let's go somewhere decent, like Fasika this ti—" Bea stopped; she was staring in the direction of our basement door. The ancient hinges creaked ominously as the door slowly swung open. Elias emerged slowly into view. I tried to see him as Bea would, for the first time. But I saw only familiar smile lines on a friendly, if angular, face. His short dark hair was ruffled by sleep, and his clothes had taken on a decidedly slept-in look. The silk showed spots of cobwebs and smudges of dust. However, rest had returned the sparkle in his eye, and he no longer seemed quite so stooped by his injuries. I thought he looked terrific. Bea, meanwhile, seemed to find his appearance hilarious. She laughed wildly. "This . . . You're a vampire? He just looks like a guy! With that entrance I expected at least a long cloak and a 'good evthing,'" she drawled in a passable if ridiculously thick accent.

"Good evening," Elias obliged, with a slight tip of his head. To me, he asked, "Bea, I presume?"

I nodded, though I would have been just as happy to deny knowing her, the way she kept smirking at Elias. I kind of wished Elias would transform his eyes and drop his fangs just to show her what vampires could really look like. But it would be hard to get service at the restaurant like that and I was starving. "Can we go?"

Bea sniggered the whole way out to Elias's car.

"You didn't drive?" I asked her.

"No. Mom dropped me off."

I took Elias's elbow and pulled him close so I could speak softly in his ear. "I'll catch you up on everything. Bea has some interesting theories about the talisman."

"I look forward to it," Elias said.

It was weird not having Elias in the driver's seat, and even stranger to see him at a restaurant. Fasika was this hole-in-the-wall on Snelling Avenue with cramped seating and sticky plastic tablecloths, but the scent of Ethiopian spices made my mouth water. Neon signs advertising Summit beer flashed in the window, above rows of dusty plastic potted plants. A college student with a goatee and round-rimmed Harry Potter glasses showed us to a table. "Hamline," Bea guessed, spotting the tattoos on his forearms as he set out service and water glasses. We liked to play a game where we tried to guess which college waiters/waitresses went to, since there were so many in Minneapolis/St. Paul.

I shook my head. "No way. Macalester." Macalester was a much hipper school, in my opinion.

The waiter laughed, "Actually, Augsburg. I'll be back in a minute to take your order." He gave the bandage on my arm a quick nod. "Looks like you got a new tat, huh?"

"Oh." My hand automatically reached to pull the sleeve down to hide it. Damn, my cuff must have come unbuttoned. "Um, something like that."

As soon as the waiter walked away, I knew I'd have Bea to answer to. Sure enough, she was staring in horror at where my hand covered the bandage. It didn't take long for her to put two and two together either. She gave Elias a nasty look.

"You . . . ," she snarled at Elias. She put her hand over her mouth and said to me, "You didn't!"

All sorts of responses flitted through my head, but they all sounded like the kinds of excuses a battered wife might use. *It's not a big deal. He didn't mean to hurt me. I wanted him to. This was a special circumstance; it won't happen again.* So I just shrugged.

"The lamb looks good," Elias said drily.

Bea crossed her arms in front of her chest and frowned at him. "Don't try to change the subject, leech," she said.

"Really? Because that'd be cool with me," I said. I really, really had to clamp down on my desire to explain the bite to

Bea. It *had* been an emergency. I *wasn't* planning to make it a habit. But it was also our business. And, more to the point, no matter how accurately and honestly we explained the circumstances, nothing would be good enough for Bea.

Elias's lips pressed together. "Leech?"

"Could everyone just let this go?" I asked. Just once I'd like to get through a meal without feeling a keen desire to run away. "It's hardly a news flash. Guess what, Bea? Vampires bite."

My outburst shocked a laugh out of Bea. Even Elias smiled a bit from behind the menu.

"Okay, good. Now that that's out of the way," I said, taking charge, "we came here to talk about the talisman."

Bea laid out everything she knew. I told Elias the details he might not have heard during last night's break-in. Bea seemed to delight in the story and had me retell the part where I defiantly told Nik's dad to replace the jar.

"Let me see if I understand correctly," Elias said, as he tore off a piece of injera. "The hunter doesn't have it or he wouldn't be looking for it at your house. Your mother says she doesn't have it, though she may just mean not with her." Turning to Bea, he said, "Your father, an Elder, thinks a vampire is in possession and also sent you to try to find out who might have it. So, at the very least, he doesn't know where it is, which may imply the rest of the Elders don't either."

Nods of agreement were shared all around.

"Vampires make good thieves," Elias continued around a mouthful of lentils. It occurred to me that I'd never seen him eat before. He certainly did it with relish, savoring every bite. "We were often employed as such during the time of servitude."

"What are you saying?" Bea asked. She sat back, her hands resting on her stomach, clearly stuffed.

I didn't think I could eat another bite myself.

Elias, on the other hand, continued as if there was no limit to his appetite. "Unless your kind has perfected the spell of invisibility to electronic devices, then perhaps a servant *was* involved."

Bea looked to me for a translation. "He means a vampire still loyal to the witches," I supplied.

"There are witches who still keep vampires?" Bea sounded appropriately horrified. A least I thought she did, until she added, "Why doesn't my family have one? How come we don't rate?"

"Perhaps this tragedy will be rectified soon," Elias said coolly.

"They could clean the house while we slept," she leaned in to tell me excitedly. "Can you imagine? No more house chores!"

"Awesome," I said, but she didn't seem to notice my sarcasm.

"I suppose you'd still have to do the mowing and gardening," Bea said, looking into her red plastic water glass and finding it empty. "Although there's that guy in my neighborhood who always starts his engine up in the middle of the night—"

I couldn't tell whether Bea was joking, so, ignoring her, I turned to Elias. "Mom doesn't have any servants."

"But she has command over others who do," he reminded me.

"There can't be that many of these servants, as you call them," Bea said, abruptly joining our conversation. "*I* would have heard of it before now."

Bea took pride in the fact that she'd been invited to all the prominent-witch households. Her father's position as an Elder meant that they had a very active social life, and at an early age,

Bea had decided to collect them all, like some sort of game. She kept note of every family she met in a diary—actually, *diaries* at this point.

Elias nodded. "If we knew how many, it would narrow down our search."

"Our?" Bea snapped. "Don't consider me part of your little scheme, witch biter."

Witch biter? That had to be the lamest insult yet. "You want me to be a slave?" I asked her. Bea wasn't in my honors class, but I was pretty sure the horrors of slavery were covered in most standard American history textbooks. "Really? You're okay with that?"

"Don't be stupid," she said. "This situation is totally different. Vampires aren't human."

Of course, that was the moment the waiter came with the check. We all looked at him nervously, but he gave a knowing smile. "Neither are zombies, I hear," he said.

The three of us found that enormously funny. Perhaps even a bit too funny, given the look the waiter gave us as he retreated, having deposited the check in front of Elias.

"I guess they don't teach feminism at Augsburg," Bea said, taking the brown plastic tray and looking over the bill.

"Mom isn't an adjunct there," I said seriously. "So probably not."

Bea scrutinized the bill for a long time, looking vaguely dissatisfied. I was about to ask her if they'd overcharged us for something, when she put the tray down with a determined slap. "You pay for this," she said to me, "and I'll give you my best guesses as to who has vampire help around the house, as it were."

"Deal," I said without hesitation. I'd taken more than forty dollars from the cookie jar, so I was confident I could cover the total.

"All right," she said, never looking at Elias. She counted off on her fingers, "Franklin, Stewart, Nelson, Keillor, Ramsey, and Jones for sure. They're all traditionalists in the worst way. Oh, and the Hills, of course."

My eyebrows rose. Most normal people didn't know it, but the old money of Minneapolis and St. Paul were all True Witch families. In one way, they wouldn't be hard to find. Most of them owned palatial residences in my neighborhood or in nearby Cathedral Hill. The problem would be getting in unnoticed. "They're going to have wicked wards," I told Elias. "With vampire backup."

"We are in your debt." Elias bowed slightly to Bea, who still refused to look at him.

"I'm doing this for you," Bea said, jabbing a finger at me. "Nobody else."

"Thanks," I told her.

"You'd make a crappy slave anyway, Ana." She gave me a crooked smile.

Before we parted ways, Bea grabbed my elbow and pulled me aside. I'd sat in the front seat this time. We'd stopped for a quick scouting expedition before taking Bea home. Elias was already in the trees, surveying the security system surrounding the Summit Avenue house of a very famous radio-show host.

"Do you remember the Initiation?" she asked me in a hushed tone.

"Of course," I said. My Initiation Fail. The worst night of my life—it was hard to forget.

"Remember my gift?"

Bea's aunt Diane, who had been acting high priestess that night, had proclaimed each initiate's special area of witchcraft at the end of the ceremony. I remembered jealously that a friend of ours, Shannon, had gotten to be a bard, a talent I'd been secretly hoping for. But what had Bea gotten?

"Prophecy," she supplied when I hesitated too long. "I've got a bad feeling in my gut. It's early stages, but—well, be careful."

That was her prophecy? Bad stuff could happen? "You should get a refund," I joked. "Your superpower sucks."

"I'm serious," she insisted, but then let my arm go. "You're right. My gift totally blows. It's taken forever for me to understand how to read these strange sensations I get. But I'll go home and do a spread. That will tell me more."

Yeah, like tarot cards were never vague. But I appreciated the sentiment. "Thanks, Bea."

Elias came back to the car, and we drove Bea home. We said our good-byes and he waited until she got inside the house before starting the engine.

It didn't take very long to come to the conclusion that I wasn't much help to Elias. If I were willing to go vamp, I could scale the brick walls or use superspeed to baffle motion detectors. The problem turned out to be more mental than physical. I couldn't get over the idea of whose house we were about to illegally trespass into. "This isn't right," I whispered. "We're going to get so busted. I mean, he must be one of the most famous Minnesotans ever."

Elias, of course, slept through much of daily popular culture. "Do you think the former vice president has softer security?"

"Probably," I nearly shouted.

Elias hushed me with a frantic hand motion. We could see a beat-up station wagon in the parking space next to the garage. Someone was home.

"This is such a bad idea," I repeated for the hundredth time. I hugged my arms around my chest, ostensibly to keep warm in the evening chill, but really to steady my nerves.

Elias's eyes tracked something, like a cat getting ready to pounce. He pointed to something I couldn't see in the darkness. "The security cameras have a small blind spot. If we move quickly enough, we can make it to the roof before they finish the sweep."

He must have seen the doubt in my still-untransformed eyes, because he put an arm on my shoulder.

"You can be the lookout, my lady," he said kindly.

"Yeah, that's probably good," I agreed. It was only after he'd disappeared in a blur that I wondered exactly how I was supposed to contact him in an emergency. I watched the darkened house through the budding branches with my breath held, but if any alarms sounded, they were silent. After a few minutes, I let my butt sink onto the clammy dirt. What was going on in there? Where was Elias? Were the police already on their way?

When a car moved down the street behind me, I almost had a heart attack.

But when I turned back around, Elias appeared at my side, so silent it was almost like magic. I grabbed him in a grateful bear hug. He rose, gently coaxing me along back down the cliffside approach we'd used to get behind the house. When the floodlights receded behind us, he finally spoke.

"There is a safe in the house," he said. We came out of the bushes onto a rough asphalt road that circled the few more moderate houses that clung to the cliffside behind the Summit mansions. "I wasn't willing to risk trying to crack it."

My eyebrows rose at that. Maybe Elias had firsthand experience being "used" as a thief by a witch master. That might explain how he got in and out of the History Center without raising any alarms. "Did you run into any nonhuman servants?"

"I doubt my survey of the house would have been so quick if I had."

He had a good point. "Do you really think that a vampire servant stole the talisman?"

"I do," he said, after a moment's consideration. The stars shone brightly in a clear, dark sky. His eyes were drawn up to the glowing orb of the mostly full moon. "Magic is powerful, but there's a reason witches kept vampire slaves—and why they might want us back."

I'd just seen him break into a house, search it, and come out in about ten minutes, so I could easily imagine what he meant. Still, I couldn't shake this feeling I'd been having since the moment I knew the talisman was possibly in witch hands. "Why do you think no one has—you know—activated it or whatever?"

Elias shook his head. "It is a mystery, my lady."

I left Elias to scout out the other houses, since it was clear I wasn't much help. For the second time in so many days, I sneaked into the house well after midnight. The place was quiet, no late-night baking surprises waiting in the kitchen. It didn't even look like Mom had been home, but I'd stopped worrying about her now that I knew she had supersecret witch stuff going on.

I couldn't believe I had school tomorrow. I was going to need a double espresso.

Especially since I kept turning things over in my mind. Somebody had the talisman, but who? Would they use it? Why hadn't they so far?

I was still awake when my phone vibrated on my bedside table at three a.m. I was sleepy enough to first think it might be Elias with news, but then I remembered he didn't have a damn cell phone. Instead, it was a two-word text from Bea that caused chills to run down my spine.

"High Priestess," was all she'd written.

The tarot High Priestess was often equated with witchcraft, a kind of Queen of Witches. My mom.

Despite the hour, I called Bea's cell. She answered in a hushed whisper, "Are you still breaking and entering?"

"No," I told her. "I sucked at it. I was a total nervous wreck. Elias is on his own."

"You got my text, huh?" Bea didn't wait for my answer. "I don't want you to freak out. The High Priestess could also mean an initiate."

The tarot tended to be vague, but apparently, in this case, it was clear on one thing: "So a witch has the talisman for sure."

"The only question is, is it your mom or someone else?"

Since neither of us had an answer to that, we chatted a bit about other things, and then said our good-byes.

It was a long time before I finally fell asleep.

When I woke up, I could tell instantly that I was late, as in a you're-going-to-need-a-tardy-slip late. I quickly threw on the first thing my fingers lit on in my closet, brushed my teeth, ran a comb through my hair, touched up my makeup, and ran. I had to skip the coffee shop and head straight to the city bus stop.

I made it to school in time to hear the first-period dismissal bell ring. Crap, I'd missed math entirely. I loved math.

As I stood in line in the office with the other deadbeat kids straggling in, it occurred to me to wonder why the hell Mom hadn't woken me up. More all-hours witch business, I supposed. I was going to have to learn to be more self-sufficient if this was the new norm. My stomach was already complaining about the lack of breakfast and the grim prospect of cafeteria lunch.

Though she'd written slip after slip as if on automatic pilot, the office lady stopped when she saw me. Her voice became noticeably cheerier. "Oh, Ms. Parker? What can I do for you?"

"I overslept," I said sheepishly.

Her face crumpled into disapproval. She wrote the note with brisk strokes of her pen. Before handing it over, she said, "You know this goes on your record? I trust this is the last time we'll see you here for this?"

"Yes, ma'am," I said, because it was clear that was the only sane response.

For the rest of the day, I struggled to catch up. Even though I was on time for everything else, it was like I never got into the rhythm. Plus, I realized I'd neglected to do any work on the extra-credit project that was due in American history this Wednesday. I had three days to pick a subject, do the research, and write ten pages. I went right to the library.

Thompson was there with his tutor. He jumped up the moment he saw me. With a huge smile on his face, he swept me into a waltz. As distracted and surprised as I was, I couldn't follow and tripped over his feet.

"You're going to have to do better than that, Ms. Eliza Doolittle." He beamed.

I was about to remind him that I didn't have the part yet, when I suddenly remembered that today was the day Mr. Martinez was supposed to post the cast list. "Oh my God!" I shouted. "Does that mean? Are you . . . ?"

He nodded vigorously. "You are. I am. How awesome is that?"

I screamed with joy.

The librarian was coming around her desk when I remembered where I was and clamped a hand over my mouth. The last thing I needed was detention on top of everything else today. "Sorry," I mouthed.

She seemed to take pity and waved her finger at us. "Thompson. Parker. Keep it down," she said. "Your first warning."

"Yes, ma'am," I said. Thompson was apparently used to warnings, however, because he ignored her. Instead, he took my hand and pulled me over to his table.

"Where were you this morning?" he asked. "I thought you'd be one of the first in line."

"I would have been, but I kind of overslept."

Thompson's eyes widened. "You? Today?"

What could I say? I'd surprised myself by sleeping in so much lately. Having a secret life as a vampire princess messed up my biorhythms something fierce. "I guess it's sort of, you know, trouble at home."

Thompson nodded like he completely related to late nights in underground caves, traipsing through famous people's yards, and the constant stress of knowing you could become someone's slave any minute.

"Plus, I'm behind on this extra-credit project," I said, and I probably shouldn't have gone for the final sympathy points. I could tell by the sudden glazing over of his eyes I'd lost him with this one.

"Must be rough," he said, sarcasm sneaking into his tone.

I was too tired to try to make nice, and so I just hefted my backpack over my shoulder and said, "See you at first rehearsals."

That brought his huge, almost-stupid-with-happy smile back. "Yeah." But then he ruined the moment by pointing to my forearm. "New tattoo? Hope Mr. Martinez doesn't see that."

Walking quickly to the stacks, I pretended I didn't hear. Back at my favorite desk, I peeked under the bandage. If anything, the bite looked worse.

I put my head down and flipped uselessly through the books that I'd grabbed on my way. How was I going to make it through today?

Especially when I found out that Bea didn't get into the show. At all.

She sulked through lunch, hardly saying a word. I tried a cheery, "Understudy is good," only to be met with a snarl.

Cafeteria lunch wasn't too bad. The fried chicken was rendered mostly edible by the incredible amount of salt marinated into the meat. The mashed potatoes, however, were a big mushy pile of goop. String beans had been overcooked to the point of being slimy. But I filled up on chocolate milk and spinach salad, which, with enough dressing, passed for tasty.

I enviously eyed the sandwich Bea picked at disconsolately. Turkey, mayo, and crisp red-leaf lettuce on whole wheat topped with a thick slice of tomato. Her mom had also packed a Baggie of carrots, snap peas, and kohlrabi, clearly freshly picked up at the farmers' market.

My mouth watered. But I didn't dare ask for a trade with the mood she was in. Besides, what did I have to offer? Maybe if I told her she could be Eliza, she'd give me a couple of carrots. . . .

The bell rang and we hadn't exchanged more than three words. My head was starting to hurt from lack of caffeine.

I found myself reacting very self-consciously to all the shouts in the hallways between classes of "Hey, Doolittle!" and "You go!" and other such congratulations, especially with Bea beside me looking more and more depressed. Every time I thought Bea and I had a chance of being friends again, something like this happened.

At least in American history, the subject of my paper finally hit me. I decided that what I wanted to focus on was all the rationalizations people came up with to justify slavery. I hadn't even realized how much what Bea joked about last night bothered me until Mr. Shultz explained that a lot of slave owners sincerely considered their African captives subhuman. They'd even come up with a lot of bogus science to prove racial superiority.

You could make the case that vampires *really* weren't human, of course. Elias kept saying weird things about when he was "created," which sounded not at all natural. But one thing I remembered from studying natural selection in biology was that you couldn't breed animals that weren't essentially the same species. You might be able to mate a lion and a tiger and get a viable baby, but you couldn't, for instance, cross a lion and a zebra.

The fact that I was alive meant that vampires were at least a related species to Homo sapiens. It was a start. Maybe if I could understand slavers' mind-sets a little better, I could help change the opinions of Bea and Nikolai and Mr. Kirov and all the other witches.

I didn't think I'd have much luck. It took a massive paradigm shift for people to "judge by the content of a person's character, not the color of their skin," to paraphrase Martin Luther King Jr., and it's not like there wasn't still racism in America. I'd experienced my own racism just the other day when I'd initially been scared of the guys who ended up protecting me from the red-haired vampire.

Who was that vamp, anyway? Could he be a servant to whoever had the talisman? I made a mental note to try to engage him in conversation if I ever met up with him again.

"I know my teaching is exceptional, but are you planning on staying for the next period as well?" Mr. Shultz asked, tapping his pencil on my notebook, breaking my reverie. I looked up, stunned. The room was empty. Somehow I'd missed the bell.

Crap.

I quickly shoved everything into my backpack and rushed out. I ran down the hall and up the stairs. I couldn't afford another tardy slip. If I got too many in one day, it was an automatic detention.

By some miracle, I managed to survive the rest of the day. At least until drama, that was.

I stood at the bottom of the stairs, letting everyone move around me. I just didn't want to face all the attention and the jealousy and that crap. The situation was so ironic. I mean,

I'd wanted to be the lead since forever, you know? It finally happened.

At the worst possible time.

So now I stared up at the wide staircase swarming with students hurrying to the last class of the day and seriously considered telling Mr. Martinez I couldn't do it. How could I? There was so much uncertainty. What if Elias didn't get the talisman? What if I woke up tonight as someone's slave . . . ?

Then I remembered Bea was understudy. The show, quite literally, could go on without me.

Okay, I could do this.

Drama was nearly as bad as I imagined. The room was filled to capacity with jealous, irritable, sullen, bitter theater geeks. Lane was deliriously happy because he'd scored the role of my suitor, Freddy. Taylor was in the play, but only as an extra, but I guess being in a relationship with someone in the show was enough to keep her spirits up.

Mr. Martinez gave his traditional lecture about how it was the effort that counted and how theater, just like life, was full of all sorts of rejections.

I wished Martinez would realize how no one appreciated this patronizing postcasting speech. I was sure he was trying to do the right thing by all the losers, but it just made everyone, even those of us who got in, feel worse.

To survive, I alternated micro-napping with taking notes about my American history paper. I was never more happy in my entire life for the ring of the bell.

No Mom when I got home, but I was getting used to having an empty house to myself. The first thing I did was raid the cupboards for the makings of a sandwich like the one Bea had at lunch. I found moldy bread and peanut butter. With a frustrated grunt, I wedged the bread into an overfilled garbage can.

I sat down at the kitchen table to eat peanut butter from the jar. Damn, I was going to starve to death if Mom didn't finish up her witchy stuff soon. Luckily, I still had a few bucks left from our night out at Fasika. I'd pick up something fast on my way to tonight's rehearsals.

After putting the peanut butter away and the spoon in the sink, I texted Mom to let her know I'd gotten into the play and that I'd be out late basically from now until opening night.

Keeping a careful eye on the time, I tackled my homework. I had to leave early, since I was city busing it back to school, so I finished only three-quarters of it. I ended up bringing along a few math problems and some English lit to read in the house seats when other people had the stage.

At Burger King, I noticed the red-haired vampire.

Chapter Eleven

Before becoming the vampire princess of St. Paul, I never spent much time scanning trees for people. I mean, who lounges on branches, besides panthers? We don't have a lot of those in Minnesota—though I guess we do have the occasional mountain lion, but that's not the point.

The point, and I do have one, was that I happened to be looking out the window as I stood in line for my cheeseburger. I spotted him in an upper fork of the trunk of a rangy silver maple. Honestly, I think I noticed him because he was wearing cute cowboy boots. Maybe there was a method to the vampires' nakedness madness, after all. There was something particularly striking about seeing a fully clothed dude hanging out in a tree, especially when he had awesome taste in footwear.

He tucked his feet up, which made me suspect that he'd noticed my attention.

I grabbed my burger the second the server put it on the counter, and ran out the door toward the treed vamp. Unless he wanted to squirrel it by tightrope walking the telephone wires, he didn't really have a place to go. "Hey," I shouted up to where he tried to blend into the hand-shaped leaves. "Those are great boots! Where'd you get them?"

"Uh . . ." I heard a rustling from the branches. "DSW."

"Oh! I love that place." I wasn't much of a clotheshorse, but Bea was, and I'd spent a lot of time with her browsing stores like that. "Why don't you come down? You're going to follow me anyway, right? We might as well walk together."

He hopped down gracefully, the heels of those lovely boots clicking softly on the cement. A helicopter seed stuck into one of the reddish curls that fell across his pale forehead. His eyes were a mossy green, and his features held a slight broadness to them that made me think he might be Irish.

"Shall we go?" he asked.

That was the moment I started to suspect that this vampire wasn't "friendly." All the vampires allied with my dad do this deep bow and formally introduce themselves or otherwise act, well, like I'm some kind of princess. Of course, I was exiled now, so maybe they wouldn't anymore. Still, there was something about how completely unimpressed he seemed with me that made me wary. "Oh, yeah. Sure," I said, looking at him more carefully now.

Falling into step beside me, he walked with his hands clasped behind his back. It made me think that instead of a blue Windbreaker he should be wearing one of those frilly frock coats men wore in the seventeenth century.

After my embarrassing attempts at espionage with Mom and Bea, I decided on the direct approach. "Who are you working for? Why are you following me?"

"I agreed to walk, not talk."

Touché. "Come on," I said with a smile. "At least tell me your name."

"Aiden West."

"West?" I asked as we waited at the corner for a break in the traffic. It seemed like a strangely mundane name for a vampire.

"Richard West was the lord chancellor of Ireland when I came over."

"Oh, so you get your surnames from whoever was ruler in the place where you came over?" I asked. "Khan" made sense, I supposed. "Ramses," though . . . Did that mean my dad came over in the time of a pharaoh? "So if I was a vampire, I'd be Ana Clinton."

He joined me in a chuckle. "Except no vampires have been made since the end of the secret war around the time of the American Civil War," he pointed out. "The last American vampire is named Grant."

The traffic slowed enough for us to venture out into the street. In St. Paul, drivers often stopped for pedestrians in crosswalks, but you couldn't count on it. In fact, not far from here one of my classmates had gotten run over by a recycling truck. On the corner, people had planted a cross and plastic memorial flowers, teddy bears, and other tokens.

"Why do you say 'made,' anyway? 'Came over' makes more sense, doesn't it?"

Aiden raised his eyebrows. "I'm not sure I should be the one to educate you on this. Suffice it to say, it's a combination."

I wanted to keep him talking with the hopes I might learn something about why he'd been following me around. Besides, this was something I'd always been curious about. "What do you mean? Are you formed from clay or something?"

"Only in the biblical sense."

"Which means what? I mean, my friend Bea says vampires aren't human. But I say they have to be related, otherwise you couldn't have dhampyrs, like me."

"Our flesh is human. Our spirit is not. The human who was born into this body is no more. His soul left when the body was transformed to contain me. I took his body and his first name."

When I'd first met Elias, I asked if he was undead. He'd said, "No. Not yet, anyway." I'd always wondered about that "yet" part. I suppose if your spirit animated someone else's corpse, you weren't the one dead—or undead, as the case may be—especially since the body stayed "alive" during the transference.

It took the rest of the walk to school for me to completely digest this information. I wanted to be grossed out, horrified that vampires were dead people. But they weren't dead, not in the traditional sense. Hearts had never stopped beating. Brains kept functioning. Blood flowed. Yet, when a vampire was created, someone else had occupied that mysterious spot where the soul resided.

In all the time I was studying to be a witch, no one ever talked about the fact that the First Witch had created vampires, much less that she'd apparently sacrificed someone's soul to do it.

Aiden seemed unfazed that I continued to gape and mutter incoherently as he held the door open for me. It was only when we pushed open the door to the darkened theater did I realize that he'd been wandering around in the daylight. "Hey," I said, poking him in the chest. "Why didn't you go poof or melty or whatever is supposed to happen to you in the sun?"

He smiled, moving around me to take a seat in the far back. "I'm very young. Only a couple of hundred years old. I can stand everything but high noon." When he settled back against the fake crushed velvet, his features took on a sinister cast. Only the black irises of otherwise hooded eyes dully reflected the stage lights.

"So why *are* you following me?"

He just gave me a Cheshire cat grin.

"Hey, Ana!" Taylor said, coming in the door behind me.

"Oh, hey. So, this is—" I thought maybe I should introduce Aiden, though I didn't know how I would explain who he was. But when I looked for him, he was gone. I scanned the theater, just in time to see those cowboy boots retreat into the catwalk. "Never mind."

Taylor watched me like she wasn't certain about the state of my sanity. She looked like she might ask something I couldn't answer, but then her eyes lit on the paper sack in my hand and she held up one of her own. "I brought dinner too."

Neither Mr. Martinez nor Todd was even here yet. Taylor and I took our food to the front row. "So, you and Lane, huh?" I asked as I bit into the lukewarm burger. The cheese had congealed, but tart pickles and Goddess knew what chemicals satisfied something intense. I took another large chomp hungrily.

Her lashes fluttered shyly. Who does that for real? Still, it was sort of sweet on her. "Yeah," she said, "it just started. Did you know he was a gamer?"

I told her I hadn't, and I finished the last of my fries as she enumerated all his charms. Mr. Martinez came in just as she got to the good stuff, and she promised to tell me more about his kisses after rehearsal.

Taylor offered to clean up our wrappers, and I helped Todd set out the scripts and the song sheets. I looked at all the markings on the music, wondering if I could really read anything this complex.

"I'll help you figure out all that," said a familiar voice at my elbow. It was Nikolai. Somehow I hadn't heard him come in.

It'd been so long since I'd seen him I forgot how cute he was. An acoustic guitar was slung over his shoulders. His amber eyes glinted warmly as they gazed into my own, and I had to shove my hand in my pocket to keep from fixing a stray lock of hair that hung over his forehead. I felt myself get all trembly at his nearness. After I'd just mocked Taylor for being all girly, a blush colored my cheeks.

"Wow," he said, gently grabbing my wrist to turn over my forearm. "Your mom actually let you get a tattoo? What is it?"

My protests came too late. By the time I jerked my hand away, he'd already peeled the edge of the bandage to take a peek. Nikolai no longer looked so pleased to see me. His energy prickled angrily to the surface.

"Oh," was all he said before he turned and walked away.

I wanted to run after him and explain, but everyone started arriving and Mr. Martinez was calling for people to find a seat so we could begin. Thompson plopped down right beside me. Nik, meanwhile, chose the spot farthest away. Bea joined him.

Mr. Martinez explained how the evening would go. We'd read through the entire script. We'd sing each song through one time, to get a hang of the tune. Nik would provide simple backup. Nik stood up and held up a bunch of flash drives on strings.

"The band made a special recording of all the songs for everyone, so you can listen to the new arrangements all you like," he said.

Everyone oohed and aahed, but I just felt sad. I used to get files like that all the time. I never realized how special they really were.

Out of the corner of my eye, I detected movement. I glanced up at the light bar to see the vampire adjusting his view. He seemed awfully relaxed with a hunter so near; it made me wonder if he was a servant. Also, it struck me as very odd that Nik never seemed to notice him. He was usually so hyperaware of vampires and even their Igors. But then, maybe he was distracted by me or by having to teach us his music. Scripts were passed out, we all took seats at the edge of the stage, and we began.

Thompson, it turned out, was a terrible reader. Some people are, even veteran actors, because, well—because they're kind of energy vampires. They feed off audience reaction. When the house is empty, their enthusiasm bottoms out too.

It was hard to believe, but Thompson was one of those. I could see Mr. Martinez trying to do the eyebrow coach. You know, where he tries to model the emotional response with his own overly exaggerated expressions while mouthing the lines? His eyebrows nearly wagged off his face while Thompson continued to drone on like he was reading the most boring essay ever.

Things were better when it was time to sing. Malcolm was playing Eliza's father, and it was fun to watch Nikolai coach him through the version of "Get Me to the Church on Time." Malcolm got really into it and let out his inner rock star. Everyone started to loosen up after that.

Back to the words, and, finally, Mr. Martinez's contorting face must have gotten tired reacting to Thompson's lackluster performance, because he broke his own one-time-only rule by begging Thompson to try it again, "Only with a little feeling."

I felt sort of sorry for Thompson. He was out of his element, and clearly nervous. Worse than that, our theater clique began sharing snotty, intolerant looks. When it was someone else's turn, I pressed my shoulder up to Thompson's and whispered, "Don't worry. It's *just* the read-through."

That seemed to cheer him a little. Anyway, soon enough it was time for me to sing.

Nikolai came to stand next to me. I didn't really want to even look at him, but he shoved the musical score into my hand and started in on some technical explanation of the arrangement. He pointed at symbols and was close enough that I could smell his aftershave. I didn't really understand what he was saying, and so instead luxuriated in his nearness.

"Ready?" he asked.

I wasn't really, it turned out. It was incredibly difficult to change such a familiar tune. Despite Nik's coaching, I kept screwing up. His frustration jabbed at me like the sting of his blade. Even though we hadn't made it through all the lyrics, he stopped. "You'll just have to listen to that one," he snapped impatiently.

Mr. Martinez asked him if he'd sing it through one time so everyone else could hear how it was *supposed* to go. Meanwhile, I looked around wishing for a rock to crawl under, shame burning all the way up to my ears.

Thompson nudged me sympathetically.

It was a long night.

When Mr. Martinez finally called it a wrap, my eyes were blurry from exhaustion. And while I'd managed to get some

English lit reading done during the breaks, I still had three math problems left. If I hadn't slept through first period, I probably would understand them better. Man, I hoped Mom was finally home. I was seriously going to need her help making sure I got up in time for school tomorrow. With a tired groan, I slid off the stage.

Lane and Malcolm excitedly recruited people for the usual postrehearsal gathering at IHOP. Though neither of them approached Thompson, he perked up and said loudly, "I'll join you. Where is it?"

Though he was greeted with a not very enthusiastic chorus of "Sure" and "Sounds great," everyone ignored his question about the location of the gathering. I pulled him aside. "You know they want to gossip about you, right?"

We stood in the funny L-shaped area between the first row of seats and the edge of the thrust.

He scratched his chin. The emotions that had been lacking all night were etched in his face and nearly broke my heart. Like a little boy, he said, "I just want to be friends."

"I know," I said. "Just give them time. They'll warm up to you."

"Are you going?"

"Nah," I said, looking over to where Nikolai packed up his guitar. Bea loitered beside him, ostensibly organizing sheet music, but clearly flirting. "I'm not up for it tonight." I showed Thompson my precalc book. "Besides, I haven't finished this."

He nodded. Looking over his shoulder at the group gathered with Malcolm and Lane under the exit sign, he sighed. "Did I really suck that much?"

"Yeah," I said, but I softened it with a smile and my theory about how some people just need an audience. "You were in-credible at auditions," I reminded him. "Trust me, Mr. Martinez doesn't give away roles. You wouldn't have gotten the part if Mr. Martinez didn't think you were right for it."

Thompson nodded slowly, and I could tell by the way he stood a little less stooped that his confidence was returning. "This theater stuff is hard."

"I warned you," I said with a wag of my finger. "We work really hard to make it seem effortless."

The rest of the cast was heading out. Stealing a glance at the rafters, I wondered where the vampire was hidden. Would he slip out before the doors locked? Why was he following me, anyway? I should have pressed him more, but I'd been so dis-tracted to learn how vampires were "made."

Thompson lingered, not saying anything. Not knowing what to do with his attention, I packed up my books. I felt eyes on me. Looking up, I expected the vampire, but it was Nikolai. "Hey," he said, with a man-nod at Thompson. "You need a ride home, Ana?"

Thompson's chest puffed out in the I-was-here-first, testos-terone-fueled defensive posture.

"Um," I said, with a glance between them. I really didn't want to hurt Thompson's feelings, and he seemed on the verge of of-fering to take me home as well. Sensing my hesitation, Nikolai squared his shoulders, as if he was ready to fight for me.

"Actually, I'm giving her a ride," said Bea, sweeping in and taking my arm. "Right, hon?"

"Right," I said. "Sorry. Prearranged."

Thompson seemed to buy it, but Nik looked a bit miffed, like he knew he'd been punked. I shouldered my pack and followed

Bea out to the parking lot. As soon as we were out of earshot, I said, "Thanks for saving me."

"Saving you? I was thinking of the music industry," she said, as she turned the key in her Buick. It didn't have automatic locks, so I had to wait until she could lean across the bucket seat to pop open the door. "If you got back together with Nik, what would happen to his creativity? Do you want to be Courtney Love or whoever?"

"I think you mean Yoko Ono," I said, fishing around for the buckle. "And I think you're making sure we don't have an opportunity to talk."

"Busted," she said cheerfully, like I wasn't seriously irritated. The engine sprang to life with a cough. She turned on the radio to cover the rattling sound. With a knuckle, she twisted the volume up high, which cut my reply short. Fine. She didn't want to talk.

I stared pointedly out the window.

In the shadow of the school building, I saw Nikolai talking to someone. I recognized Nik from the guitar, but I couldn't quite make out the other person. As Bea swung the car out of the parking lot, the headlights skipped across the building and I saw the glint of red hair.

Chapter Twelve

"Stop the car," I shouted. "Let me out."

"What? Why?"

"Just do it, Bea," I said, with my hand on the door, clutching the handle. The car slowed as Bea pulled over to the curb.

"What's going on?"

"I don't know, but I'm beginning to think Nikolai does." I jumped out as soon as the car came to a stop. Slamming the door shut behind me, I ran back toward school as fast as I could. My fangs began to drop. I tried to remember everything I'd seen in the brief second of illumination. Aiden seemed relaxed, like he had in the theater. Nik wasn't hunting; I was sure of it. He hadn't had the right posture, had he?

No, they'd seemed like friends chatting.

I was running faster now, weaving around the cars parked in the lot, like a wildcat. Despite the burst of speed, when I got to the spot where Nikolai and Aiden had been, they were already gone. I was too late.

"Damn it," I said, my teeth aching and my eyes bright.

Bea was turning back into the parking lot. Her headlights nearly blinded me. I blinked the spots from my eyes. My fangs were still out. Using breathing techniques I learned as a witch-in-training, I brought my heart rate down. My teeth slid back into place just as she was trotting up beside me.

"What the hell was that about?"

"I thought I saw . . ." But what had I seen? I had a lot of suspicions, but no real proof. Aiden might just be the very servant that a witch used to steal the talisman. The fact that he had been talking to Nikolai might mean that Nikolai knew exactly where it was and who had it.

. . . Or not.

Because Aiden might also just be some random servant sent to follow me to see if I could lead the Elders to the vampire *they* thought stole the talisman.

"Never mind." I shrugged. "It was probably nothing."

"Damn, girl. You scared the shit out of me," Bea said.

"I'm sorry. Thanks for coming back for me."

Her lips pursed together like she wasn't so sure she should have, but then she waved me to where the car sat idling noisily. "Come on. Let's go home."

My house was dark. According to my cell, it was just after ten thirty. Late for a school night, but not so late that Mom would have gone to bed. There was this talk show she liked to stay up to watch, and most nights I fell asleep listening to the muffled sounds of it from the other room. "That's weird," I said.

Bea shrugged. "She could be asleep. She's got school in the morning too, you know."

"No, this is starting to freak me out." I told Bea about how much Mom had gone missing lately.

"You seriously thought she had a boyfriend?"

I wasn't sure I liked Bea's incredulous tone. "She can be cute . . . in a schoolmarm sort of way." Okay, no, that was weird. I didn't want to think about Mom that way. I shook my head. "Listen, do you think I could stay over at yours? I can't take another night in this house all by myself."

"My folks would never go for it," Bea said. I understood. There were pretty strict rules about school nights. "But I don't have to go home yet. Do you want me to drive you around? Maybe she's working late at one of her universities?"

I double-checked my phone for a message. She hadn't even answered my text about getting the part with a congratulations. That wasn't like her at all. Nor was all this sneaking around without telling me where she was. "The last thing she told me was that she was going to an Elders' meeting."

Bea fished her cell out of her purse. The phone's cover glittered red and had rhinestones that spelled "diva." Her thumbs worked like mad. I tried to see what she was writing, but she pulled the screen close to her chest, like concealing a hand of cards.

She snapped the phone closed dramatically. Quickly, she slipped it back into her purse as if just having it in my sight might reveal some seekrit information. "There's no meeting right now," she said, certain. "If your mom isn't home, it's got to be school related."

"Okay," I said. I wanted to doubt her, but if anyone knew what was happening in the Inner Circle, it was Bea. That was why Elias and I tapped her to begin with. "I'll just check the house and make sure. You want to come in or wait in the car?"

Bea started to reach for the buckle, but stopped. "Depends. Is there still a vampire in the basement?"

Good question. If Elias had slipped in before dawn this morning, I never even felt a twinge of the wards. "I don't know. Maybe?"

Sitting back, she retrieved an iPod from her purse. Tucking a bud in each ear, she said, "I'll wait."

The second I saw the dirty dishes still in the sink, I knew Mom wasn't home. I double-checked upstairs, but just as I suspected, her bed was empty. No sign of Elias either.

On my way back up from the basement, I spied the spare keys to the carriage house hanging on their usual hook. Mom kept the main key on the ring in her purse. I'd forgotten about these. I grabbed them. Finally, I could see what she'd been hiding back there.

I headed out the side door, and hesitated when I saw the baseball bat leaning against the wall. Once, after watching a horror film, I became convinced we should have backup in case the wards failed. Mom rolled her eyes, but when I found the Louisville Slugger at a rummage sale the next day, she relented, agreeing it must be fate. I took it now, pleasantly surprised by its weight. After all, who knew what might be waiting for me in the carriage house?

Even before I reached the carriage house, I could feel the wards, like a knotty tangle of thorns brushing against my skin. The closer I got, the denser the imaginary thicket became. I came to a halt, unable to move, about an arm's length from the door. Suffocating under the oppressive magical jungle, my limbs pressed close to my body, I couldn't even lift my hand to try the key.

What I needed was a psychic machete.

Or an invitation.

But Mom wasn't home; who could let me in? Another witch in the Inner Circle, perhaps, but who?

Bea.

I turned around. Letting the baseball bat clatter onto the sidewalk, I dashed through the side yard to the front. Under the streetlamp, I could see Bea in her car, her head bent over her phone's keyboard.

I tapped on the window, startling her. She squeaked and her phone dropped to the floor. "Hey," I said, once she'd recovered and pulled a bud free from her ear. "Can you go into the carriage house for me? It's warded."

She frowned uncertainly. "I don't know if I should get involved. I've probably helped your vampire friends too much already. I mean, if your vamp boyfriend gets caught breaking into one of the old families' houses and rats me out—"

"Who said this had anything to do with vampires?"

"Um." Bea's face couldn't look guiltier. "You did?"

But I hadn't. I'd only said the carriage house was warded, not that it was set to keep out vampires, specifically. "You already know what Mom is hiding in there, don't you?"

Bea eyed the stick shift, like she was considering putting the car in gear and running away. I pulled open the car door, and sat down in the passenger seat.

"How deep in this are you?" I asked.

"It's not me," she insisted, dropping the hand that had begun to reach for the gear shift into her lap with a sigh. "It's my dad. I was honest with you guys the other night. I don't know where the talisman is or who has it."

"So what do you know?"

She stared out the window, biting her bottom lip.

"Bea, we've been best friends since kindergarten. I'd hate to have to bite you." The threat was pretty hollow at this point, but if I got frustrated enough, my fangs would pop out.

Bea's frown darkened. "You wouldn't."

"Do you know that for sure?" I tried to sound menacing, but failed when Bea didn't back down. I'd forgotten that she'd seen my patented spook eye too many times. When I tried to use it on her, she just laughed. I couldn't resist joining in; my tough-girl act was pretty mock-worthy. After we'd settled down, I said, "Please, Bea. This is important."

"I don't know where the talisman is. I swear on our friend-ship."

"But you do know what my mom has stashed in the carriage house, don't you?"

"Yeah, I think so, but you're going to freak out."

"I'm already freaked-out!" And as if to prove my point, my eyes changed. At least, I assumed that was why the interior of the car suddenly seemed brighter.

Bea shrank away from me and put up her hands in surren-der. "Okay, once everyone was sure it was the talisman that was stolen, they've been . . . preparing."

I didn't like the sound of this. "Preparing what?"

"There's only two things you can do with the talisman," Bea said, with a look that said, *Think it through.*

Enslave vampires . . .

Or make more.

"Holy shit, we've got to get in there!"

Even though she told me she couldn't feel the wards at all, Bea approached the carriage house slowly, her steps labored. She got about as far as I had, then stopped dead.

"Whoa! Neat trick," she said, her eyes darting around as if looking for something.

"What happened? Why did you stop?"

"The carriage house just disappeared."

"Can you still move?"

She took a hesitant step, her hands groping in the air blindly. "It's weird. Now I feel like I'm walking through a thick fog. I can't see anything."

"I'll guide you through it."

Though we looked about as stupid as some kind of elimination challenge on a reality-TV show, I was able to get Bea to the door after only a few missteps. One of them literal. As in, she tripped on a crack in the sidewalk I hadn't noticed, and ended up sprawling on the grass.

Her hand pressed to the door, she felt for the keyhole with the other. "I can feel the wards here," she said. "I'll try a dampening spell."

The moment Bea's power started to swell, I felt the wards drop. They must be keyed to magic use. Damn, if we'd known that, we could've skipped all the stumbling and swearing.

Bea blinked rapidly. "I guess that worked. Except I didn't really do anything."

"I'll explain it later," I said. Cautiously, I took a single step forward. I didn't know if the wards had been completely disarmed, or whether they'd snap back on once I tried to approach. My foot hit the ground with no zip, no sensation of barbed wire or jungle vines—nothing but normal.

Or at least what passed for normal around here.

Quickly, I caught up to Bea, who was mounting the stairs. The carriage house apartment was completely separate from the stable/garage. The steps had an old-fashioned velvet runner down the middle that cushioned our footfalls, but they were narrow. There wasn't room for me next to Bea on the landing. She used the key at the second door at the top.

"Hello?" she ventured, peeping around the door.

When no one answered, she gave me a shrug and walked through. I followed. The ceilings were low and angled like in an attic. The beams had intentionally been left exposed, and an ornate, tulip-shaped light fixture hung from the center. Bea didn't need to switch on the main light, however, because a table lamp had been left on. A folding chair, a ratty recliner, and a fancy high-back chair sat in a circle near the table and lamp. Though someone clearly had been using the place, it smelled of mothballs and old books.

Bea checked the water closet. I couldn't really call the side room a bathroom since the plumbing was pretty decrepit, having last been updated in the early 1900s. "No one here," she said.

All this security for nothing besides an impromptu meeting room? I didn't buy it.

"There's one more place to check," I said. Once, when I was little and decided to run away from home, I spent an entire day and most of the night in the carriage house. I would have lasted until morning too, except for the thunderstorm that scared me back into Mom's waiting arms. But while I was checking out what I hoped to be my new permanent home, I'd found a trapdoor.

"Help me move the rug out of the way," I said. Soon we had the floor exposed. The handle was little more than a notch in the floorboards, but I found it. When I reached to open the door, an electric current shocked through me. I fell back on my heels, shaking the prickles out of my hand. "Ow! Son of a gun!"

"I'll do it," Bea offered. But before touching the trap, she took in a deep breath. Her power bubbled just under the surface. With a defiant flip of her hair, she slid her hand into the groove and gave the trap a heave. The door creaked open with a rain of dust.

I knelt beside her. Inside the hidden compartment was a book—an old hand-stitched vellum book. Bea looked at me for an explanation. "Is this the talisman?"

"It's supposed to be a snake-headed Nile goddess figurine," I said. "So I don't think so. But maybe this book contains the spells for binding and creating vampires."

Bea picked it up and cradled it gently in her lap. The cover was a moldy brown. If there had been anything written on it, the ink had long ago faded. Slowly, she turned the yellowed and crumbly pages. The script inside reminded me of calligraphy, like the kind you might imagine medieval monks used to copy the Bible or the Book of Kells or something. Except this was completely unreadable. I wasn't even sure if it was in English.

"Latin," Bea said, pointing to a word. "Here it says something about demons. You were right. This is the spell book."

"We have to destroy it," I said.

Before I could grab for it, Bea slammed the book shut and hugged it protectively against her chest. "Are you insane? This is witch history!"

"Yeah, but if they don't have the spell, they can't use it against us."

"Us? They? *I'm* a witch, Ana. *I'm* 'them,' and so are you," Bea said, still clutching the grimoire. She stood up, backing away from me with an expression of pure horror. "Besides, there's clearly more than one spell here. This could be one of the only spell books to survive the Burning Times. I won't let you do it."

Though most of the people accused had been innocent, True Witches had died during the Inquisition too. Those who survived had destroyed all evidence of their practice. In fact, we still lived under the shadow of the Burning Times, which was why we were supposed to keep our witchcraft secret from the general populace, the mundanes.

Almost like another electric blast, Bea's words shocked me. I had to stop taking sides. I wasn't a vampire. I wasn't a witch. I was both.

And I needed to start acting like it.

Bea had been right about so many things. Maybe it was time for me to trust her, *really* trust her. "Okay," I said, not getting up from where I knelt on the floor. "But you take the book, and you hide it. Don't tell anyone, not even me, where it is. Ever."

Chapter Thirteen

For once, Bea didn't protest. She seemed to understand the gravity of the situation because she bundled the book up in an old sweater we found in the apartment and scurried down the stairs without a single word.

I'd just finished putting the rug back in place when I heard a bloodcurdling scream.

Adrenaline brought me to the backyard in no time flat. Bea held the book squeezed tightly against her chest. A figure loomed over her. I bared my teeth and pushed myself between them.

"Ana, thank Goddess." It was Elias. "I've been looking for you."

I glanced over my shoulder at the terrified Bea. Her eyes glistened with surprise when she noticed my transformation. I waved off her reaction, and instead jerked my head in the direction of her car. She looked confused for a second, but then seemed to catch my drift. I didn't want Elias to know what she had either. It was best if no vampire did.

Not even me.

Bea gave Elias a brief nod as she slunk past him. "Thanks for the fright of my life, asshole," she said.

"My pleasure, lady." He bowed. Thankfully, he didn't seem to wonder why Bea was sneaking around our backyard clutching an orange sweater. As soon as she was around the corner of the house, he said, "Your mother is in danger, I'm afraid."

"What? How?"

"I wanted to confirm before coming, but it was surprisingly difficult to find a colleague willing to speak with an outcast about such matters."

"Would you cut to the chase and tell me what's going on?"

"Yes, of course. When I awoke, I felt the hunger building. A hunt has been called."

"Vampires are hunting Mom? Are you sure?" He nodded. My stomach dropped. I shifted my feet, not knowing which way to run, feeling overwhelming panic. "But . . . it makes no sense!"

"I think your father is becoming increasingly desperate. Your public denouncement of him as a 'do-nothing' ruler put his back against the wall. My source tells me the people have been demanding action, *any* action," Elias said. "Perhaps the prince believes that if they attack so openly, the witches will be forced to show their hand as well, and we—er, they—can seize the talisman when it surfaces."

"Oh my God, Mom!"

"Yes, I thought at the very least we should warn her," Elias said.

I was near hysteria. "But I don't know where she is!"

His hand on my shoulder calmed me. "I can find her."

Gulping back tears, I asked, "How?"

"I was only exiled yesterday. I can still catch her essence, and I'll feel the feeding frenzy building." He glanced around like a wolf, scenting the wind. "We should hurry."

I couldn't agree more.

Luckily, Elias had his car, since Bea had already driven off in hers. We didn't talk much, since I didn't know how much concentration Elias needed in order to find Mom. I wouldn't have had anything helpful to say anyway. Wordless dread roiled in my gut. I chewed my fingernails.

Elias drove down University Avenue, over Highway 280, and past the blinking red lights of the KSTP radio tower. Soon the buildings looked less industrial and took on a more collegiate flare. The dead, empty streets of St. Paul fell behind us, replaced by vibrant Minneapolis. The closer we got to the university, the more restaurants advertised student discounts and late hours. By the time we turned onto Washington Avenue, students traveled the streets in packs, loitered outside of bars or bookstores or coffeehouses, laughing, and generally being loud.

It felt very alien and only managed to agitate me further.

"Why?" I asked again. "Why would Dad want to kill Mom?"

"As I said, I think he's hoping to flush the talisman out into the open, but I also suspect that after banishing me, he felt the need to unite the kingdom in a common purpose. I had my supporters, but a hunt would wipe all thought of mutiny from their minds." He snorted, "Or any thought, really, since we become more like dumb animals when we're caught in the frenzy of a feed."

That wasn't what I'd meant by my question, but Elias got

that faraway look that made me think he was doing his tracking thing. What I'd wanted to know was, how could Dad do it? How could he basically take out a hit on Mom? I knew it was foolish to think that there was any love left between them, but to send hungry vampires after your former—no, if I remembered correctly, they'd never officially divorced—current wife? It seemed inhumane. It was hard to believe Dad had been driven to this kind of crazy desperation, but it seemed he had. And maybe even my little rebellion in front of his court had pushed him to it.

I felt so guilty. "Can you stop a hunt once it's started?"

"I couldn't, but you could," Elias said. His foot came off the gas as we approached Folwell Hall. "I need to get out for a moment," he explained, pulling the car into a metered space.

Cracking open his door, he partially stood, as if inspecting the windshield. I wondered if I should get out, but before I'd begun to unbuckle, he was back in. We pulled back out into the street. "She's near. A little closer, and we'll walk."

We pulled into an underground ramp near the Bell Museum. "I hope she's not in there," I said, pointing at the brass elk statue that guarded the museum's front entrance. Even though I'd been to the Bell once in sixth grade, the memories haunted me. I shivered. "All those taxidermy dioramas will be especially spooky at night."

"She's not there. From what I can guess, she's probably in Walter Library."

Hiding in the stacks, I'd bet, just like I do at Stassen High. I nodded. "Let's go."

But instead of taking the stairs up to the sidewalk, Elias went through another door that opened to a tunnel. Glossy white paint covered the walls, and the ceiling curved slightly as if the channel had been dug by a giant worm. The place smelled of wet and basement. Bare bulbs in metal cages cast bright, artificial light. "And I thought the Bell Museum was creepy?"

Elias frowned. "I prefer the subterranean route myself."

"Oh, right. Sorry."

He certainly seemed to know where to turn and which forks to follow. We moved along the passageway so fast that when he stopped suddenly, I bumped into him. I apologized, but Elias didn't respond. His whole body stretched taut, and he turned slowly, like an antenna seeking a signal.

Without a word, he backtracked several paces to a door I hadn't noticed. We came out into a grand hallway lined with classrooms. Polished marble flooring gleamed in the moonlight eking through arched stone windows.

"Come," Elias said, taking my hand to urge me forward. I hadn't even realized I'd slowed down to peer through an open door at the swivel-arm desks lined up in attentive rows facing the long chalkboard filled with impressive scribbles. Down a shallow, open stair and out double doors, we emerged at the far end of Northrup Mall.

A swath of nearly treeless manicured grass, probably as long as, if not longer than, a football field, stretched between several buildings, including the library. With towering white Doric columns, Walter looked majestic, even in the dimly lit evening.

The doors were locked.

"Are you sure she's in there?"

"Positive," he said, shaking the brass handles again. "I could break the locks."

"There's probably an alarm," I said, though as I stared up at the walls in frustration, I spotted an open window. I pointed to it. "Could you get up there?"

"Yes," he said.

I pulled my cell phone out of my pocket. Mom hadn't been answering any of my calls or texts, but I had an idea. I typed "911. We're @Walter. A hunt called on u. Elias coming 2 help."

"Do you think the hunt would risk the alarm?" I asked. "I mean, is she safe in there if you close the window behind you?"

"The hunger will make them insane," he said, pacing the length of the building, judging the best route to the window. "And desperate. I'd also wager there's a sewer or other maintenance access to the building."

"Okay," I said, trying to think. "How long before they get here?"

"The hunt is building." He looked at me. When he blinked, his eyes flickered between human and cat-slit irises. "We don't have much time."

"Will you get . . . you know, swept up?"

"I don't know," he admitted.

I needed nonvamp help. "You try to protect her until I can come back."

"Where are you going?"

"If we're going to fend off vampires, we're going to need someone skilled in fighting them. I know just the guy."

Nikolai used to live on the upper floor of a duplex near the Witch's Hat Tower in Prospect Park, but the rent had gotten too high and the neighbors too irritated by the loud music. He and a bandmate, John, now shared a place in Dinkytown, the student-focused area right around the U's campus.

If I used my superpowers, I could be there in less than a minute.

Elias, however, wasn't so sure. He put a hand on my shoulder. "The hunter's apprentice? It'll be a bloodbath."

"Isn't it going to be anyway? What if you turn? What if *I* start looking at Mom like she's something good to eat? We need him. Admit it."

He couldn't quite. Not out loud, anyway, but he did muster a curt nod.

That was all I needed. I abandoned myself to panic and started to run. The spike in fear brought my eyes out first. My feet began to skip across the pavement. I crossed University at a gallop, easily sliding through the heavy traffic. My passage elicited a honk and a rude comment from a car full of frat boys.

Dinkytown's lights blazed, slowing me somewhat. I blinked away tears from the brightness and wove through a queue of people waiting for a show to start at the Varsity Theater. Luckily, the epicenter of the neighborhood was only a few blocks in length, and soon I left the fluorescent glow behind and returned to the moderate darkness of a busy street.

As I got closer, it occurred to me that I should have called ahead. Even though it was a Monday night, there was no guarantee he'd be home. He could be over at a friend's or out on a date.

My fangs dropped. In a burst of speed, I found myself on the sidewalk directly in front of Nikolai's apartment. Like a lot of student housing, Nik's place needed repairs and a paint job. The salmon pink trim flaked and peeled off in large chunks, and the stucco was smudged and worn. A rusty bicycle leaned against a listing stoop. A cracked planter grew stinging nettle and milkweed.

But lights were on, and I breathed a sigh of relief when I saw Nik's Toyota parked down the block. A figure moved in front of the large window, cracked open to let in the breeze. I raised my hand to wave, but it wasn't Nik.

It was the red-haired vampire, Aiden.

When I heard Nik saying something, I shrank back against an overgrown rhododendron to listen. I couldn't make out his words, but I heard Aiden's response. "Master," he said, "the hunt begins. Surely, we are discovered."

Discovered? So they were working together on something?

Okay, I'd had enough sneaking around in bushes. Besides, it sounded like I didn't have time for this kind of subterfuge. Standing up, I rapped on the window. "They're not after you guys. They're after my mom."

Aiden clutched at his chest like I'd given him a heart attack. Nik jumped to his feet and into view. I saw a black, onyx figurine shaped like a Nile goddess in his hand.

Holy shit. I suddenly understood Bea's tarot prophecy. It wasn't referring to the High Priestess in her role as witch queen, like I thought. Instead, the High Priestess card meant the initiate, like Bea said it could. As in one of the people who were with me during Initiation Fail.

Nikolai had the talisman.

Chapter Fourteen

Too late, Nikolai hid the talisman behind his back. At the same time, Aiden moved to block my line of sight.

"What are you doing here?" Nikolai asked. "I call you all the time and you can't be bothered. But tonight, of all nights, you show up unannounced at my house? What the hell?"

"I need your help," I said, peering in through the screen like a Peeping Tom. "My dad seems to think that Mom is the one hiding the talisman, not you."

Nik and Aiden exchanged nervous looks. Aiden reached over and slammed the window down in front of my face. Now their voices were a muffled jumble of argument. I pushed through the branches of the bush to the door. Just as I reached for the knob, Nikolai pulled the door open. "You're sure the hunt was called on Amelia?"

"Please don't call her that, and yes. Elias confirmed it."

"Master, they're on the move," Aiden warned.

"You've got to come," I said. "I don't know how to stop the hunt."

Nikolai looked down at the figurine he held. "I don't know either," he said. "I've been trying to destroy this thing ever since Aiden brought it to me. It's like Excalibur or something. I can't even chip it."

"Maybe Dad would call off the hunt if we traded Mom for it." I tried to snatch the statue, but he pulled his hand back before I could.

"I compelled Aiden to steal it for me because I don't want anybody to have it," he said. "It was for you, you know. For us. I couldn't stand the idea that it might kill you."

"Kill me?" No one had brought up that possibility. "How do you have that figured?"

"If it was used to push everyone back through the Veil," Aiden piped up from just beyond Nik's shoulder, "half of you would die."

But would I? I was neither witch nor vampire, but something else in between. I had a sudden thought. "What if we pretended to trade the talisman for Mom, and then I destroyed it?"

Nik snorted incredulously. "I tried everything, even sulfuric acid from the chemistry department. What makes you think you can do it?"

"I've got some magic I haven't tried yet."

As it turned out, Aiden had been at the big showdown between Mom and Dad last semester and had firsthand experience with the ice-wave-time-shift thing that happened the last time I tried to raise power. His account convinced Nikolai to trust my plan, even though I wasn't entirely sure if it would work myself.

The three of us raced back to Walter Library in Nik's car, totally ignoring the speed limit, not to mention all the one-way and pedestrian-only signs. A cascade of beeps and rude gestures followed us.

"You did it for yourself too," I said from the backseat. I kept glancing between Nik and Aiden, my mind busily trying to process this whole turn of events. I never expected Nikolai to work with a vampire—I mean, besides me. But some clues started to fall into place. "You said you had this plan to graduate, a game changer. You were talking about the talisman."

He nodded. "Are you sure you can destroy it?"

I started to shake my head, but Aiden said, "If anyone can, Master, it will be the half-breed."

I didn't much like being called a half-breed, but I appreciated Aiden's vote of confidence enough to keep my opinion to myself. Instead, I asked him another question that was on my mind. "How come you've been helping destroy the talisman? I mean, aren't you on the side of the slavers?"

Aiden glanced at Nikolai as if looking for permission to speak. Nikolai rolled his eyes irritably, which apparently was a "yes," because Aiden answered, "A slave can't marry whom he pleases. I'm in love with a free vampire, who recently used a royal decree to break her betrothal—"

He didn't need to finish. "Khan," I supplied. Oh, when Dad finally put this all together, I'd be in double trouble. Luckily, I didn't have much opportunity to consider the details. We'd arrived.

Just in time too.

From where Nik parked, we could see their approach. Under the Washington Avenue Bridge, a swarm of vampires rose into view along the riverbank. Fifty or more pale and naked forms ran low through the grass. Every so often, a figure popped up, like a prairie dog, as if scouting a new direction. The pack twisted and moved around the scouts, pulling them back under. Reaching the bridge, they climbed over the pylons and one another. At this distance, their speed was deceptive. They'd covered a lot of ground in only a few seconds.

"Go!" I shouted, grabbing hold of Nikolai's shoulder and giving him a little squeeze.

"Oh. Yeah," he said, shaking off the shock of seeing the hunt.

"More approach from the front, Master," Aiden said.

We hurried through the narrow gap between the buildings, ducking around a rusty fire escape.

"He keeps calling you that," I said to Nik between breaths.

"What?"

"Master," I repeated, even though I was sure he knew what I'd meant.

"Yes, he does." The chains of his leather jacket clanked as we ran.

"Do you own him?"

We came out the other side. Whatever Nikolai's answer might have been was choked off by the sight of the vampires coming across the mall. A line advanced, leaping on all fours.

Nikolai tossed the talisman to me. I grabbed it out of the air. As he ran toward the line of vampires, his blade shot out of his fist. He yowled like a banshee. After a second's hesitation, Aiden followed after. If they'd hoped to get the attention of the vampires, it worked. Sort of. A group broke off to meet him. The rest continued, unfazed.

Mom stood behind Walter's locked front doors, her face filled with horror. Elias stood solemnly beside her, his eyes cast down. He clasped his hands in front of him, like he was holding himself in check.

I dashed up the steps of the library. Mom's eyes nearly popped out of her head when she saw me and what I was carrying. Elias looked up, his irises slits.

The column of approaching vampires reached the first step. Glancing up, I could see the heads of those who had come from behind hanging over the rooftop. I brandished the talisman high over my head.

"Stop!" I commanded.

I'm not sure if the advance halted at the power of my words or from sheer confusion.

The hand that held the talisman prickled, like the nerves had fallen asleep. A few steps below me, vampires tangled around one another's nude forms like a scene from Dante's *Inferno*. Pale skin of all hues twisted this way and that, reaching for me. Now and again, a limb would stretch beyond the invisible barrier that surrounded me only to shoot back as if burned.

Nikolai and Aiden attacked from behind, pushing aside a swath of bodies with a slash of psychic blade. But for every one they knocked down, more filled the gap.

I had to do something. Even without a particular incantation, the talisman appeared to impart some control over the vampires. Despite the pain, I held it tightly, and shouted, "The hunt is off."

"Nice try." Dad's voice rose over the soft moans of the vampires. He stood up from the center of the mass, an unmoving pillar in a sea of writhing flesh. "But only I can call off a hunt."

"Then I offer a trade," I said. My hand was slowly losing feeling, and I had to check to make sure I still grasped the talisman. "The artifact for Mom's life."

"Did you have it all along, my daughter?" Dad asked. "Is the traitor your loyal lapdog?"

I tried not to glance in Nikolai's direction, but it was instinct. Dad tracked immediately.

"The apprentice, I see," Dad said silkily. "Your other lover."

The talisman dropped to the step with a clatter, my hand completely deadened. The vampire heap lurched forward. I knelt down and grabbed the figurine with my other hand, and wielded it in front of me like a cross.

Now my fingers burned as the goddess figure began to heat. This standoff couldn't last. "Call it off," I screamed, though Ramses stood just over a yard away. "Call off the hunt now."

"Or what?" he purred. His eyes glinted with something dark, as if he was feeding off the desire and approval of the vampires consumed by the hunt. "If you destroy it, you'll be doing us a favor. And we can still continue our feast."

Feast of Mom? Whoa. What a prick! The surge of anger dropped my fangs. The heat of the talisman spiked, but I willed myself to hold on.

"I'll use the spell of binding," I bluffed. "Mom had the spell book in our carriage house. I saw the words."

A frightened hiss skittered through the hunt.

Dad and I locked in a stare-down. Doubt played across his face, even as he said, "You wouldn't. It could destroy you."

"Are you saying I wouldn't sacrifice myself to save Mom?"

"Ana, no!" Nikolai shouted.

My dad glanced back for a split second, distracted by Nikolai's shout. Impulsively, I smacked the back of his head with the talisman. His hair burst into flame. Vampires leaped up to douse the fire as he shouted in pain.

"Do it," I said. I took a step closer, forcing the vampires to slither back. "Call off the damn hunt."

Dad looked seriously pissed. Gingerly, he rubbed the spot on his head.

I waited, but he didn't do it. Meanwhile, the talisman grew hotter and hotter in my own hand. I had to destroy the statuette now, if I could. But how? I hadn't really thought out the details of my big plan. I had to figure a way to trigger my internal electromagnetic pulse or whatever the heck it was.

In the meantime, I needed to stall.

So I decided to punk Dad as I considered my options. I began to spout nonsense words that I thought sounded Latin, "Invictus memoralli," I intoned.

The vampires recoiled instinctively at my words. True Witch magic was the antithesis of all things vampire.

Hmmm, magic.

I hadn't practiced a lick of magic since my failed Initiation earlier this school year. Since my power seemed to come whenever I used my opposing vampire and witch sides in combination, I wondered what would happen if I tried it now. As I continued spouting vaguely Latin-sounding nonsense, I reached into that stillness I cultivated when I was practicing to be a witch. My breath evened out and something began to awaken deep inside, churning and spinning. The whirling sensation felt exactly like when I drank magical blood before.

It was working!

Maybe I didn't need blood if I could tap into both parts of my dhampyr nature at once. But I'd never successfully cast a spell in my entire life. Bea could zap people and make messages unreadable, but the best I'd ever done was act as a placeholder in a circle.

I might as well try. I didn't see a lot of other options, unless I could bite myself. And anyway, I was running out of convincing Latin words.

Facing east, I imagined the goddess statue as the athame, the ritual knife, which was supposed to symbolically cut a space between the Veil and the world. Ironically, this statue had been used to do that, literally.

Almost instantly I began to feel a spinning pressure, like the opposite poles of a magnet repulsing each other. A cold wind lifted my hair and swirled around the white-hot artifact in my hand, relieving some of the pain.

The vampires moaned louder now. Some shielded their faces. My dad's yellow eyes narrowed determinedly.

When I turned south, hot air blasted me. It was harder to concentrate on the words as the magic grew, but I continued to speak. I slipped into complete gibberish. "Julius Caesar. Rigor mortis."

The sensation of spinning made me feel faint. My entire body shook with the effort to stay conscious. I still had two more directions before the circle was complete. I wasn't sure I could make it without an infusion of blood, so I cautiously bit the inside of my cheek.

When the familiar coppery taste filled my mouth, I felt a corresponding jolt of energy.

Turning to the west, I imagined water quenching the fire of the talisman. Steam hissed on my hand, surprising me. Wow. That was Real Magic. I'd never done anything like it before. My own blood and the talisman must augment whatever tiny spark of witchiness I possessed.

The circle of vampires around me widened suddenly as if giant hands pushed them back a pace. Dad recovered from a stumble, and his expression had changed to one of panic. I could see Dad mouthing a spell or prayer of his own. But it had no effect. The strange power inside me continued to rise. My hair stood on end.

Like an electromagnet was spinning in my core, tiny flashes of lightning arced outward. Bolts jumped any gap. It leaped the space between my legs, between my side and my arms, and, finally, between each finger.

When I faced north and completed the circle, a spark hit the talisman.

Like a clap of thunder, a deafening boom rattled the air. A spiderweb crack appeared on the hip of the goddess. More sparks flashed across my skin, widening the fracture.

An eerie reddish glow filled the night. Wind whipped wildly at my hair, and a strong, inexplicable compulsion caused me to look up. A vortex of spinning clouds in a perfect celestial mirror of the circle I'd cast below appeared above my head. Through the hole rent in the sky, I saw flame tongues flitting across an alien sky.

Somehow I knew it was the Other Side of the Veil.

Outside the circle, vampires began to look up, drawn by the same strange desire that had me reaching upward as though to try to dive into welcoming waters. *Home,* begged a part of my mind, but my internal rotation reached a fever pitch. I couldn't hold back the massive energy I'd created. It burst from me like a wave of light.

The clay of the talisman began to splinter. A black, ancient dust coughed out. I breathed in the scent of frankincense.

The core of the talisman flashed bright, like I had. The vampires shouted in pain and scattered at the sudden intense burst of sunlight. The passage to the Veil slammed shut with an audible, earsplitting snap.

Then the talisman was gone, crumbled to clay fragments in my fist.

The only vampire who remained was Dad. He'd fallen to his knees; his watery eyes appeared filmy and clouded.

Behind me, the door burst open to the sound of shrieking alarms. Even as spent and exhausted as I was, I felt Mom's power building as she rushed to my side. Nikolai, Aiden, and Elias joined, and the four of them stood just outside the circle I'd cast, facing outward at the cardinal points, like guardians.

But there was nothing and no one to defend me from anymore. Dad must have used whatever strength he had left to rush blindly away.

Sirens wailed in the distance. The feeling in my arm returned painfully. My other palm looked like it had a bad case of sunburn.

We were an odd and unlikely group—a free vampire, a servant, a hunter, the Queen of Witches, and me—all of us momentarily united in our determination to stop the hunt and destroy the talisman. "I guess that's it, then." Mom's voice sounded shaky. She looked at the granite under my feet, which had been burned black in a perfect circle.

Elias and Nikolai faced each other menacingly. My gaze returned to the lifeless bodies on the lawn. I said to Nikolai, "Looks like you found a way to graduate after all."

He broke from his stony posture, clearly shaken by the realization of what he'd done. I wondered if he knew that he'd killed living bodies that had once been human. Given the look on his pale, horrified face, I hardly needed to remind him.

"Oh. Shit," he said, looking at his hands as if they were stained with blood. His psychic dagger crumbled instantly. "It wasn't like that. I didn't mean to—"

I raised my hand. "I know, Nik. You were defending me. All of you were. That was awesome."

It wasn't exactly a group hug, but my words were enough for us to form an uneasy alliance for the time being. Nik drove Mom and me home, and Elias met us there. Mom looked surprised to see him, but I explained Elias had no other place to stay. Before I could even argue my case, Mom threw up her hands and agreed he could continue to stay in the basement, but only until other arrangements could be made. "You saved my life, I guess," Mom sniffed. "I suppose I owe you a couple of weeks for that."

Nik, meanwhile, seemed completely shell-shocked. He hadn't said a single word on the drive back. When I looked around to invite him in for a soda, he'd already taken off. I guessed he had a lot on his mind.

I abandoned the strange scene in the parlor of Mom explaining the "house rules" to Elias, to head to my room. I could hardly keep my eyes open, I was so physically drained.

But before I collapsed into bed, I opened my desk drawer to look for something and saw that the snake-headed goddess figurine had shattered into a million pieces. I cut my finger on one of the shards. The blood rolled down my finger. Instinctively, I put it in my mouth, tasting copper and salt and residual magic, intensely sweet, like honey.

A thought brought me instantly awake. We'd avoided the hunt tonight, but how much longer could we put it off?

With that worry skittering around my brain I slept fitfully, but I awoke happily to the sound of Mom's weather radio. She'd packed my lunch and she even gave me a peck on the cheek before I headed out the door. My days quickly fell into a routine: classes, homework, and rehearsals. Bea and I didn't talk much, nor did Nik and I. But I wanted space from her and allowed him to have what he seemed to need.

Meanwhile, when I returned home in the late evening, I'd sometimes find Elias in the dusty front room reading one of my manga series in the dark. Mom would come in and turn on a light for him or place a cup of tea at his elbow. The house was a lot less empty, but the tension was still more of a cease-fire than a truce.

One night over a late dinner, Elias told us that he'd heard that the guard had found Ramses and taken him back to the kingdom. He was blinded, though Elias seemed to think that a steady diet of blood would eventually heal him. Mom offered her opinion, which involved rotting in hell.

"Except no one can return to hell now," I pointed out. "Rotting or not."

"Return? No one has ever returned home," Elias said. "Not even on the hunter's blade."

A month later, I sat in my chair in the greenroom. Though the bruise on my arm had finally healed, I still had to smear a ton of pancake on my sunburned palm. Around me, everyone chattered excitedly. Thompson very seriously applied eyeliner. Bea buzzed around, happily practicing lines because the girl playing the nanny had come down with strep.

Through the intercom, the sounds of a full house drifted in. The band struck a few practice chords and adjusted sound.

My stomach fluttered, even though I dreamed the lines of this play, I knew it so well. I'd finally gotten the hang of the new arrangements, especially when Stevie came over to tutor me. She'd assured me that Nikolai would come around when he was good and ready, but in the meantime I'd let myself get lost in the work of rehearsals and flirting/fighting with Thompson.

A knock on the greenroom door startled me from my thoughts. Since everyone else was occupied, I got up to answer it. A florist stood in the doorway with a huge bouquet of bloodred roses. "Are you Ana Parker?"

"I am."

"For you," he said. I took them and read the note: "Break a leg, from Elias."

He had a few other deliveries, so I let him through. Bea squealed at her bouquet of daisies, and even Thompson got a single yellow rose. I took my vase back to my spot. That was when I noticed the mysterious envelope. It had my name printed on it, so I opened it. Inside was a brief note and a flash drive that fell into my palm.

"Even if we never figure out how to make things work," the card read, "you will always be my muse. With all my love, Nik."

I wiped a tear from my eye and fixed my makeup, and then Thompson and I brought the house down.

About the Author

Tate Hallaway lives in St. Paul, Minnesota. She is also the author of the Garnet Lacey novels. Visit her on the Web at www.tatehallaway .com or check out her blog at tatehallaway.blogspot.com.